THE VALLEY OF FEAR

Arthur Conan Doyle

Biography of Sir Arthur Conan Doyle

Sir Arthur Conan Doyle, maximum famed for his 4 novels and fifty-six quick stories approximately the "consulting detective" Sherlock Holmes, become born on May 22, 1859 in Edinburgh to a Catholic family of ten. His father, Charles Altamont Doyle, changed into an architect and an artist. Unfortunately, his skills have been shadowed by alcoholism and epilepsy. He sooner or later died in an asylum wherein he became institutionalized. As an end result, the family suffered financially, even though Arthur Conan Doyle's mom, Mary, turned into capable of pay for his schooling at a Jesuit institution.

Doyle decided to pursue clinical research at Edinburgh University, and needed to take a task as a physician's assistant to pay for his school charges. He was already writing and publishing testimonies by way of this time, but his installation an exercise in South Sea in the early Eighteen Eighties. During this era, he finished the primary Sherlock Holmes novel, A Study in Scarlet, which was published in Beeton's Christmas Annual in 1887. Sherlock Holmes became modeled after Doyle's college professor, Joseph Bell, whom he substantially favorite. Doyle wrote to Bell, "It is maximum simply to you that I owe Sherlock Holmes. ... [R]found the center of deduction and inference and observation which I even have heard you inculcate I have tried to build up a man."

However, there has been also plenty of Doyle himself inside the man or woman of Sherlock Holmes, as Bell once remarked. Doyle is thought to had been analytical, responsive to detail, methodical (though once in a while absentminded and clumsy), inventive, and reserved. He even solved a mystery of a lacking person in 1907 in only one hour's time. This case concerned a countrywoman who turned into afraid that her cousin had been murdered; Doyle deduced from the man's bank records, but, that he had actually long past to Scotland.

In Doyle's autobiographical works, The Stark Munro Letters and Memories and Adventures, he executed little evaluation of either his personal personality or religious troubles. Like Holmes, then, Doyle concealed his personal self. Similar to Holmes, too, Doyle changed into called an active and prodigious character, who additionally would disappear into his have a look at for days. As his son, Adrian, remarked: "My memories as an adolescents are mottled with sudden, silent intervals while, following a few agitated stranger, or missive, my father might disappear into his look at for two or 3 days on stop."

Doyle posted other historic works as he endeavored to write down severe, "higher things." However, he took gain of the up-and-coming Strand Magazine (1891) with the aid of publishing quick stories there for economic gain. The Holmes quick stories that he contributed have become very popular with the reading public. The editor of the mag, George Newness, became dedicated to tremendous manufacturing and lots of illustrations, along with the memorable visual photo of Sherlock Holmes designed by using Sidney Paget.

The reputation of the Holmes tales secured Doyle financial comfort and fame, but he soon bored with his hero and killed him off in The Final Problem (1893). However, he later lower back to tales approximately his hero while the general public clamor proved too hard to disregard. All the even as, though, Doyle wrote other works and took a post as a conflict correspondent in Egypt; supported the British control of the Boer War; he oversaw an area sanatorium in South Africa; and he became knighted in 1902. In 1902, Doyle penned one of his most famous Sherlock Holmes works, The Hound of the Baskervilles.

In 1912, Doyle wrote one in every of his different maximum enduring works, The Lost World. This technology fiction story targeted on the man or woman Professor Challenger's adventure to the Amazon, wherein he determined an area wherein dinosaurs and different prehistoric beasts still survived.

During World War I, Doyle became immensely inquisitive about spiritualism, and he wrote many works at the concern. This new awareness of his produced a great deal complaint, particularly regarding his guide for the photographs of the Cuttingly Fairies. Throughout this time, he persevered to jot down poetry, quick stories, pamphlets, and journey novels. Some of his paintings treated humanitarian causes, along with The Crime of the Congo (1909), which excoriated the brutality of the Belgians within the Congo.

Sir Arthur Conan Doyle died on July 7, 1930 of a heart attack; he changed into 71 years vintage. He changed into married twice; his first spouse Louise died from tuberculosis in 1906, and his 2nd spouse Jean survived him. He had five kids in total. He turned into buried in an anonymous grave in unconsecrated floor outside a churchyard fence, attributable to his avowedly Spiritualist non secular beliefs. The graveyard was later extended and now carries his grave; there are still no public headstones, but.

The Valley of Fear Study Guide

Arthur Conan Doyle posted The Valley of Fear in serial form in Strand Magazine between September 1914 and May 1915. A book shape accompanied the British serialization in 1915. The manuscript, 176 folio pages with Doyle's deletions and revisions, suggests that Watson changed into not meant to be the unique narrator. It is the handiest Holmes story to deal directly with Irish issues.

Like A Study in Scarlet, one of the more well-known Holmes testimonies, The Valley of Fear features a flashback phase inserted after Holmes has put his deductive electricity to work solving the thriller. This places the reader throughout the Atlantic Ocean and firmly on the stable floor of real American history. The historic impetus behind the plot of The Valley of Fear turned into the actual war of words among the Pinkerton Detective Agency and contributors of an Irish secret society referred to as the Molly Maguires who had immigrated to Pennsylvania. Depending on one's point of view, the Molly Maguires have been either only a collection of mindlessly violent vigilantes who in order that occurred to have centered the anti-union owners of coal mines, or they had been guerrilla warriors in the struggle for honest and sincere treatment of coal miners with the aid of an possession class that wasn't above engaging Pinkerton Detective to dispense their similarly violent methods for retaining the unions beneath control.

Conan Doyle had visited America on a lecture tour to exquisite acclaim in the Nineties and returned to New York City in May of 1914. It is possibly he mentioned The Valley of Fear with his American editor. It is likewise likely that his editor advocated that the American book elide 3 phrases from the second part of the story: "coal and iron" from the sentence "Captain Marvin is my call—of the Coal and Iron Police." A more impartial word, "mine," was substituted (264).

Like The Sign of Four, The Hound of the Baskervilles, and the foundation of Sherlock Holmes (A Study in Scarlet), The Valley of Fear isn't any mere brief tale, however alternatively a completely fleshed out, novel-duration engagement with the most famous resident of Baker Street. This description of the work is far more appropriate than, say, "Sherlock Holmes novel," because the paintings stocks with A Study in Scarlet and The Sign of Four one of the much less famous factors of the complete Holmes canon: that explanatory section in flashback. This arguably goes on longer than it probable wishes to, although, to its merit, it's far indeed a charming read. It may additionally sense needlessly extended for positive readers (it consists of more phrases than the whole section) but it is actually a quite wonderful example of just how imaginative an author Conan Doyle will be when his coronary heart turned into without a doubt in it.

How lots one enjoys The Valley of Fear likely relies upon whether one enjoys the alternative 3 novels offering Sherlock more than one enjoys the various short testimonies. Even what is arguably the most well-known Holmes mystery of all of them—The Hound of the Baskervilles—is as light on actual Sherlock-centric scenes as the novels that have many Holmes-much less flashback sections (Hound fills time with Watson's interaction with different characters, however). Doyle got to work building The Valley of Fear in a very deliberate style, with two elements and an additional coda; these are literary conventions subtly hired through the author as a means of manipulating the tale's very palpable tension. Readers who enjoy historic context to their fiction as a means of increasing their understanding of the significant narrative have to discover The Valley of Fear one of the greater rewarding surprises in their adventure in the course of the Sherlock Holmes canon.

The biggest mystery right here may be, in fact, just why The Valley of Fear is much less recognized, anthologized, and filmed than The Hound of the Baskervilles. Ultimately, once the flashback explanatory segment is placed into context and The Valley of Fear is approached extra on Conan Doyle's intended phrases rather than as simply any other episode in the Holmes catalogue, it should start to grow to be clean that the radical is more similar to an Edwardian psychological thriller than to a Sherlock Holmes detective story.

The Valley of Fear Themes

Deception

There is a first-rate deal of deception in this paintings, starting with Porlock and Moriarty. The significant deception, of direction, is John Douglas, who's in reality McMurdo, who's simply Birdy Edwards. Edwards deceives all the Scowrers as well as Ettie first of all; then in England he deceives Cecil and his wife. The deception deepens along with his faked loss of life, but even then it is not sufficient to fool Moriarty (or Holmes, of course). Deception is used for each ethical and immoral reasons. Moriarty deceives to benefit power; Edwards deceives so that you can advantage access to a society of murderers whom he seeks to bring down. Doyle suggests that deception may be beneficial but that one must be very cautious to no longer lose himself in the disguise.

Authority

Sherlock Holmes possesses an excellent deal of authority thru mind, capability, and performance. The different characters on this work, primarily the Scowrers, possess authority thru greater deleterious means: they threaten, terrorize, wound, kill, and are seeking for to establish their authority on the idea of being capable of do all of this stuff without retribution. Authority within the company is not based totally on sound thoughts or intellect; instead, its miles hooked up and maintained through pressure. Doyle indicates that this kind of authority is doomed to fail eventually because it is not sustainable.

Power

Power manifests itself in lots of ways within the text, but Doyle definitely appears to signify that the type of electricity Sherlock Holmes possesses is good. This power is rooted in mind, logical and deductive reasoning, thoughtfulness and care, perspicacity, open-mindedness, and clarity of notion and expression. Holmes is able to remedy the case thru all of those developments, restoring Douglas to his wife, exonerating him from punishment, and, even though in the end failing, protective him relatively from the danger of Moriarty. Doyle explores different styles of electricity like traditional regulation enforcement, which he depicts as beneficial however restricted, and energy primarily based in violence and terror, which he depicts as putatively absolute but ultimately doomed to fail.

Observation

One of the most critical issues of the radical is commentary, which is what readers are advocated to exercise in conjunction with Holmes. Doyle sets out the particulars of the case without sparing any details if you want to set off his readers to reflect on consideration on what they see and attempt to shape connections. Holmes is highly clever, however all of the proof he has is the identical proof that readers have at the start. Doyle teaches his readers to do not forget each element regardless of how small, to no longer allow one's preconceptions take prominence, and to be open-minded.

Faith

One of the maximum compelling elements of the Holmes stories is the relationship among Holmes and Watson. If this is the only Holmes tale readers have ever read, then it nevertheless does a super process at portraying the connection and demonstrating how both guys benefit from it. Watson's faith in Holmes's capabilities is ever-apparent here, as it's far in other stories. Holmes's ideas sometimes appear wild or impossible, however Holmes always offers his pal credit. Watson's faith may be tested however it by no means falters; this is the recipe for now not best a good friendship but also a dynamic detective duo.

Fear

The title of the radical shows how plenty fear plays a role inside the events depicted inside. The "Valley of Fear" is each a bodily location—Vermissa Valley, coronary heart of the Pennsylvania coal mines—and a symbolic place. In the latter feel it's far a mental valley in which Douglas finds himself stuck without a method of get away. He is menaced and harassed via his worry and knows that he can never break out it. It permeates all aspects of his existence. Ultimately, fear keeps Douglas on his ft. and alive loads longer than if he were complacent, however it can't absolutely keep him.

Morality

On the one hand, Doyle is apparent approximately morality inside the tale. The Scowrers are practically irredeemable, characterized by using near-mindless violence. They tolerate no threat to their authority and menace harmless human beings. However, McMurdo poses an extra thrilling ethical conundrum for readers. While he is undercover with the Scowrers, he beats, threatens, lies, and most possibly kills humans. He additionally watches and says not anything in many of these situations, even though he does warn Wilcox and saves Stanger from being beaten to death. One wonders if he is simply as horrific because the Scowrers even though he ultimately places them away. It is perhaps less complicated to say that he is doing an awesome aspect, but without knowing just how completely he participated of their bloody deeds, it's miles impossible to mention so definitively.

The Valley of Fear Symbols, Allegory and Motifs

The Valley (Symbol)

Vermissa Valley itself is an image, one which is basically explained with the aid of the name of the unconventional. The reader learns early on that John Douglas lived in a literal valley inside the western United States. However, even after leaving America, Douglas' wife refers to residing in a valley of worry. Thus it isn't only a literal valley, but also a looming entrapment from which Douglas cannot pretty break out.

Encirclement (Motif)

Encirclement is a robust motif in The Valley of Fear, meant to illustrate Douglas' war to get away entrapment with the aid of the Scowrers. This motif is may be seen in numerous bureaucracy: the moat surrounding Douglas house; the triangle inscribed in a circle, that is the mark of the Scowrers; even Douglas' wedding ceremony ring, which he claims he has worn see you later that he cannot bodily eliminate it. Even the "valley of fear" itself is an instance of this motif, as a valley is a geographically sunken area, normally encircled through mountains.

Struggle against the Unseen (Allegory)

Douglas' struggle in "The Valley of Fear" can be seen as an allegory of struggle against the unseen. Fear itself is unseen and faceless, and in lots of ways, so are the Scowrers. Existing as a big and odious agency with many contributors, it changed into impossible for Douglas to protect himself absolutely from their plots. The e-book tells us that the crimes the Scowrers commit before they are apprehended by Birdy Edwards move completely unpunished, commonly due to the incapacity of the sufferer to become aware of his attacker.

Moriarty is simply as removed and unseen, with men below him acting as invisible retailers. An interesting addition to this allegory is the reality that the frame determined at the start of the radical (concept before everything to be Douglas) has been almost decapitated by means of a shotgun blast. The corpse, then, can be visible as figuratively and actually "faceless."

The Shotgun (Symbol)

The shotgun, that's the homicide weapon described at the start of the tale, is a critical symbol. Its most on the spot reason is plain: as Holmes factors out, it's miles most virtually an American weapon. The sawed-off shotgun is utilized by Doyle to truly underline the American connection. The weapon is also symbolic of the Scowrers themselves, however. It is the whole thing the Scowrers are: bloodless, brutal, and extraordinarily deadly. As Holmes factors out, the triggers are wired collectively, making sure both barrels discharge immediately, maximizing the impact.

The shotgun embodies the ironic paradox of the Scowrers as properly. It is sawn off so it could be carried underneath a coat—in other phrases, hid. However, the loud discharge of the weapon could make a stealthy crime not possible. This is just like the Scowrers: a "secret" society that everybody is aware of approximately.

Moriarty's Note

Perhaps one of the cleverest portions of writing in The Valley of Fear is Moriarty's be aware. It is a really quick message, together with best sentences: "Dear me, Mr. Holmes. Dear me!" (319.) it is thru this observe that Holmes deduces Douglas' death at the arms of his arch-rival, making it by hook or by crook odious in its simplicity. Moriarty's notice is symbolic of the professor himself: this message, if viewed by means of a stranger, appears absolutely harmless, almost polite. Likewise, Professor Moriarty is viewed with the aid of the public as a banal math professor. To Holmes, the message approach something an awful lot more sinister: it scoffs from a distance.

The Valley of Fear Metaphors and Similes

Chain of Criminality (Metaphor)

Holmes describes the criminal international and his relation to it as if it were a series, everybody representing a hyperlink. He identifies Porlock particularly as a weak link in that crook chain: this weak spot is what makes Porlock Holmes' ideal factor of get entry to the chain as an entire.

Chemistry (Simile)

When Holmes hears about the murder of Douglas right after he has simply deciphered the observe alluding to this very aspect, he is not especially amazed. In fact, he shows almost no emotion. Instead, as Watson says, "his face confirmed as a substitute the quiet and involved composure of the chemist who sees the crystals falling into position from his oversaturated answer" (171). This assessment to a scientist is a superb because Holmes is commonly emotionless, cerebral, meticulous, and quiet. His cases are like clinical experiments, his hypotheses just like the ones of scientists.

Moriarty's deceptive character (Simile)

MacDonald describes his assembly with Moriarty in the following way: "When he positioned his hand on my shoulder as we were parting, it become like a father's blessing before you exit into the cold, cruel international" (173). This simile expresses one of the most disconcerting elements of Moriarty's character: the fact that he can be so apparently sagacious and heat. Clearly he's a grasp of legerdemain and manipulation; MacDonald is aware of this, but he can't shake his superb impressions of the awesome professor.

Holmes's brain as a tool (Metaphor)

Watson makes use of the metaphor of a device to describe Holmes's mind. He says, "A long series of sterile weeks lay behind us, and right here at final there has been a fitting object for those awesome powers which, like several unique gifts, come to be irksome to their owner when they're no longer in use. That razor brain blunted and rusted with state of no activity" (178). When Holmes isn't the use of his mind, its miles rusty and stupid; when he's the usage of it, it comes alive and hums along with energy and strength. The past weeks dulled Holmes's first rate brain, and now its miles kicking into high tools once more. The rust is long past, and the edge is sharp once more.

The fly-like press (Simile)

White Mason states "We'll have the pressmen down like flies after they recognize it" (189) whilst he tells MacDonald, Holmes, and Watson approximately the case. This simile works well as it implies just how terrific and compelling this situation is.

The Valley of Fear Irony

"Fatherly" Moriarty (Dramatic Irony)

When Inspector MacDonald is talking with Holmes of his interview with Professor Moriarty, he says that once the professor placed his hand on his shoulder before leaving "it became like a father's blessing before you go out into the cruel, merciless, global" (173) This is ironic because, given that MacDonald is a policeman, Moriarty absolute confidence holds not anything however hatred for the person; also, given Moriarty's deeds, it's miles in all likelihood that he has significantly contributed to the evil in MacDonald's "cruel, merciless global."

The missing dumb-bell (Dramatic Irony)

In this situation, the police find themselves overrun with clues that everyone appear equally critical: bloody footprints, the uncommon weapon, a card inscribed 'V.V.' subsequent to the body, the ordinary burn on the dead guy's arm, and so on. The one commentary that Holmes makes that seems to be of no result whatsoever is that there may be only one dumbbell inside the room. This oddity is typically regarded on as unimportant by using the alternative detectives, but, as it turns out, it's far the most revealing clue. As Holmes says later, "Dear me, Watson, is it feasible that you haven't penetrated the truth that the case hangs upon the lacking dumb-bell?" (213.)

The Scowrers' love of song (Situational Irony)

The Scowrers are defined as a brutal and heartless gang of murderers, who take pleasure in their bloody work with a complete absence of shame. Yet when describing certainly one of their conferences, the reader unearths that "the smooth or pathetic in music ought to flow them to tears" (274) this nicely positioned irony makes the men even greater twisted and vile within the eyes of the reader. The Scowrers have sympathy and feeling for the fictional characters in songs, but not for the lives of their victims.

Douglas' dying (Dramatic Irony)

John Douglas, in any other case referred to as either Jack McMurdo or Birdy Edwards, escapes death a couple of instances. Indeed, at the start of the tale we consider he is useless. We study that the Scowrers of Vermissa Valley hunted him for years earlier than in the end catching up with him. It is best after he has shaken them off, seemingly safe for the first time in years, that he finally ends up assembly his dying on the fingers of Professor Moriarty. This piece of cruel irony affords a poignant ending to the novel, and additionally intensifies the odious personality of Holmes' nemesis, Moriarty.

The Valley of Fear Character List

Sherlock Holmes

Arguably the maximum famous fictional character in history, Sherlock Holmes is synonymous with "brilliant detective." His place as the most excellent detective in all of literature is challenged simplest likely through Agatha Christie's Poirot. Sherlock Holmes is defined as tall, skinny, and reserved, with an aquiline nose and penetrating eyes. He is notably first rate, fairly vain, and often impatient with those who are not able to keep up with his speedy deductions. This specific novel, sarcastically enough, probable contains less of Holmes than any of the others, with the exceptional sleuth being contained in large part to Part I. In The Valley of Fear, we do no longer see as tons of the "bloodhound" Holmes; as an alternative, he seems to penetrate the mystery as a substitute quickly, and the actual heart of the tale rather lies within the 2nd element. Still, he stays intellectually superior absolutely, even when surrounded with the aid of other successful detectives.

Dr. John Watson

Perhaps simply as well-known as his terrific companion, Dr. John Watson is the dependable sidekick of Sherlock Holmes, performing in almost each Sherlock Holmes tale ever written with the aid of Conan Doyle. Through almost the complete canon, we see the entirety thru Watson's eyes: the story is provided as though written firsthand by the best doctor himself. Such is the case in an awful lot of The Valley of Fear, even though Conan Doyle departs from this attitude for an awful lot of Part II. Watson, fairly intelligent in his very own right, appears to stay in a steady country of stupor over

Holmes' brilliance, and regularly voices the reader's personal confusions regarding the detective's speedy deductions. Watson's presence is fairly insignificant on this specific novel, acting in only some scenes in which Holmes became now not gift as properly. Watson is regularly described as stout and quite withdrawn, as well as being very smooth-going in nature.

Professor James Moriarty

Every outstanding fictional hero has an equally exquisite nemesis. Sherlock Holmes is not any exception. One of the most notorious characters in literature, Moriarty satirically seems in handiest Sherlock Holmes testimonies. Indeed, he does not ever virtually appear in The Valley of Fear: he's simplest referenced, and, at the give up of the e-book, Holmes receives a brief note from him. Nonetheless, Moriarty remains one of the central characters of this novel, and he's revealed to be the mastermind at the back of Douglas' dying.

John Douglas/Jack McMurdo/Birdy Edwards

This crucial and multi-dimensional person (to whom we will refer as Douglas for the sake of readability) ought to actually be taken into consideration 3 unique characters contained in one man. Introduced at the start of the tale as John Douglas, this guy seems to be a faceless sufferer, truly the object of Holmes' investigation. Towards the quit of Part I, however, Douglas is revealed to be very lots alive, and he commences to share his history, which contains nearly everything of Part II. During this "story inside a story," we study that Douglas once bore the call "Jack

McMurdo," and that he became a part of an infamous gang inside the United States, which turned into not unlike the Mafia. At the give up of Part II, however, we examine that "McMurdo" is actually a Pinkerton detective named "Birdy Edwards." Throughout all three of his "identities," Douglas is described as fearless, wise, and proper-humored. Douglas is an instance of Conan Doyle's ability as a writer, in that the reader is able to be given with little trouble the composition of the "three-in-one" man or woman.

Boss (Body master) McGinty

Mentioned in Part I, but now not absolutely brought until Part II, Boss McGinty is one of the principal villains of this novel. The merciless and brutal leader of "the Scowrers," a murderous society now not unlike the Mafia, McGinty is a fearsome chief, defined as looking nearly like a lion, with fierce eyes and a mane-like beard. McGinty is the undisputed lord of Vermissa Valley, which many call the "Valley of Fear." The Body master (the title of the head of the Scowrers) regulations over the valley with an iron fist, crushing all and sundry who gets in his way thru the marketers underneath him. McGinty could be visible as an American Moriarty, although neither as sensible nor as powerful.

Inspector MacDonald

Scotland Yard's most important regulation enforcement official at the Douglas case, and a pal of Holmes's. MacDonald is sensible, efficient, young, dour, and stoic.

White Mason

The nearby regulation enforcement guy at the Douglas case. Friendly and useful, he nonetheless looks like he is in over his head.

Mrs. Douglas

John Douglas's second wife, Mrs. Douglas (Ivy) is young and beautiful. She suspects something is wrong together with her husband concerning his past, but he keeps her ignorant. She and Cecil determine to fabricate the crime scene, however then they confess to Holmes and the others.

Cecil Barker

The wealthy and good-looking American friend of the Douglasses who enables orchestrate the crime scene to shield Douglas. He is first of all arrogant and standoffish, however ultimately he comes round to letting the detectives assist.

Ames

The elderly and constant butler at Manor House.

Mrs. Allen

The elderly and deaf housekeeper at Manor House.

Scanlan

He is the Scowrer whom McMurdo meets on the train into coal country. Scanlan is amiable, useful, and a loyal member of the E.O.F., but he does now not like violence as a whole lot as some of the others do.

Ettie Shafter

The lovable daughter of Jacob Shafter, the man with whom McMurdo forums. She and McMurdo fall in love, however their dating is strained by way of 1st earl baldwin of bewdley's declare on her, along with the dangerous situations McMurdo faces because of his status as a brother. When McMurdo famous himself as Birdy Edwards, she flees the valley with him. She later dies in California.

Jacob Shafter

Ettie's father and a stout foe of the E.O.F.

Teddy Baldwin

The young and hotheaded brother who wants to marry Ettie and resents McMurdo stepping into his manner. He usually butts heads with McMurdo; however, he grudgingly accepts him, till his actual identity is revealed. He tracks McMurdo to England and attempts to kill him; alternatively, McMurdo/Douglas kills 1st Earl Baldwin of Bewdley in self-defense.

Morris

An aged brother who disapproves of the Scowrers' violent processes and warns that they need to be cautious in their targets. He seeks out McMurdo as a best friend and later provides the facts approximately the Pinkerton undercover agent to McMurdo, thereby unwittingly imparting it to the undercover agent himself.

Evans Pott

The bold County Delegate and E.O.F. Leader, of whom even McGinty is wary.

Lawler and Andrews

The assassins dispatched via Evans Pott to perform the murders at the mine.

Chester Wilcox

A nearby mine owner focused through the Scowrers.

James Stanger

The newspaper editor important of the Scowrers; McGinty orders him to be crushed.

Captain Marvin

The new member of the Iron and Coal Police who initially seems to be an enemy of McMurdo; later, but, him's discovered to be in on McMurdo's genuine identification as a Pinkerton spy.

The Valley of Fear Summary

The Valley of Fear starts with Sherlock Holmes, the famous detective, and Dr. Watson, his comrade and roommate at 221B Baker Street, in mid-conversation. Holmes is confusing over an encrypted message that he obtained from Porlock, a companion of Holmes' nemesis, Professor Moriarty. A 2d message from Porlock, which changed into imagined to incorporate the important thing to the coded message, quickly arrives, declaring that he (Porlock) is afraid of Moriarty's wrath and will no longer screen the cause of his correspondence. Holmes quickly deciphers the message regardless, and discovers that it warns that Douglas of Birlstone is in forthcoming danger. The two are quickly visited through MacDonald, a policeman buddy of Holmes, who informs them that this equal Douglas has been murdered.

Upon inspection of the lifeless guy, its miles discovered that he has been killed with a sawed off shotgun, an American weapon. Beside the disfigured frame lies a card inscribed 'V.V. 341'. Other clues in the room include a bloody footprint on the windowsill, a missing dumb-bell, and the truth that the man's wedding ring is lacking. Another clue found quickly after is a bicycle, concealed just outdoor the house grounds. Interrogation of the residence servants exhibits little, and after Mrs. Douglas, wife of the murdered guy, and Cecil Barker, a pal of the family, are questioned, Holmes reveals to Watson that he believes the 2 are in a conspiracy together.

Although the opposite detectives at the scene share their own theories, Holmes informs Watson that he believes the case hangs totally on the missing dumb-bell, the one piece of evidence deemed trivial by the police force. Holmes broadcasts that he is going to spend the night alone in the room in which Douglas became murdered, taking nothing with him but Watson's umbrella. The day after Holmes' vigil, he reveals to the police pressure investigating Douglas' murder that he has solved the case, and asks them to sign up for him in a stakeout that night time.

During the stakeout, which takes location inside the trees outdoor of the room wherein the crime become devoted, Holmes, Watson, and the other detectives witness a man lean out the window and fish something out of the moat that surrounds the house. When the organization confronts the determine, they find out it's far Cecil Barker, and that the item he has taken from the moat is a bag, weighed down with the lacking dumb-bell. Within the bag is a suit of clothing, boots, and a knife. During his stay within the room, Holmes located this equal bag the use of the criminal of Watson's umbrella, and positioned it returned to watch for Barker to retrieve it. To the astonishment of the others, Holmes famous that Douglas is still alive. Upon pronouncing this, a hidden compartment within the room opens, and Douglas himself steps out.

Douglas proceeds to provide an explanation for that he have been sought for some time with the aid of a man named 1st Earl Baldwin of Bewdley, who later attempted to kill him. The two struggled, and 1st earl baldwin of bewdley died when the shotgun went off in his face. With the help of his spouse and Barker, Douglas concocted a plan to fake his personal loss of life, taking benefit of the reality that Baldwin's disfigured face might save you an accurate identity. Douglas explains that there are others who would are looking for his life, and his obvious demise could permit him to shake them off forever. Douglas offers Watson a manuscript, which he says details his beyond existence, and tells of the guys who wish him lifeless. After this, the novel shifts to Part II, which deals with Douglas' lifestyles in America.

Part II starts with a person named Jack McMurdo, (whom we later discover is Douglas). McMurdo journeys to Vermissa Valley, a coal mining district in the western United States. McMurdo expresses a severe hatred of policemen, which draws the eye of a man named Scanlan. Scanlan exhibits himself to be a member of the order of the Freemen, a society to which McMurdo also belongs. McMurdo quickly joins the local motel of Freemen, headed up by way of a cruel, violent man named Boss McGinty. It is revealed that the Freemen of this district move by means of another name: the Scowrers, a Mafia-like society that oppresses the people of Vermissa Valley. McMurdo proves to be simply as violent as the rest, and he quickly turns into an outstanding member of the Scowrers.

The gang maintains their reign of terror without being challenged, till they learn that Birdy Edwards, a Pinkerton detective, is on their trail. McMurdo informs the inn that he knows who Birdy Edwards is, and he lays a plan to capture him. McMurdo lures Edwards to his rental, where Boss McGinty and numerous of the alternative prominent contributors of the gang are concealed. McMurdo all of sudden turns the tables on the Scowrers through revealing that he himself is Birdy Edwards, and that he joined the resort most effective to gain data to use towards them. McGinty and several of the others are hanged primarily based on McMurdo's testimony, and the others are dispatched to jail. Edwards, understanding the vindictive nature of the crowd, disappears, ultimately ending up in England, in which occasions play out as unique in Part I.

After Douglas' incredible tale, Holmes warns the person to stay on his shield, as Moriarty, whom Baldwin contacted to locate Douglas' whereabouts, will no question attempt to kill Douglas himself. Douglas agrees and is going again into hiding.

Sometime after Douglas flees England, Holmes gets a cryptic message which reads best "Dear me, Mr. Holmes, expensive me!" Watson and McDonald speculate as to whether or not or not Moriarty will ever be added to justice. Holmes assures them that he'll seize the Professor, but he wishes time for you to achieve this.

PART 1—The Tragedy of Birlstone

Chapter 1—The Warning

"I am inclined to think—" said I.

"I should do so," Sherlock Holmes remarked impatiently.

I believe that I am one of the most long-suffering of mortals; but I'll admit that I was annoyed at the sardonic interruption. "Really, Holmes," said I severely, "you are a little trying at times."

He was too much absorbed with his own thoughts to give any immediate answer to my remonstrance. He leaned upon his hand, with his untasted breakfast before him, and he stared at the slip of paper which he had just drawn from its envelope. Then he took the envelope itself, held it up to the light, and very carefully studied both the exterior and the flap.

"It is Porlock's writing," said he thoughtfully. "I can hardly doubt that it is Porlock's writing, though I have seen it only twice before. The Greek e with the peculiar top flourish is distinctive. But if it is Porlock, then it must be something of the very first importance."

He was speaking to himself rather than to me; but my vexation disappeared in the interest which the words awakened.

"Who then is Porlock?" I asked.

"Porlock, Watson, is a nom-de-plume, a mere identification mark; but behind it lies a shifty and evasive personality. In a former letter he frankly informed me that the name was not his own, and defied me ever to trace him among the teeming millions of this great city. Porlock is important, not for himself, but for the great man with whom he is in touch. Picture to yourself the pilot fish with the shark, the jackal with the lion—anything that is insignificant in companionship with what is formidable: not only formidable, Watson, but sinister—in the highest degree sinister. That is where he comes within my purview. You have heard me speak of Professor Moriarty?"

"The famous scientific criminal, as famous among crooks as—"

"My blushes, Watson!" Holmes murmured in a deprecating voice.

"I was about to say, as he is unknown to the public."

"A touch! A distinct touch!" cried Holmes. "You are developing a certain unexpected vein of pawky humour, Watson, against which I must learn to guard myself. But in calling Moriarty a criminal you are uttering libel in the eyes of the law—and there lie the glory and the wonder of it! The greatest schemer of all time, the organizer of every deviltry, the controlling brain of the underworld, a brain which might have made or marred the destiny of nations—that's the man! But so aloof is he from general suspicion, so immune from criticism, so admirable in his management and self-effacement, that for those very words that you have uttered he could hale you to a court and emerge with your year's pension as a solatium for his wounded character. Is he not the celebrated author of The Dynamics of an Asteroid, a book which ascends to such rarefied heights of pure mathematics that it is said that there was no man in the scientific press capable of criticizing it? Is this a man to traduce? Foul-mouthed doctor and slandered professor—such would be your respective roles! That's genius, Watson. But if I am spared by lesser men, our day will surely come."

"May I be there to see!" I exclaimed devoutly. "But you were speaking of this man Porlock."

"Ah, yes—the so-called Porlock is a link in the chain some little way from its great attachment. Porlock is not quite a sound link—between ourselves. He is the only flaw in that chain so far as I have been able to test it."

"But no chain is stronger than its weakest link."

"Exactly, my dear Watson! Hence the extreme importance of Porlock. Led on by some rudimentary aspirations towards right, and encouraged by the judicious stimulation of an occasional ten-pound note sent to him by devious methods, he has once or twice given me advance information which has been of value—that highest value which anticipates and prevents rather than avenges crime. I cannot doubt that, if we had the cipher, we should find that this communication is of the nature that I indicate."

Again Holmes flattened out the paper upon his unused plate. I rose and, leaning over him, stared down at the curious inscription, which ran as follows:

534 C2 13 127 36 31 4 17 21 41 DOUGLAS 109 293 5 37 BIRLSTONE 26 BIRLSTONE 9 47 171

"What do you make of it, Holmes?"

"It is obviously an attempt to convey secret information."

"But what is the use of a cipher message without the cipher?"

"In this instance, none at all."

"Why do you say 'in this instance'?"

"Because there are many ciphers which I would read as easily as I do the apocrypha of the agony column: such crude devices amuse the intelligence without fatiguing it. But this is different. It is clearly a reference to the words in a page of some book. Until I am told which page and which book I am powerless."

"But why 'Douglas' and 'Birlstone'?"

"Clearly because those are words which were not contained in the page in question."

"Then why has he not indicated the book?"

"Your native shrewdness, my dear Watson, that innate cunning which is the delight of your friends, would surely prevent you from inclosing cipher and message in the same envelope. Should it miscarry, you are undone. As it is, both have to go wrong before any harm comes from it. Our second post is now overdue, and I shall be surprised if it does not bring us either a further letter of explanation, or, as is more probable, the very volume to which these figures refer."

Holmes's calculation was fulfilled within a very few minutes by the appearance of Billy, the page, with the very letter which we were expecting.

"The same writing," remarked Holmes, as he opened the envelope, "and actually signed," he added in an exultant voice as he unfolded the epistle. "Come, we are getting on, Watson." His brow clouded, however, as he glanced over the contents.

"Dear me, this is very disappointing! I fear, Watson, that all our expectations come to nothing. I trust that the man Porlock will come to no harm.

"DEAR MR. HOLMES [he says]:

"I will go no further in this matter. It is too dangerous—he suspects me. I can see that he suspects me. He came to me quite unexpectedly after I had actually addressed this envelope with the intention of sending you the key to the cipher. I was able to cover it up. If he had seen it, it would have gone hard with me. But I read suspicion in his eyes. Please burn the cipher message, which can now be of no use to you.

"FRED PORLOCK."

Holmes sat for some little time twisting this letter between his fingers, and frowning, as he stared into the fire.

"After all," he said at last, "there may be nothing in it. It may be only his guilty conscience. Knowing himself to be a traitor, he may have read the accusation in the other's eyes."

"The other being, I presume, Professor Moriarty."

"No less! When any of that party talk about 'He' you know whom they mean. There is one predominant 'He' for all of them."

"But what can he do?"

"Hum! That's a large question. When you have one of the first brains of Europe up against you, and all the powers of darkness at his back, there are infinite possibilities. Anyhow, Friend Porlock is evidently scared out of his senses—kindly compare the writing in the note to that upon its envelope; which was done, he tells us, before this ill-omened visit. The one is clear and firm. The other hardly legible."

"Why did he write at all? Why did he not simply drop it?"

"Because he feared I would make some inquiry after him in that case, and possibly bring trouble on him."

"No doubt," said I. "Of course." I had picked up the original cipher message and was bending my brows over it. "It's pretty maddening to think that an important secret may lie here on this slip of paper, and that it is beyond human power to penetrate it."

Sherlock Holmes had pushed away his untasted breakfast and lit the unsavoury pipe which was the companion of his deepest meditations. "I wonder!" said he, leaning back and staring at the ceiling. "Perhaps there are points which have escaped your Machiavellian intellect. Let us consider the problem in the light of pure reason. This man's reference is to a book. That is our point of departure."

"A somewhat vague one."

"Let us see then if we can narrow it down. As I focus my mind upon it, it seems rather less impenetrable. What indications have we as to this book?"

"None."

"Well, well, it is surely not quite so bad as that. The cipher message begins with a large 534, does it not? We may take it as a working hypothesis that 534 is the particular page to which the cipher refers. So our book has already become a LARGE book, which is surely something gained. What other indications have we as to the nature of this large book? The next sign is C2. What do you make of that, Watson?"

"Chapter the second, no doubt."

"Hardly that, Watson. You will, I am sure, agree with me that if the page be given, the number of the chapter is immaterial. Also that if page 534 finds us only in the second chapter, the length of the first one must have been really intolerable."

"Column!" I cried.

"Brilliant, Watson. You are scintillating this morning. If it is not column, then I am very much deceived. So now, you see, we begin to visualize a large book printed in double columns which are each of a considerable length, since one of the words is numbered in the document as the two hundred and ninety-third. Have we reached the limits of what reason can supply?"

"I fear that we have."

"Surely you do yourself an injustice. One more coruscation, my dear Watson—yet another brain-wave! Had the volume been an unusual one, he would have sent it to me. Instead of that, he had intended, before his plans were nipped, to send me the clue in this envelope. He says so in his note. This would seem to indicate that the book is one which he thought I would have no difficulty in finding for myself. He had it—and he imagined that I would have it, too. In short, Watson, it is a very common book."

"What you say certainly sounds plausible."

"So we have contracted our field of search to a large book, printed in double columns and in common use."

"The Bible!" I cried triumphantly.

"Good, Watson, good! But not, if I may say so, quite good enough! Even if I accepted the compliment for myself I could hardly name any volume which would be less likely to lie at the elbow of one of Moriarty's associates. Besides, the editions of Holy Writ are so numerous that he could hardly suppose that two copies would have the same pagination. This is clearly a book which is standardized. He knows for certain that his page 534 will exactly agree with my page 534."

"But very few books would correspond with that."

"Exactly. Therein lies our salvation. Our search is narrowed down to standardized books which anyone may be supposed to possess."

"Bradshaw!"

"There are difficulties, Watson. The vocabulary of Bradshaw is nervous and terse, but limited. The selection of words would hardly lend itself to the sending of general messages. We will eliminate Bradshaw. The dictionary is, I fear, inadmissible for the same reason. What then is left?"

"An almanac!"

"Excellent, Watson! I am very much mistaken if you have not touched the spot. An almanac! Let us consider the claims of Whitaker's Almanac. It is in common use. It has the requisite number of pages. It is in double column. Though reserved in its earlier vocabulary, it becomes, if I remember right, quite garrulous towards the end." He picked the volume from his desk. "Here is page 534, column two, a substantial block of print dealing, I perceive, with the trade and resources of British India. Jot down the words, Watson! Number thirteen is 'Mahratta.' Not, I fear, a very auspicious beginning. Number one hundred and twenty-seven is 'Government'; which at least makes sense, though somewhat irrelevant to ourselves and Professor Moriarty. Now let us try again. What does the Mahratta government do? Alas! the next word is 'pig's-bristles.' We are undone, my good Watson! It is finished!"

He had spoken in jesting vein, but the twitching of his bushy eyebrows bespoke his disappointment and irritation. I sat helpless and unhappy, staring into the fire. A long silence was broken by a sudden exclamation from Holmes, who dashed at a cupboard, from which he emerged with a second yellow-covered volume in his hand.

"We pay the price, Watson, for being too up-to-date!" he cried. "We are before our time, and suffer the usual penalties. Being the seventh of January, we have very properly laid in the new almanac. It is more than likely that Porlock took his message from the old one. No doubt he would have told us so had his letter of explanation been written. Now let us see what page 534 has in store for us. Number thirteen is 'There,' which is much more promising. Number one hundred and twenty-seven is 'is'—'There is' "—Holmes's eyes were gleaming with excitement, and his thin, nervous fingers twitched as he counted the words—"'danger.' Ha! Ha! Capital! Put that down, Watson. 'There is danger— may—come—very soon—one.' Then we have the name 'Douglas'—'rich—country—now—at Birlstone— House—Birlstone—confidence—is—pressing.' There, Watson! What do you think of pure reason and its fruit? If the green-grocer had such a thing as a laurel wreath, I should send Billy round for it."

I was staring at the strange message which I had scrawled, as he deciphered it, upon a sheet of foolscap on my knee.

"What a queer, scrambling way of expressing his meaning!" said I.

"On the contrary, he has done quite remarkably well," said Holmes. "When you search a single column for words with which to express your meaning, you can hardly expect to get everything you want. You are bound to leave something to the intelligence of your correspondent. The purport is perfectly clear. Some deviltry is intended against one Douglas, whoever he may be, residing as stated, a rich country gentleman. He is sure—'confidence' was as near as he could get to 'confident'—that it is pressing. There is our result—and a very workmanlike little bit of analysis it was!"

Holmes had the impersonal joy of the true artist in his better work, even as he mourned darkly when it fell below the high level to which he aspired. He was still chuckling over his success when Billy swung open the door and Inspector MacDonald of Scotland Yard was ushered into the room.

Those were the early days at the end of the '80's, when Alec MacDonald was far from having attained the national fame which he has now achieved. He was a young but trusted member of the detective force, who had distinguished himself in several cases which had been intrusted to him. His tall, bony figure gave promise of exceptional physical strength, while his great cranium and deep-set, lustrous eyes spoke no less clearly of the keen intelligence which twinkled out from behind his bushy eyebrows. He was a silent, precise man with a dour nature and a hard Aberdonian accent.

Twice already in his career had Holmes helped him to attain success, his own sole reward being the intellectual joy of the problem. For this reason the affection and respect of the Scotchman for his amateur colleague were profound, and he showed them by the frankness with which he consulted Holmes in every difficulty. Mediocrity knows nothing higher than itself; but talent instantly recognizes genius, and MacDonald had talent enough for his profession to enable him to perceive that there was no humiliation in seeking the assistance of one who already stood alone in Europe, both in his gifts and in his experience. Holmes was not prone to friendship, but he was tolerant of the big Scotchman, and smiled at the sight of him.

"You are an early bird, Mr. Mac," said he. "I wish you luck with your worm. I fear this means that there is some mischief afoot."

"If you said 'hope' instead of 'fear,' it would be nearer the truth, I'm thinking, Mr. Holmes," the inspector answered, with a knowing grin. "Well, maybe a wee nip would keep out the raw morning chill. No, I won't smoke, I thank you. I'll have to be pushing on my way; for the early hours of a case are the precious ones, as no man knows better than your own self. But—but—"

The inspector had stopped suddenly, and was staring with a look of absolute amazement at a paper upon the table. It was the sheet upon which I had scrawled the enigmatic message.

"Douglas!" he stammered. "Birlstone! What's this, Mr. Holmes? Man, it's witchcraft! Where in the name of all that is wonderful did you get those names?"

"It is a cipher that Dr. Watson and I have had occasion to solve. But why—what's amiss with the names?"

The inspector looked from one to the other of us in dazed astonishment. "Just this," said he, "that Mr. Douglas of Birlstone Manor House was horribly murdered last night!"

Chapter 2—Sherlock Holmes Discourses

It was one of those dramatic moments for which my friend existed. It would be an overstatement to say that he was shocked or even excited by the amazing announcement. Without having a tinge of cruelty in his singular composition, he was undoubtedly callous from long overstimulation. Yet, if his emotions were dulled, his intellectual perceptions were exceedingly active. There was no trace then of the horror which I had myself felt at this curt declaration; but his face showed rather the quiet and interested composure of the chemist who sees the crystals falling into position from his oversaturated solution.

"Remarkable!" said he. "Remarkable!"

"You don't seem surprised."

"Interested, Mr. Mac, but hardly surprised. Why should I be surprised? I receive an anonymous communication from a quarter which I know to be important, warning me that danger threatens a certain person. Within an hour I learn that this danger has actually materialized and that the person is dead. I am interested; but, as you observe, I am not surprised."

In a few short sentences he explained to the inspector the facts about the letter and the cipher. MacDonald sat with his chin on his hands and his great sandy eyebrows bunched into a yellow tangle.

"I was going down to Birlstone this morning," said he. "I had come to ask you if you cared to come with me—you and your friend here. But from what you say we might perhaps be doing better work in London."

"I rather think not," said Holmes.

"Hang it all, Mr. Holmes!" cried the inspector. "The papers will be full of the Birlstone mystery in a day or two; but where's the mystery if there is a man in London who prophesied the crime before ever it occurred? We have only to lay our hands on that man, and the rest will follow."

"No doubt, Mr. Mac. But how do you propose to lay your hands on the so-called Porlock?"

MacDonald turned over the letter which Holmes had handed him. "Posted in Camberwell—that doesn't help us much. Name, you say, is assumed. Not much to go on, certainly. Didn't you say that you have sent him money?"

"Twice."

"And how?"

"In notes to Camberwell post office."

"Did you ever trouble to see who called for them?"

"No."

The inspector looked surprised and a little shocked. "Why not?"

"Because I always keep faith. I had promised when he first wrote that I would not try to trace him."

"You think there is someone behind him?"

"I know there is."

"This professor that I've heard you mention?"

"Exactly!"

Inspector MacDonald smiled, and his eyelid quivered as he glanced towards me. "I won't conceal from you, Mr. Holmes, that we think in the C.I.D. that you have a wee bit of a bee in your bonnet over this professor. I made some inquiries myself about the matter. He seems to be a very respectable, learned, and talented sort of man."

"I'm glad you've got so far as to recognize the talent."

"Man, you can't but recognize it! After I heard your view I made it my business to see him. I had a chat with him on eclipses. How the talk got that way I canna think; but he had out a reflector lantern and a globe, and made it all clear in a minute. He lent me a book; but I don't mind saying that it was a bit above my head, though I had a good Aberdeen upbringing. He'd have made a grand meenister with his thin face and gray hair and solemn-like way of talking. When he put his hand on my shoulder as we were parting, it was like a father's blessing before you go out into the cold, cruel world."

Holmes chuckled and rubbed his hands. "Great!" he said. "Great! Tell me, Friend MacDonald, this pleasing and touching interview was, I suppose, in the professor's study?"

"That's so."

"A fine room, is it not?"

"Very fine—very handsome indeed, Mr. Holmes."

"You sat in front of his writing desk?"

"Just so."

"Sun in your eyes and his face in the shadow?"

"Well, it was evening; but I mind that the lamp was turned on my face."

"It would be. Did you happen to observe a picture over the professor's head?"

"I don't miss much, Mr. Holmes. Maybe I learned that from you. Yes, I saw the picture—a young woman with her head on her hands, peeping at you sideways."

"That painting was by Jean Baptiste Greuze."

The inspector endeavoured to look interested.

"Jean Baptiste Greuze," Holmes continued, joining his finger tips and leaning well back in his chair, "was a French artist who flourished between the years 1750 and 1800. I allude, of course to his working career. Modern criticism has more than indorsed the high opinion formed of him by his contemporaries."

The inspector's eyes grew abstracted. "Hadn't we better—" he said.

"We are doing so," Holmes interrupted. "All that I am saying has a very direct and vital bearing upon what you have called the Birlstone Mystery. In fact, it may in a sense be called the very center of it."

MacDonald smiled feebly, and looked appealingly to me. "Your thoughts move a bit too quick for me, Mr. Holmes. You leave out a link or two, and I can't get over the gap. What in the whole wide world can be the connection between this dead painting man and the affair at Birlstone?"

"All knowledge comes useful to the detective," remarked Holmes. "Even the trivial fact that in the year 1865 a picture by Greuze entitled La Jeune Fille a l'Agneau fetched one million two hundred thousand francs—more than forty thousand pounds—at the Portalis sale may start a train of reflection in your mind."

It was clear that it did. The inspector looked honestly interested.

"I may remind you," Holmes continued, "that the professor's salary can be ascertained in several trustworthy books of reference. It is seven hundred a year."

"Then how could he buy—"

"Quite so! How could he?"

"Ay, that's remarkable," said the inspector thoughtfully. "Talk away, Mr. Holmes. I'm just loving it. It's fine!"

Holmes smiled. He was always warmed by genuine admiration—the characteristic of the real artist. "What about Birlstone?" he asked.

"We've time yet," said the inspector, glancing at his watch. "I've a cab at the door, and it won't take us twenty minutes to Victoria. But about this picture: I thought you told me once, Mr. Holmes, that you had never met Professor Moriarty."

"No, I never have."

"Then how do you know about his rooms?"

"Ah, that's another matter. I have been three times in his rooms, twice waiting for him under different pretexts and leaving before he came. Once—well, I can hardly tell about the once to an official detective. It was on the last occasion that I took the liberty of running over his papers—with the most unexpected results."

"You found something compromising?"

"Absolutely nothing. That was what amazed me. However, you have now seen the point of the picture. It shows him to be a very wealthy man. How did he acquire wealth? He is unmarried. His younger brother is a station master in the west of England. His chair is worth seven hundred a year. And he owns a Greuze."

"Well?"

"Surely the inference is plain."

"You mean that he has a great income and that he must earn it in an illegal fashion?"

"Exactly. Of course I have other reasons for thinking so—dozens of exiguous threads which lead vaguely up towards the center of the web where the poisonous, motionless creature is lurking. I only mention the Greuze because it brings the matter within the range of your own observation."

"Well, Mr. Holmes, I admit that what you say is interesting: it's more than interesting—it's just wonderful. But let us have it a little clearer if you can. Is it forgery, coining, burglary—where does the money come from?"

"Have you ever read of Jonathan Wild?"

"Well, the name has a familiar sound. Someone in a novel, was he not? I don't take much stock of detectives in novels—chaps that do things and never let you see how they do them. That's just inspiration: not business."

"Jonathan Wild wasn't a detective, and he wasn't in a novel. He was a master criminal, and he lived last century—1750 or thereabouts."

"Then he's no use to me. I'm a practical man."

"Mr. Mac, the most practical thing that you ever did in your life would be to shut yourself up for three months and read twelve hours a day at the annals of crime. Everything comes in circles—even Professor Moriarty. Jonathan Wild was the hidden force of the London criminals, to whom he sold his brains and his organization on a fifteen per cent. commission. The old wheel turns, and the same spoke comes up. It's all been done before, and will be again. I'll tell you one or two things about Moriarty which may interest you."

"You'll interest me, right enough."

"I happen to know who is the first link in his chain—a chain with this Napoleon-gone-wrong at one end, and a hundred broken fighting men, pickpockets, blackmailers, and card sharpers at the other, with every sort of crime in between. His chief of staff is Colonel Sebastian Moran, as aloof and guarded and inaccessible to the law as himself. What do you think he pays him?"

"I'd like to hear."

"Six thousand a year. That's paying for brains, you see—the American business principle. I learned that detail quite by chance. It's more than the Prime Minister gets. That gives you an idea of Moriarty's gains and of the scale on which he works. Another point: I made it my business to hunt down some of Moriarty's checks lately—just common innocent checks that he pays his household bills with. They were drawn on six different banks. Does that make any impression on your mind?"

"Queer, certainly! But what do you gather from it?"

"That he wanted no gossip about his wealth. No single man should know what he had. I have no doubt that he has twenty banking accounts; the bulk of his fortune abroad in the Deutsche Bank or the Credit Lyonnais as likely as not. Sometime when you have a year or two to spare I commend to you the study of Professor Moriarty."

Inspector MacDonald had grown steadily more impressed as the conversation proceeded. He had lost himself in his interest. Now his practical Scotch intelligence brought him back with a snap to the matter in hand.

"He can keep, anyhow," said he. "You've got us side-tracked with your interesting anecdotes, Mr. Holmes. What really counts is your remark that there is some connection between the professor and the crime. That you get from the warning received through the man

Porlock. Can we for our present practical needs get any further than that?"

"We may form some conception as to the motives of the crime. It is, as I gather from your original remarks, an inexplicable, or at least an unexplained, murder. Now, presuming that the source of the crime is as we suspect it to be, there might be two different motives. In the first place, I may tell you that Moriarty rules with a rod of iron over his people. His discipline is tremendous. There is only one punishment in his code. It is death. Now we might suppose that this murdered man—this Douglas whose approaching fate was known by one of the arch-criminal's subordinates—had in some way betrayed the chief. His punishment followed, and would be known to all—if only to put the fear of death into them."

"Well, that is one suggestion, Mr. Holmes."

"The other is that it has been engineered by Moriarty in the ordinary course of business. Was there any robbery?"

"I have not heard."

"If so, it would, of course, be against the first hypothesis and in favour of the second. Moriarty may have been engaged to engineer it on a promise of part spoils, or he may have been paid so much down to manage it. Either is possible. But whichever it may be, or if it is some third combination, it is down at Birlstone that we must seek the solution. I know our man too well to suppose that he has left anything up here which may lead us to him."

"Then to Birlstone we must go!" cried MacDonald, jumping from his chair. "My word! it's later than I thought. I can give you, gentlemen, five minutes for preparation, and that is all."

"And ample for us both," said Holmes, as he sprang up and hastened to change from his dressing gown to his coat. "While we are on our way, Mr. Mac, I will ask you to be good enough to tell me all about it."

"All about it" proved to be disappointingly little, and yet there was enough to assure us that the case before us might well be worthy of the expert's closest attention. He brightened and rubbed his thin hands together as he listened to the meagre but remarkable details. A long series of sterile weeks lay behind us, and here at last there was a fitting object for those remarkable powers which, like all special gifts, become irksome to their owner when they are not in use. That razor brain blunted and rusted with inaction.

Sherlock Holmes's eyes glistened, his pale cheeks took a warmer hue, and his whole eager face shone with an inward light when the call for work reached him. Leaning forward in the cab, he listened intently to MacDonald's short sketch of the problem which awaited us in Sussex. The inspector was himself dependent, as he explained to us, upon a scribbled account forwarded to him by the milk train in the early hours of the morning. White Mason, the local officer, was a personal friend, and hence MacDonald had been notified much more promptly than is usual at Scotland Yard when provincials need their assistance. It is a very cold scent upon which the Metropolitan expert is generally asked to run.

"DEAR INSPECTOR MACDONALD [said the letter which he read to us]:

"Official requisition for your services is in separate envelope. This is for your private eye. Wire me what train in the morning you can get for Birlstone, and I will meet it—or have it met if I am too occupied. This case is a snorter. Don't waste a moment in getting started. If you can bring Mr. Holmes, please do so; for he will find something after his own heart. We would think the whole had been fixed up for theatrical effect if there wasn't a dead man in the middle of it. My word! it IS a snorter."

"Your friend seems to be no fool," remarked Holmes.

"No, sir, White Mason is a very live man, if I am any judge."

"Well, have you anything more?"

"Only that he will give us every detail when we meet."

"Then how did you get at Mr. Douglas and the fact that he had been horribly murdered?"

"That was in the inclosed official report. It didn't say 'horrible': that's not a recognized official term. It gave the name John Douglas. It mentioned that his injuries had been in the head, from the discharge of a shotgun. It also mentioned the hour of the alarm, which was close on to midnight last night. It added that the case was undoubtedly one of murder, but that no arrest had been made, and that the case was one which presented some very perplexing and extraordinary features. That's absolutely all we have at present, Mr. Holmes."

"Then, with your permission, we will leave it at that, Mr. Mac. The temptation to form premature theories upon insufficient data is the bane of our profession. I can see only two things for certain at present—a great brain in London, and a dead man in Sussex. It's the chain between that we are going to trace."

Chapter 3—The Tragedy of Birlstone

Now for a moment I will ask leave to remove my own insignificant personality and to describe events which occurred before we arrived upon the scene by the light of knowledge which came to us afterwards. Only in this way can I make the reader appreciate the people concerned and the strange setting in which their fate was cast.

The village of Birlstone is a small and very ancient cluster of half-timbered cottages on the northern border of the county of Sussex. For centuries it had remained unchanged; but within the last few years its picturesque appearance and situation have attracted a number of well-to-do residents, whose villas peep out from the woods around. These woods are locally supposed to be the extreme fringe of the great Weald forest, which thins away until it reaches the northern chalk downs. A number of small shops have come into being to meet the wants of the increased population; so there seems some prospect that Birlstone may soon grow from an ancient village into a modern town. It is the center for a considerable area of country, since Tunbridge Wells, the nearest place of importance, is ten or twelve miles to the eastward, over the borders of Kent.

About half a mile from the town, standing in an old park famous for its huge beech trees, is the ancient Manor House of Birlstone. Part of this venerable building dates back to the time of the first crusade, when Hugo de Capus built a fortalice in the center of the estate, which had been granted to him by the Red King.

This was destroyed by fire in 1543, and some of its smoke-blackened corner stones were used when, in Jacobean times, a brick country house rose upon the ruins of the feudal castle.

The Manor House, with its many gables and its small diamond-paned windows, was still much as the builder had left it in the early seventeenth century. Of the double moats which had guarded its more warlike predecessor, the outer had been allowed to dry up, and served the humble function of a kitchen garden. The inner one was still there, and lay forty feet in breadth, though now only a few feet in depth, round the whole house. A small stream fed it and continued beyond it, so that the sheet of water, though turbid, was never ditchlike or unhealthy. The ground floor windows were within a foot of the surface of the water.

The only approach to the house was over a drawbridge, the chains and windlass of which had long been rusted and broken. The latest tenants of the Manor House had, however, with characteristic energy, set this right, and the drawbridge was not only capable of being raised, but actually was raised every evening and lowered every morning. By thus renewing the custom of the old feudal days the Manor House was converted into an island during the night—a fact which had a very direct bearing upon the mystery which was soon to engage the attention of all England.

The house had been untenanted for some years and was threatening to moulder into a picturesque decay when the Douglases took possession of it. This family consisted of only two individuals—John Douglas and his wife. Douglas was a remarkable man, both in character and in person. In age he may have been about fifty, with a strong-jawed, rugged face, a grizzling moustache, peculiarly keen gray eyes, and a wiry, vigorous figure which had lost nothing of the strength and activity of youth. He was cheery and genial to all, but somewhat offhand in his manners, giving the impression that he had seen life in social strata on some far lower horizon than the county society of Sussex.

Yet, though looked at with some curiosity and reserve by his more cultivated neighbours, he soon acquired a great popularity among the villagers, subscribing handsomely to all local objects, and attending their smoking concerts and other functions, where, having a remarkably rich tenor voice, he was always ready to oblige with an excellent song. He appeared to have plenty of money, which was said to have been gained in the California gold fields, and it was clear from his own talk and that of his wife that he had spent a part of his life in America.

The good impression which had been produced by his generosity and by his democratic manners was increased by a reputation gained for utter indifference to danger. Though a wretched rider, he turned out at every meet, and took the most amazing falls in his determination to hold his own with the best. When the vicarage caught fire he distinguished himself also by the fearlessness with which he reentered the building to save property, after the local fire brigade had given it up as impossible. Thus it came about that John Douglas of the Manor House had within five years won himself quite a reputation in Birlstone.

His wife, too, was popular with those who had made her acquaintance; though, after the English fashion, the callers upon a stranger who settled in the county without introductions were few and far between. This mattered the less to her, as she was retiring by disposition, and very much absorbed, to all appearance, in her husband and her domestic duties. It was known that she was an English lady who had met Mr. Douglas in London, he being at that time a widower. She was a beautiful woman, tall, dark, and slender, some twenty years younger than her husband; a disparity which seemed in no wise to mar the contentment of their family life.

It was remarked sometimes, however, by those who knew them best, that the confidence between the two did not appear to be complete, since the wife was either very reticent about her husband's past life, or else, as seemed more likely, was imperfectly informed about it. It had also been noted and commented upon by a few observant people that there were signs sometimes of some nerve-strain upon the part of Mrs. Douglas, and that she would display acute uneasiness if her absent husband should ever be particularly late in his return. On a quiet countryside, where all gossip is welcome, this weakness of the lady of the Manor House did not pass without remark, and it bulked larger upon people's memory when the events arose which gave it a very special significance.

There was yet another individual whose residence under that roof was, it is true, only an intermittent one, but whose presence at the time of the strange happenings which will now be narrated brought his name prominently before the public. This was Cecil James Barker, of Hales Lodge, Hampstead.

Cecil Barker's tall, loose-jointed figure was a familiar one in the main street of Birlstone village; for he was a frequent and welcome visitor at the Manor House. He was the more noticed as being the only friend of the past unknown life of Mr. Douglas who was ever seen in his new English surroundings. Barker was himself an undoubted Englishman; but by his remarks it was clear that he had first known Douglas in America and had there lived on intimate terms with him. He appeared to be a man of considerable wealth, and was reputed to be a bachelor.

In age he was rather younger than Douglas—forty-five at the most—a tall, straight, broad-chested fellow with a clean-shaved, prize-fighter face, thick, strong, black eyebrows, and a pair of masterful black eyes which might, even without the aid of his very capable hands, clear a way for him through a hostile crowd. He neither rode nor shot, but spent his days in wandering round the old village with his pipe in his mouth, or in driving with his host, or in his absence with his hostess, over the beautiful countryside. "An easy-going, free-handed gentleman," said Ames, the butler. "But, my word! I had rather not be the man that crossed him!" He was cordial and intimate with Douglas, and he was no less friendly with his wife—a friendship which more than once seemed to cause some irritation to the husband, so that even the servants were able to perceive his annoyance. Such was the third person who was one of the family when the catastrophe occurred.

As to the other denizens of the old building, it will suffice out of a large household to mention the prim, respectable, and capable Ames, and Mrs. Allen, a buxom and cheerful person, who relieved the lady of some of her household cares. The other six servants in the house bear no relation to the events of the night of January 6th.

It was at eleven forty-five that the first alarm reached the small local police station, in charge of Sergeant Wilson of the Sussex Constabulary. Cecil Barker, much excited, had rushed up to the door and pealed furiously upon the bell. A terrible tragedy had occurred at the Manor House, and John Douglas had been murdered. That was the breathless burden of his message. He had hurried back to the house, followed within a few minutes by the police sergeant, who arrived at the scene of the crime a little after twelve o'clock, after taking prompt steps to warn the county authorities that something serious was afoot.

On reaching the Manor House, the sergeant had found the drawbridge down, the windows lighted up, and the whole household in a state of wild confusion and alarm. The white-faced servants were huddling together in the hall, with the frightened butler wringing his hands in the doorway. Only Cecil Barker seemed to be master of himself and his emotions; he had opened the door which was nearest to the entrance and he had beckoned to the sergeant to follow him. At that moment there arrived Dr. Wood, a brisk and capable general practitioner from the village. The three men entered the fatal room together, while the horror-stricken butler followed at their heels, closing the door behind him to shut out the terrible scene from the maid servants.

The dead man lay on his back, sprawling with outstretched limbs in the center of the room. He was clad only in a pink dressing gown, which covered his night clothes. There were carpet slippers on his bare feet. The doctor knelt beside him and held down the hand lamp which had stood on the table. One glance at the victim was enough to show the healer that his presence could be dispensed with. The man had been horribly injured. Lying across his chest was a curious weapon, a shotgun with the barrel sawed off a foot in front of the triggers. It was clear that this had been fired at close range and that he had received the whole charge in the face, blowing his head almost to pieces. The triggers had been wired together, so as to make the simultaneous discharge more destructive.

The country policeman was unnerved and troubled by the tremendous responsibility which had come so suddenly upon him. "We will touch nothing until my superiors arrive," he said in a hushed voice, staring in horror at the dreadful head.

"Nothing has been touched up to now," said Cecil Barker. "I'll answer for that. You see it all exactly as I found it."

"When was that?" The sergeant had drawn out his notebook.

"It was just half-past eleven. I had not begun to undress, and I was sitting by the fire in my bedroom when I heard the report. It was not very loud—it seemed to be muffled. I rushed down—I don't suppose it was thirty seconds before I was in the room."

"Was the door open?"

"Yes, it was open. Poor Douglas was lying as you see him. His bedroom candle was burning on the table. It was I who lit the lamp some minutes afterward."

"Did you see no one?"

"No. I heard Mrs. Douglas coming down the stair behind me, and I rushed out to prevent her from seeing this dreadful sight. Mrs. Allen, the housekeeper, came and took her away. Ames had arrived, and we ran back into the room once more."

"But surely I have heard that the drawbridge is kept up all night."

"Yes, it was up until I lowered it."

"Then how could any murderer have got away? It is out of the question! Mr. Douglas must have shot himself."

"That was our first idea. But see!" Barker drew aside the curtain, and showed that the long, diamond-paned window was open to its full extent. "And look at this!" He held the lamp down and illuminated a smudge of blood like the mark of a boot-sole upon the wooden sill. "Someone has stood there in getting out."

"You mean that someone waded across the moat?"

"Exactly!"

"Then if you were in the room within half a minute of the crime, he must have been in the water at that very moment."

"I have not a doubt of it. I wish to heaven that I had rushed to the window! But the curtain screened it, as you can see, and so it never occurred to me. Then I heard the step of Mrs. Douglas, and I could not let her enter the room. It would have been too horrible."

"Horrible enough!" said the doctor, looking at the shattered head and the terrible marks which surrounded it. "I've never seen such injuries since the Birlstone railway smash."

"But, I say," remarked the police sergeant, whose slow, bucolic common sense was still pondering the open window. "It's all very well your saying that a man escaped by wading this moat, but what I ask you is, how did he ever get into the house at all if the bridge was up?"

"Ah, that's the question," said Barker.

"At what o'clock was it raised?"

"It was nearly six o'clock," said Ames, the butler.

"I've heard," said the sergeant, "that it was usually raised at sunset. That would be nearer half-past four than six at this time of year."

"Mrs. Douglas had visitors to tea," said Ames. "I couldn't raise it until they went. Then I wound it up myself."

"Then it comes to this," said the sergeant: "If anyone came from outside—IF they did—they must have got in across the bridge before six and been in hiding ever since, until Mr. Douglas came into the room after eleven."

"That is so! Mr. Douglas went round the house every night the last thing before he turned in to see that the lights were right. That brought him in here. The man was waiting and shot him. Then he got away through the window and left his gun behind him. That's how I read it; for nothing else will fit the facts."

The sergeant picked up a card which lay beside the dead man on the floor. The initials V.V. and under them the number 341 were rudely scrawled in ink upon it.

"What's this?" he asked, holding it up.

Barker looked at it with curiosity. "I never noticed it before," he said. "The murderer must have left it behind him."

"V.V.—341. I can make no sense of that."

The sergeant kept turning it over in his big fingers. "What's V.V.? Somebody's initials, maybe. What have you got there, Dr. Wood?"

It was a good-sized hammer which had been lying on the rug in front of the fireplace—a substantial, workmanlike hammer. Cecil Barker pointed to a box of brass-headed nails upon the mantelpiece.

"Mr. Douglas was altering the pictures yesterday," he said. "I saw him myself, standing upon that chair and fixing the big picture above it. That accounts for the hammer."

"We'd best put it back on the rug where we found it," said the sergeant, scratching his puzzled head in his perplexity. "It will want the best brains in the force to get to the bottom of this thing. It will be a London job before it is finished." He raised the hand lamp and walked slowly round the room. "Hullo!" he cried, excitedly, drawing the window curtain to one side. "What o'clock were those curtains drawn?"

"When the lamps were lit," said the butler. "It would be shortly after four."

"Someone had been hiding here, sure enough." He held down the light, and the marks of muddy boots were very visible in the corner. "I'm bound to say this bears out your theory, Mr. Barker. It looks as if the man got into the house after four when the curtains were drawn, and before six when the bridge was raised. He slipped into this room, because it was the first that he saw. There was no other place where he could hide, so he popped in behind this curtain. That all seems clear enough. It is likely that his main idea was to burgle the house; but Mr. Douglas chanced to come upon him, so he murdered him and escaped."

"That's how I read it," said Barker. "But, I say, aren't we wasting precious time? Couldn't we start out and scout the country before the fellow gets away?"

The sergeant considered for a moment.

"There are no trains before six in the morning; so he can't get away by rail. If he goes by road with his legs all dripping, it's odds that someone will notice him.

Anyhow, I can't leave here myself until I am relieved. But I think none of you should go until we see more clearly how we all stand."

The doctor had taken the lamp and was narrowly scrutinizing the body. "What's this mark?" he asked. "Could this have any connection with the crime?"

The dead man's right arm was thrust out from his dressing gown, and exposed as high as the elbow. About halfway up the forearm was a curious brown design, a triangle inside a circle, standing out in vivid relief upon the lard-coloured skin.

"It's not tattooed," said the doctor, peering through his glasses. "I never saw anything like it. The man has been branded at some time as they brand cattle. What is the meaning of this?"

"I don't profess to know the meaning of it," said Cecil Barker; "but I have seen the mark on Douglas many times this last ten years."

"And so have I," said the butler. "Many a time when the master has rolled up his sleeves I have noticed that very mark. I've often wondered what it could be."

"Then it has nothing to do with the crime, anyhow," said the sergeant. "But it's a rum thing all the same. Everything about this case is rum. Well, what is it now?"

The butler had given an exclamation of astonishment and was pointing at the dead man's outstretched hand.

"They've taken his wedding ring!" he gasped.

"What!"

"Yes, indeed. Master always wore his plain gold wedding ring on the little finger of his left hand. That ring with the rough nugget on it was above it, and the twisted snake ring on the third finger. There's the nugget and there's the snake, but the wedding ring is gone."

"He's right," said Barker.

"Do you tell me," said the sergeant, "that the wedding ring was BELOW the other?"

"Always!"

"Then the murderer, or whoever it was, first took off this ring you call the nugget ring, then the wedding ring, and afterwards put the nugget ring back again."

"That is so!"

The worthy country policeman shook his head. "Seems to me the sooner we get London on to this case the better," said he. "White Mason is a smart man. No local job has ever been too much for White Mason. It won't be long now before he is here to help us. But I expect we'll have to look to London before we are through. Anyhow, I'm not ashamed to say that it is a deal too thick for the likes of me."

Chapter 4—Darkness

At three in the morning the chief Sussex detective, obeying the urgent call from Sergeant Wilson of Birlstone, arrived from headquarters in a light dog-cart behind a breathless trotter. By the five-forty train in the morning he had sent his message to Scotland Yard, and he was at the Birlstone station at twelve o'clock to welcome us. White Mason was a quiet, comfortable-looking person in a loose tweed suit, with a clean-shaved, ruddy face, a stoutish body, and powerful bandy legs adorned with gaiters, looking like a small farmer, a retired gamekeeper, or anything upon earth except a very favourable specimen of the provincial criminal officer.

"A real downright snorter, Mr. MacDonald!" he kept repeating. "We'll have the pressmen down like flies when they understand it. I'm hoping we will get our work done before they get poking their noses into it and messing up all the trails. There has been nothing like this that I can remember. There are some bits that will come home to you, Mr. Holmes, or I am mistaken. And you also, Dr. Watson; for the medicos will have a word to say before we finish. Your room is at the Westville Arms. There's no other place; but I hear that it is clean and good. The man will carry your bags. This way, gentlemen, if you please."

He was a very bustling and genial person, this Sussex detective. In ten minutes we had all found our quarters. In ten more we were seated in the parlour of the inn and being treated to a rapid sketch of those events which have been outlined in the previous chapter.

MacDonald made an occasional note; while Holmes sat absorbed, with the expression of surprised and reverent admiration with which the botanist surveys the rare and precious bloom.

"Remarkable!" he said, when the story was unfolded, "most remarkable! I can hardly recall any case where the features have been more peculiar."

"I thought you would say so, Mr. Holmes," said White Mason in great delight. "We're well up with the times in Sussex. I've told you now how matters were, up to the time when I took over from Sergeant Wilson between three and four this morning. My word! I made the old mare go! But I need not have been in such a hurry, as it turned out; for there was nothing immediate that I could do. Sergeant Wilson had all the facts. I checked them and considered them and maybe added a few of my own."

"What were they?" asked Holmes eagerly.

"Well, I first had the hammer examined. There was Dr. Wood there to help me. We found no signs of violence upon it. I was hoping that if Mr. Douglas defended himself with the hammer, he might have left his mark upon the murderer before he dropped it on the mat. But there was no stain."

"That, of course, proves nothing at all," remarked Inspector MacDonald. "There has been many a hammer murder and no trace on the hammer."

"Quite so. It doesn't prove it wasn't used. But there might have been stains, and that would have helped us. As a matter of fact there were none. Then I examined the gun. They were buckshot cartridges, and, as Sergeant Wilson pointed out, the triggers were wired together so that, if you pulled on the hinder one, both barrels were discharged. Whoever fixed that up had made up his mind that he was going to take no chances of missing his man. The sawed gun was not more than two foot long—one could carry it easily under one's coat. There was no complete maker's name; but the printed letters P-E-N were on the fluting between the barrels, and the rest of the name had been cut off by the saw."

"A big P with a flourish above it, E and N smaller?" asked Holmes.

"Exactly."

"Pennsylvania Small Arms Company—well-known American firm," said Holmes.

White Mason gazed at my friend as the little village practitioner looks at the Harley Street specialist who by a word can solve the difficulties that perplex him.

"That is very helpful, Mr. Holmes. No doubt you are right. Wonderful! Wonderful! Do you carry the names of all the gun makers in the world in your memory?"

Holmes dismissed the subject with a wave.

"No doubt it is an American shotgun," White Mason continued. "I seem to have read that a sawed-off shotgun is a weapon used in some parts of America. Apart from the name upon the barrel, the idea had occurred to me. There is some evidence then, that this man who entered the house and killed its master was an American."

MacDonald shook his head. "Man, you are surely travelling overfast," said he. "I have heard no evidence yet that any stranger was ever in the house at all."

"The open window, the blood on the sill, the queer card, the marks of boots in the corner, the gun!"

"Nothing there that could not have been arranged. Mr. Douglas was an American, or had lived long in America. So had Mr. Barker. You don't need to import an American from outside in order to account for American doings."

"Ames, the butler—"

"What about him? Is he reliable?"

"Ten years with Sir Charles Chandos—as solid as a rock. He has been with Douglas ever since he took the Manor House five years ago. He has never seen a gun of this sort in the house."

"The gun was made to conceal. That's why the barrels were sawed. It would fit into any box. How could he swear there was no such gun in the house?"

"Well, anyhow, he had never seen one."

MacDonald shook his obstinate Scotch head. "I'm not convinced yet that there was ever anyone in the house," said he. "I'm asking you to conseedar" (his accent became more Aberdonian as he lost himself in his argument) "I'm asking you to conseedar what it involves if you suppose that this gun was ever brought into the house, and that all these strange things were done by a person from outside. Oh, man, it's just inconceivable! It's clean against common sense! I put it to you, Mr. Holmes, judging it by what we have heard."

"Well, state your case, Mr. Mac," said Holmes in his most judicial style.

"The man is not a burglar, supposing that he ever existed. The ring business and the card point to premeditated murder for some private reason. Very good. Here is a man who slips into a house with the deliberate intention of committing murder. He knows, if he knows anything, that he will have a deeficulty in making his escape, as the house is surrounded with water. What weapon would he choose? You would say the most silent in the world. Then he could hope when the deed was done to slip quickly from the window, to wade the moat, and to get away at his leisure. That's understandable. But is it understandable that he should go out of his way to bring with him the most noisy weapon he could select, knowing well that it will fetch every human being in the house to the spot as quick as they can run, and that it is all odds that he will be seen before he can get across the moat? Is that credible, Mr. Holmes?"

"Well, you put the case strongly," my friend replied thoughtfully. "It certainly needs a good deal of justification. May I ask, Mr. White Mason, whether you examined the farther side of the moat at once to see if there were any signs of the man having climbed out from the water?"

"There were no signs, Mr. Holmes. But it is a stone ledge, and one could hardly expect them."

"No tracks or marks?"

"None."

"Ha! Would there be any objection, Mr. White Mason, to our going down to the house at once? There may possibly be some small point which might be suggestive."

"I was going to propose it, Mr. Holmes; but I thought it well to put you in touch with all the facts before we go. I suppose if anything should strike you—" White Mason looked doubtfully at the amateur.

"I have worked with Mr. Holmes before," said Inspector MacDonald. "He plays the game."

"My own idea of the game, at any rate," said Holmes, with a smile. "I go into a case to help the ends of justice and the work of the police. If I have ever separated myself from the official force, it is because they have first separated themselves from me. I have no wish ever to score at their expense. At the same time, Mr. White Mason, I claim the right to work in my own way and give my results at my own time—complete rather than in stages."

"I am sure we are honoured by your presence and to show you all we know," said White Mason cordially. "Come along, Dr. Watson, and when the time comes we'll all hope for a place in your book."

We walked down the quaint village street with a row of pollarded elms on each side of it. Just beyond were two ancient stone pillars, weather-stained and lichen-blotched, bearing upon their summits a shapeless something which had once been the rampant lion of Capus of Birlstone. A short walk along the winding drive with such sward and oaks around it as one only sees in rural England, then a sudden turn, and the long, low Jacobean house of dingy, liver-coloured brick lay before us, with an old-fashioned garden of cut yews on each side of it. As we approached it, there was the wooden drawbridge and the beautiful broad moat as still and luminous as quicksilver in the cold, winter sunshine.

Three centuries had flowed past the old Manor House, centuries of births and of homecomings, of country dances and of the meetings of fox hunters. Strange that now in its old age this dark business should have cast its shadow upon the venerable walls! And yet those strange, peaked roofs and quaint, overhung gables were a fitting covering to grim and terrible intrigue. As I looked at the deep-set windows and the long sweep of the dull-coloured, water-lapped front, I felt that no more fitting scene could be set for such a tragedy.

"That's the window," said White Mason, "that one on the immediate right of the drawbridge. It's open just as it was found last night."

"It looks rather narrow for a man to pass."

"Well, it wasn't a fat man, anyhow. We don't need your deductions, Mr. Holmes, to tell us that. But you or I could squeeze through all right."

Holmes walked to the edge of the moat and looked across. Then he examined the stone ledge and the grass border beyond it.

"I've had a good look, Mr. Holmes," said White Mason. "There is nothing there, no sign that anyone has landed—but why should he leave any sign?"

"Exactly. Why should he? Is the water always turbid?"

"Generally about this colour. The stream brings down the clay."

"How deep is it?"

"About two feet at each side and three in the middle."

"So we can put aside all idea of the man having been drowned in crossing."

"No, a child could not be drowned in it."

We walked across the drawbridge, and were admitted by a quaint, gnarled, dried-up person, who was the butler, Ames. The poor old fellow was white and quivering from the shock. The village sergeant, a tall, formal, melancholy man, still held his vigil in the room of Fate. The doctor had departed.

"Anything fresh, Sergeant Wilson?" asked White Mason.

"No, sir."

"Then you can go home. You've had enough. We can send for you if we want you. The butler had better wait outside. Tell him to warn Mr. Cecil Barker, Mrs. Douglas, and the housekeeper that we may want a word with them presently. Now, gentlemen, perhaps you will allow me to give you the views I have formed first, and then you will be able to arrive at your own."

He impressed me, this country specialist. He had a solid grip of fact and a cool, clear, common-sense brain, which should take him some way in his profession. Holmes listened to him intently, with no sign of that impatience which the official exponent too often produced.

"Is it suicide, or is it murder—that's our first question, gentlemen, is it not? If it were suicide, then we have to believe that this man began by taking off his wedding ring and concealing it; that he then came down here in his dressing gown, trampled mud into a corner behind the curtain in order to give the idea someone had waited for him, opened the window, put blood on the—"

"We can surely dismiss that," said MacDonald.

"So I think. Suicide is out of the question. Then a murder has been done. What we have to determine is, whether it was done by someone outside or inside the house."

"Well, let's hear the argument."

"There are considerable difficulties both ways, and yet one or the other it must be. We will suppose first that some person or persons inside the house did the crime. They got this man down here at a time when everything was still and yet no one was asleep. They then did the deed with the queerest and noisiest weapon in the world so as to tell everyone what had happened—a weapon that was never seen in the house before. That does not seem a very likely start, does it?"

"No, it does not."

"Well, then, everyone is agreed that after the alarm was given only a minute at the most had passed before the whole household—not Mr. Cecil Barker alone, though he claims to have been the first, but Ames and all of them were on the spot. Do you tell me that in that time the guilty person managed to make footmarks in the corner, open the window, mark the sill with blood, take the wedding ring off the dead man's finger, and all the rest of it? It's impossible!"

"You put it very clearly," said Holmes. "I am inclined to agree with you."

"Well, then, we are driven back to the theory that it was done by someone from outside. We are still faced with some big difficulties; but anyhow they have ceased to be impossibilities. The man got into the house between four-thirty and six; that is to say, between dusk and the time when the bridge was raised. There had been some visitors, and the door was open; so there was nothing to prevent him. He may have been a common burglar, or he may have had some private grudge against Mr. Douglas. Since Mr. Douglas has spent most of his life in America, and this shotgun seems to be an American weapon, it would seem that the private grudge is the more likely theory. He slipped into this room because it was the first he came to, and he hid behind the curtain. There he remained until past eleven at night. At that time Mr. Douglas entered the room. It was a short interview, if there were any interview at all; for Mrs. Douglas declares that her husband had not left her more than a few minutes when she heard the shot."

"The candle shows that," said Holmes.

"Exactly. The candle, which was a new one, is not burned more than half an inch. He must have placed it on the table before he was attacked; otherwise, of course, it would have fallen when he fell. This shows that he was not attacked the instant that he entered the room. When Mr. Barker arrived the candle was lit and the lamp was out."

"That's all clear enough."

"Well, now, we can reconstruct things on those lines. Mr. Douglas enters the room. He puts down the candle. A man appears from behind the curtain. He is armed with this gun. He demands the wedding ring—Heaven only knows why, but so it must have been. Mr. Douglas gave it up. Then either in cold blood or in the course of a struggle—Douglas may have gripped the hammer that was found upon the mat—he shot Douglas in this horrible way. He dropped his gun and also it would seem this queer card—V.V. 341, whatever that may mean—and he made his escape through the window and across the moat at the very moment when Cecil Barker was discovering the crime. How's that, Mr. Holmes?"

"Very interesting, but just a little unconvincing."

"Man, it would be absolute nonsense if it wasn't that anything else is even worse!" cried MacDonald. "Somebody killed the man, and whoever it was I could clearly prove to you that he should have done it some other way. What does he mean by allowing his retreat to be cut off like that? What does he mean by using a shotgun when silence was his one chance of escape? Come, Mr. Holmes, it's up to you to give us a lead, since you say Mr. White Mason's theory is unconvincing."

Holmes had sat intently observant during this long discussion, missing no word that was said, with his keen eyes darting to right and to left, and his forehead wrinkled with speculation.

"I should like a few more facts before I get so far as a theory, Mr. Mac," said he, kneeling down beside the body. "Dear me! these injuries are really appalling. Can we have the butler in for a moment?... Ames, I understand that you have often seen this very unusual mark—a branded triangle inside a circle—upon Mr. Douglas's forearm?"

"Frequently, sir."

"You never heard any speculation as to what it meant?"

"No, sir."

"It must have caused great pain when it was inflicted. It is undoubtedly a burn. Now, I observe, Ames, that there is a small piece of plaster at the angle of Mr. Douglas's jaw. Did you observe that in life?"

"Yes, sir, he cut himself in shaving yesterday morning."

"Did you ever know him to cut himself in shaving before?"

"Not for a very long time, sir."

"Suggestive!" said Holmes. "It may, of course, be a mere coincidence, or it may point to some nervousness which would indicate that he had reason to apprehend danger. Had you noticed anything unusual in his conduct, yesterday, Ames?"

"It struck me that he was a little restless and excited, sir."

"Ha! The attack may not have been entirely unexpected. We do seem to make a little progress, do we not? Perhaps you would rather do the questioning, Mr. Mac?"

"No, Mr. Holmes, it's in better hands than mine."

"Well, then, we will pass to this card—V.V. 341. It is rough cardboard. Have you any of the sort in the house?"

"I don't think so."

Holmes walked across to the desk and dabbed a little ink from each bottle on to the blotting paper. "It was not printed in this room," he said; "this is black ink and the other purplish. It was done by a thick pen, and these are fine. No, it was done elsewhere, I should say. Can you make anything of the inscription, Ames?"

"No, sir, nothing."

"What do you think, Mr. Mac?"

"It gives me the impression of a secret society of some sort; the same with his badge upon the forearm."

"That's my idea, too," said White Mason.

"Well, we can adopt it as a working hypothesis and then see how far our difficulties disappear. An agent from such a society makes his way into the house, waits for Mr. Douglas, blows his head nearly off with this weapon, and escapes by wading the moat, after leaving a card beside the dead man, which will, when mentioned in the papers, tell other members of the society that vengeance has been done. That all hangs together. But why this gun, of all weapons?"

"Exactly."

"And why the missing ring?"

"Quite so."

"And why no arrest? It's past two now. I take it for granted that since dawn every constable within forty miles has been looking out for a wet stranger?"

"That is so, Mr. Holmes."

"Well, unless he has a burrow close by or a change of clothes ready, they can hardly miss him. And yet they HAVE missed him up to now!" Holmes had gone to the window and was examining with his lens the blood mark on the sill. "It is clearly the tread of a shoe. It is remarkably broad; a splay-foot, one would say. Curious, because, so far as one can trace any footmark in this mud-stained corner, one would say it was a more shapely sole. However, they are certainly very indistinct. What's this under the side table?"

"Mr. Douglas's dumb-bells," said Ames.

"Dumb-bell—there's only one. Where's the other?"

"I don't know, Mr. Holmes. There may have been only one. I have not noticed them for months."

"One dumb-bell—" Holmes said seriously; but his remarks were interrupted by a sharp knock at the door.

A tall, sunburned, capable-looking, clean-shaved man looked in at us. I had no difficulty in guessing that it was the Cecil Barker of whom I had heard. His masterful eyes travelled quickly with a questioning glance from face to face.

"Sorry to interrupt your consultation," said he, "but you should hear the latest news."

"An arrest?"

"No such luck. But they've found his bicycle. The fellow left his bicycle behind him. Come and have a look. It is within a hundred yards of the hall door."

We found three or four grooms and idlers standing in the drive inspecting a bicycle which had been drawn out from a clump of evergreens in which it had been concealed. It was a well used Rudge-Whitworth, splashed as from a considerable journey. There was a saddlebag with spanner and oilcan, but no clue as to the owner.

"It would be a grand help to the police," said the inspector, "if these things were numbered and registered. But we must be thankful for what we've got. If we can't find where he went to, at least we are likely to get where he came from. But what in the name of all that is wonderful made the fellow leave it behind? And how in the world has he got away without it? We don't seem to get a gleam of light in the case, Mr. Holmes."

"Don't we?" my friend answered thoughtfully. "I wonder!"

The Valley of Fear Summary and Analysis of Part I Chapters 1-4

Summary

Chapter 1

Watson narrates the tale. He begins with Sherlock Holmes lost in concept, looking at a letter from 'Porlock'. Watson asks who Porlock is, and Holmes explains it is a no-de-plume; Porlock is crucial in that he's linked to an influential guy: Professor Moriarty. Moriarty is unknown as a criminal to the public, but Holmes is aware of higher; however, anybody who attempts to solid aspersions on the first rate guy might be laughed at.

Watson nods in agreement and Holmes keeps, pronouncing Porlock has been a secret help to him a couple of times. He has now dispatched a sequence of numbers and letters with two words: 'Douglas' and 'Birlstone', the latter repeated twice. It is a cipher without a code.

Watson asks why there would be no code; Holmes believes it will arrive soon. Indeed, the web page quickly arrives, however while Holmes opens the letter they see that the anxious Porlock has written that he's going to not offer the code due to the fact he is underneath suspicion.

Watson rues that there's a mystery in the cipher that they will never recognize. Holmes is quiet, after which says that it relates to an e-book; he infers that Porlock assumed he'd have it. They deduce it need to be the most usually possessed e-book—an almanac (there are too many editions of the Bible, Watson's first wager).

They discover the proper almanac and the suitable pages and words on the way to determine that someone named Douglas is in threat, and a house of Birlstone is by some means concerned. Before they are able to parse these words tons similarly than acknowledging the hazard for this gentleman named Douglas, Alec MacDonald of Scotland Yard enters; he is a friend of Holmes's whom the detective had helped a few times inside the past, thereby incomes the young, sensible Scotsman's appreciate.

MacDonald greets Holmes and Watson and says there is new mischief afoot, however earlier than he can get similarly he sees the cipher on the table. His entire countenance fills with amazement and he sputters out his question of ways Holmes were given the cipher. After Holmes asks what's amiss; MacDonald says, dazed, Mr. Douglas of Birlstone became murdered remaining night.

Chapter 2

This is the type of second Holmes lives for. He appears composed and fascinated, greater intellectually excited than taken aback or horrified. He explains the heritage of the cipher to MacDonald, and whilst MacDonald says they need to discover Porlock Holmes states that this is impossible. Porlock is connected to Moriarty, he explains.

MacDonald smiles a piece and says the Yard thinks Holmes has a bee in his bonnet over the Professor. MacDonald had long past to peer the Professor himself and changed into struck by means of his solemn mien and erudition. Holmes laughs and asks if MacDonald befell to notice the painting with the aid of Jean Baptiste Greuze behind Moriarty's table. The inspector is harassed and says no. Holmes explains who Greuze is and the way valuable his artwork are; MacDonald wonders aloud how the Professor should have enough money it. That is the point, Holmes tells him, and they speculate about the man's illegal sports that procured his extremely good wealth. Holmes knows lots about Moriarty: he has many bank accounts, and need to have extravagant wealth on the way to pay, as an instance, his leader of workforce six thousand a 12 months.

The talk turns again to the murdered man, and the guys speculate that Douglas came afoul of Moriarty, who ruled over his people with an iron fist. They all conform to visit Birlstone. Mason requested MacDonald to carry Holmes.

Holmes muses aloud that there may be an extremely good mind in London and a useless man in Birlstone, and it's far their job to hint the connection among them.

Chapter 3

Watson narrates the history of the mystery as it stood earlier than they arrived.

The village of Birlstone is small and antique, however attracted a few well-to-do citizens who built stately villas in and at the outskirts of the woods. One of those is the Manor House, part of it as vintage because the First Crusade and other components added within the 1500s and 1600s. This unique domestic changed into effectively an island, as it had a drawbridge that went over a moat and become stored raised each night.

Only John Douglas and his spouse lived there. Douglas turned into fifty, imposing however genial. He became said to have earned cash in the gold fields in California. He had a great recognition and turned into reputedly detached to chance. His more youthful spouse turned into additionally popular, but become very absorbed in her husband and obligations of the home. Some people mentioned that she regarded annoying, and that there can also had been troubles between the two of them.

Another man lodged with them as properly: Cecil James Barker of Hales Lodge, Hampstead. A rich young bachelor, he had seemingly acknowledged Douglas in America. He changed into very friendly with both Douglasses, however there have been rumors approximately his closeness to the wife.

Ames the butler and Mrs. Allen the housekeeper have been the only other two people whose presence within the residence mattered that night time.

The events of the night are as a result: Cecil Barker rushed to the small police station near nighttime and stated Douglas changed into murdered. Sergeant Wilson accompanied him to Manor House, where the drawbridge changed into down and the home windows lit up. Dr. Wood, a local doctor, joined them.

The lifeless guy was on his lower back within the look at. A sawed-off shotgun fired at close variety had killed him. He wore simplest a pink dressing gown. There was one dumbbell in the room.

Barker defined that he had simply long past to bed whilst he heard the noise of the shot and got here down and saw Douglas mendacity there. He blew out the candle and lit the lamp. When Mrs. Douglas commenced to come down, he held her off. He lowered the drawbridge at that point.

Wilson requested if perhaps Douglas shot himself, however Barker said that while he idea that too at the beginning, he had found a smudge of blood at the windowsill. It appeared a person shot Douglas after which left through the window. The man might also have waded across the moat to get away. In phrases of while he got there, he should have arrived earlier that day and concealed.

Wilson observed something at the ground and collected a card classified 'V.V.—341'. Barker had now not but visible that, and become amazed.

There were muddy boot prints close to one of the different curtains, which Ames instructed them were drawn around 4.

Barker asked if they must attempt to discover the person because he possibly did not get too far. Wilson replied that there were no trains before six, so he couldn't have left with the aid of rail. Perhaps someone else might see him whilst the hunt began.

The medical doctor bent down and mentioned a mark that have been branded on Douglas's arm. It became a brown design with a triangle internal a circle; Barker stated he had visible it on Douglas in many instances those past ten years, but did not recognize what it intended.

The butler burst out all of sudden that Douglas's wedding ring become taken. Since it turned into the center ring among others, the killer should have taken them off and positioned them back on with a purpose to take the hoop. Wilson shook his head in amazement and said it changed into time to get White Mason right here on the case.

Chapter 4

Watson picks up the narrative of the cutting-edge. White Mason is a friendly, quiet, however successful guy. He explains to Holmes how he checked the hammer that changed into located close to the frame (there has been no evidence of it being involved inside the crime) and the gun, which had the initials P, E, and N on it.

Holmes informs them it's far an American gun put out by means of the Pennsylvania Small Arms Company; this information surprises and pleases Mason.

The institution speak the opportunity of whether an outsider changed into in the house, or if the murder became staged. MacDonald proffers his interpretation. He assumes the homicide changed into premeditated, but wonders why the killer would select this type of loud weapon. Holmes asks about signs and symptoms of someone hiking out of the moat, however there were none.

The guys stroll towards Manor House and Watson contemplates that the scene seems fit for a tragedy. As they close to the residence Mason points out the window and informs Holmes of the way shallow the moat is: 3 ft. at the inner most.

Ames admits the organization to the house. The verbal exchange returns to the murder. Suicide is dominated out, however the problem of the loud weapon remains. It appears not likely that the man or woman made the muddy footprint, opened the window, marked the sill, took the hoop off, and left before Cecil observed Douglas. Surely someone got here in in advance that day, concealed, after which killed Douglas, the use of the sawed-off shotgun because the murder become non-public. Douglas in all likelihood got here in, placed down the candle, struggled, grabbed the hammer, and turned into then shot. The guy left the cardboard and escaped throughout the moat.

Holmes listens; despite the fact that the men ask for his opinion, he demurs until he has extra data. He asks for Ames, and questions him. He inquiries about the mark, and Ames stated he had visible it earlier than. Ames additionally says Douglas changed into a bit greater nervous the last day he noticed him than standard.

After this line of questioning Holmes turns to the cardboard, which MacDonald says looks as if it belongs to a mystery society; he additionally considers the strangeness of the marriage ring and the truth that there has been no arrest but.

A knock sounds, and Cecil Barker interrupts to say they've discovered the killer's bicycle hidden in a clump of evergreens now not some distance off.

Analysis

The novel begins like the various tales of Sherlock Holmes: a case is provided, Holmes gets involved, and the details of the crime are laid out before the reader. However, midway through the novel a prime shift takes vicinity in that the backstory of one of the characters takes over; now we are two decades prior, in the coalfields of Pennsylvania, and coping with a band of rapacious and murderous Irish union men. It is an abrupt shift and one that disconcerted readers looking for more of the perspicacious British detective, but Doyle became working through his own issues with his Irish identification.

In these first few chapters, even though, we see the traditional duo of Holmes and Watson. Watson narrates the tale (even though Doyle considered now not making him the narrator) and, as consistent with typical for the Holmes canon, readers fashion of a portrait of the well-known detective thru the eyes of his buddy. Holmes comes across as comfortable, confident, ever sagacious, and sharp; he welcomes the new thriller and seems energized and vitalized with the aid of it. Critic Anthony Boucher (quoted in The Annotated Sherlock Holmes) says "this is a ripe, mature Holmes, free from external eccentricities...Here is Holmes in an appropriate questioning thoughts, in crypt-evaluation, in statement, in deduction...Holmes [is] at his most completely captivating...There is extra overt humor right here than is common...there's a positive fey excellent."

The first mystery (or, the thriller-inside-the-thriller) is the identity of Porlock and what Moriarty is probably as much as. It has been advised Porlock become really Mycroft, Sherlock Holmes's elder brother, but Doyle in no way stated this definitively. Porlock is shadowed in mystery and worry, and his connection to that most cunning of Holmes's enemies, Moriarty, is also ambiguous. Moriarty by no means makes a real look in the novel; as a substitute, he's fashioned through the comments of Holmes and MacDonald; this adds to the character's mystique, particularly as it will become clean that, without nearly any proof, he's indelibly linked to this example.

The second mystery is the actual case itself. What arguably makes the Sherlock Holmes collection so attractive is that readers have the opportunity to play detectives as well, the usage of Watson as their stand-in to survey the proof and then see if they could figure the case out. Here the proof may be without difficulty summed up: the lifeless frame, shot near-range through a sawed-off American shotgun; a stain of blood at the windowsill; muddy shoeprints near the windowsill; one dumbbell; a mysterious card close to the frame; a missing wedding ceremony ring; reports of the timing of the shot; a bicycle inside the hedges. Keen readers then select up on the bluster of Barker and the unusually emotionless conduct of Mrs. Douglas. Watson's encounter with the two in the lawn only adds to the rumors of Douglas's jealousy concerning their friendship.

Still extra clues start to gift themselves in terms of Douglas's past and the sense that he turned into beneath some form of darkish cloud. It is clear he got here to England to break out some form of persecution in America, and it's far connected with the shadowy "Valley of Fear." This ominous appellation is a bodily region in addition to a symbolic one in the experience that Douglas is psychologically stuck in that infernal valley.

Chapter 5—The People of the Drama

"Have you seen all you want of the study?" asked White Mason as we reentered the house.

"For the time," said the inspector, and Holmes nodded.

"Then perhaps you would now like to hear the evidence of some of the people in the house. We could use the dining room, Ames. Please come yourself first and tell us what you know."

The butler's account was a simple and a clear one, and he gave a convincing impression of sincerity. He had been engaged five years before, when Douglas first came to Birlstone. He understood that Mr. Douglas was a rich gentleman who had made his money in America. He had been a kind and considerate employer—not quite what Ames was used to, perhaps; but one can't have everything. He never saw any signs of apprehension in Mr. Douglas: on the contrary, he was the most fearless man he had ever known. He ordered the drawbridge to be pulled up every night because it was the ancient custom of the old house, and he liked to keep the old ways up.

Mr. Douglas seldom went to London or left the village; but on the day before the crime he had been shopping at Tunbridge Wells. He (Ames) had observed some restlessness and excitement on the part of Mr. Douglas that day; for he had seemed impatient and irritable, which was unusual with him. He had not gone to bed that night; but was in the pantry at the back of the house, putting away the silver, when he heard the bell ring violently. He heard no shot; but it was hardly possible he would, as the pantry and kitchens were at the very back of the house and there were several closed doors and a long passage between. The housekeeper had come out of her room, attracted by the violent ringing of the bell. They had gone to the front of the house together.

As they reached the bottom of the stairs he had seen Mrs. Douglas coming down it. No, she was not hurrying; it did not seem to him that she was particularly agitated. Just as she reached the bottom of the stair Mr. Barker had rushed out of the study. He had stopped Mrs. Douglas and begged her to go back.

"For God's sake, go back to your room!" he cried. "Poor Jack is dead! You can do nothing. For God's sake, go back!"

After some persuasion upon the stairs Mrs. Douglas had gone back. She did not scream. She made no outcry whatever. Mrs. Allen, the housekeeper, had taken her upstairs and stayed with her in the bedroom. Ames and Mr. Barker had then returned to the study, where they had found everything exactly as the police had seen it. The candle was not lit at that time; but the lamp was burning. They had looked out of the window; but the night was very dark and nothing could be seen or heard. They had then rushed out into the hall, where Ames had turned the windlass which lowered the drawbridge. Mr. Barker had then hurried off to get the police.

Such, in its essentials, was the evidence of the butler.

The account of Mrs. Allen, the housekeeper, was, so far as it went, a corroboration of that of her fellow servant. The housekeeper's room was rather nearer to the front of the house than the pantry in which Ames had been working. She was preparing to go to bed when the loud ringing of the bell had attracted her attention. She was a little hard of hearing. Perhaps that was why she had not heard the shot; but in any case the study was a long way off. She remembered hearing some sound which she imagined to be the slamming of a door. That was a good deal earlier—half an hour at least before the ringing of the bell. When Mr. Ames ran to the front she went with him. She saw Mr. Barker, very pale and excited, come out of the study. He intercepted Mrs. Douglas, who was coming down the stairs. He entreated her to go back, and she answered him, but what she said could not be heard.

"Take her up! Stay with her!" he had said to Mrs. Allen.

She had therefore taken her to the bedroom, and endeavoured to soothe her. She was greatly excited, trembling all over, but made no other attempt to go downstairs. She just sat in her dressing gown by her bedroom fire, with her head sunk in her hands. Mrs. Allen stayed with her most of the night. As to the other servants, they had all gone to bed, and the alarm did not reach them until just before the police arrived. They slept at the extreme back of the house, and could not possibly have heard anything.

So far the housekeeper could add nothing on cross-examination save lamentations and expressions of amazement.

Cecil Barker succeeded Mrs. Allen as a witness. As to the occurrences of the night before, he had very little to add to what he had already told the police. Personally, he was convinced that the murderer had escaped by the window. The bloodstain was conclusive, in his opinion, on that point. Besides, as the bridge was up, there was no other possible way of escaping. He could not explain what had become of the assassin or why he had not taken his bicycle, if it were indeed his. He could not possibly have been drowned in the moat, which was at no place more than three feet deep.

In his own mind he had a very definite theory about the murder. Douglas was a reticent man, and there were some chapters in his life of which he never spoke. He had emigrated to America when he was a very young man. He had prospered well, and Barker had first met him in California, where they had become partners in a successful mining claim at a place called Benito Canyon. They had done very well; but Douglas had suddenly sold out and started for England. He was a widower at that time. Barker had afterwards realized his money and come to live in London. Thus they had renewed their friendship.

Douglas had given him the impression that some danger was hanging over his head, and he had always looked upon his sudden departure from California, and also his renting a house in so quiet a place in England, as being connected with this peril. He imagined that some secret society, some implacable organization, was on Douglas's track, which would never rest until it killed him. Some remarks of his had given him this idea; though he had never told him what the society was, nor how he had come to offend it. He could only suppose that the legend upon the placard had some reference to this secret society.

"How long were you with Douglas in California?" asked Inspector MacDonald.

"Five years altogether."

"He was a bachelor, you say?"

"A widower."

"Have you ever heard where his first wife came from?"

"No, I remember his saying that she was of German extraction, and I have seen her portrait. She was a very beautiful woman. She died of typhoid the year before I met him."

"You don't associate his past with any particular part of America?"

"I have heard him talk of Chicago. He knew that city well and had worked there. I have heard him talk of the coal and iron districts. He had travelled a good deal in his time."

"Was he a politician? Had this secret society to do with politics?"

"No, he cared nothing about politics."

"You have no reason to think it was criminal?"

"On the contrary, I never met a straighter man in my life."

"Was there anything curious about his life in California?"

"He liked best to stay and to work at our claim in the mountains. He would never go where other men were if he could help it. That's why I first thought that someone was after him. Then when he left so suddenly for Europe I made sure that it was so. I believe that he had a warning of some sort. Within a week of his leaving half a dozen men were inquiring for him."

"What sort of men?"

"Well, they were a mighty hard-looking crowd. They came up to the claim and wanted to know where he was. I told them that he was gone to Europe and that I did not know where to find him. They meant him no good—it was easy to see that."

"Were these men Americans—Californians?"

"Well, I don't know about Californians. They were Americans, all right. But they were not miners. I don't know what they were, and was very glad to see their backs."

"That was six years ago?"

"Nearer seven."

"And then you were together five years in California, so that this business dates back not less than eleven years at the least?"

"That is so."

"It must be a very serious feud that would be kept up with such earnestness for as long as that. It would be no light thing that would give rise to it."

"I think it shadowed his whole life. It was never quite out of his mind."

"But if a man had a danger hanging over him, and knew what it was, don't you think he would turn to the police for protection?"

"Maybe it was some danger that he could not be protected against. There's one thing you should know. He always went about armed. His revolver was never out of his pocket. But, by bad luck, he was in his dressing gown and had left it in the bedroom last night. Once the bridge was up, I guess he thought he was safe."

"I should like these dates a little clearer," said MacDonald. "It is quite six years since Douglas left California. You followed him next year, did you not?"

"That is so."

"And he had been married five years. You must have returned about the time of his marriage."

"About a month before. I was his best man."

"Did you know Mrs. Douglas before her marriage?"

"No, I did not. I had been away from England for ten years."

"But you have seen a good deal of her since."

Barker looked sternly at the detective. "I have seen a good deal of HIM since," he answered. "If I have seen her, it is because you cannot visit a man without knowing his wife. If you imagine there is any connection—"

"I imagine nothing, Mr. Barker. I am bound to make every inquiry which can bear upon the case. But I mean no offense."

"Some inquiries are offensive," Barker answered angrily.

"It's only the facts that we want. It is in your interest and everyone's interest that they should be cleared up. Did Mr. Douglas entirely approve your friendship with his wife?"

Barker grew paler, and his great, strong hands were clasped convulsively together. "You have no right to ask such questions!" he cried. "What has this to do with the matter you are investigating?"

"I must repeat the question."

"Well, I refuse to answer."

"You can refuse to answer; but you must be aware that your refusal is in itself an answer, for you would not refuse if you had not something to conceal."

Barker stood for a moment with his face set grimly and his strong black eyebrows drawn low in intense thought. Then he looked up with a smile. "Well, I guess you gentlemen are only doing your clear duty after all, and I have no right to stand in the way of it. I'd only ask you not to worry Mrs. Douglas over this matter; for she has enough upon her just now. I may tell you that poor Douglas had just one fault in the world, and that was his jealousy. He was fond of me—no man could be fonder of a friend. And he was devoted to his wife. He loved me to come here, and was forever sending for me. And yet if his wife and I talked together or there seemed any sympathy between us, a kind of wave of jealousy would pass over him, and he would be off the handle and saying the wildest things in a moment. More than once I've sworn off coming for that reason, and then he would write me such penitent, imploring letters that I just had to. But you can take it from me, gentlemen, if it was my last word, that no man ever had a more loving, faithful wife—and I can say also no friend could be more loyal than I!"

It was spoken with fervour and feeling, and yet Inspector MacDonald could not dismiss the subject.

"You are aware," said he, "that the dead man's wedding ring has been taken from his finger?"

"So it appears," said Barker.

"What do you mean by 'appears'? You know it as a fact."

The man seemed confused and undecided. "When I said 'appears' I meant that it was conceivable that he had himself taken off the ring."

"The mere fact that the ring should be absent, whoever may have removed it, would suggest to anyone's mind, would it not, that the marriage and the tragedy were connected?"

Barker shrugged his broad shoulders. "I can't profess to say what it means," he answered. "But if you mean to hint that it could reflect in any way upon this lady's honour"—his eyes blazed for an instant, and then with an evident effort he got a grip upon his own emotions—"well, you are on the wrong track, that's all."

"I don't know that I've anything else to ask you at present," said MacDonald, coldly.

"There was one small point," remarked Sherlock Holmes. "When you entered the room there was only a candle lighted on the table, was there not?"

"Yes, that was so."

"By its light you saw that some terrible incident had occurred?"

"Exactly."

"You at once rang for help?"

"Yes."

"And it arrived very speedily?"

"Within a minute or so."

"And yet when they arrived they found that the candle was out and that the lamp had been lighted. That seems very remarkable."

Again Barker showed some signs of indecision. "I don't see that it was remarkable, Mr. Holmes," he answered after a pause. "The candle threw a very bad light. My first thought was to get a better one. The lamp was on the table; so I lit it."

"And blew out the candle?"

"Exactly."

Holmes asked no further question, and Barker, with a deliberate look from one to the other of us, which had, as it seemed to me, something of defiance in it, turned and left the room.

Inspector MacDonald had sent up a note to the effect that he would wait upon Mrs. Douglas in her room; but she had replied that she would meet us in the dining room. She entered now, a tall and beautiful woman of thirty, reserved and self-possessed to a remarkable degree, very different from the tragic and distracted figure I had pictured. It is true that her face was pale and drawn, like that of one who has endured a great shock; but her manner was composed, and the finely moulded hand which she rested upon the edge of the table was as steady as my own. Her sad, appealing eyes travelled from one to the other of us with a curiously inquisitive expression. That questioning gaze transformed itself suddenly into abrupt speech.

"Have you found anything out yet?" she asked.

Was it my imagination that there was an undertone of fear rather than of hope in the question?

"We have taken every possible step, Mrs. Douglas," said the inspector. "You may rest assured that nothing will be neglected."

"Spare no money," she said in a dead, even tone. "It is my desire that every possible effort should be made."

"Perhaps you can tell us something which may throw some light upon the matter."

"I fear not; but all I know is at your service."

"We have heard from Mr. Cecil Barker that you did not actually see—that you were never in the room where the tragedy occurred?"

"No, he turned me back upon the stairs. He begged me to return to my room."

"Quite so. You had heard the shot, and you had at once come down."

"I put on my dressing gown and then came down."

"How long was it after hearing the shot that you were stopped on the stair by Mr. Barker?"

"It may have been a couple of minutes. It is so hard to reckon time at such a moment. He implored me not to go on. He assured me that I could do nothing. Then Mrs. Allen, the housekeeper, led me upstairs again. It was all like some dreadful dream."

"Can you give us any idea how long your husband had been downstairs before you heard the shot?"

"No, I cannot say. He went from his dressing room, and I did not hear him go. He did the round of the house every night, for he was nervous of fire. It is the only thing that I have ever known him nervous of."

"That is just the point which I want to come to, Mrs. Douglas. You have known your husband only in England, have you not?"

"Yes, we have been married five years."

"Have you heard him speak of anything which occurred in America and might bring some danger upon him?"

Mrs. Douglas thought earnestly before she answered. "Yes," she said at last, "I have always felt that there was a danger hanging over him. He refused to discuss it with me. It was not from want of confidence in me—there was the most complete love and confidence between us—but it was out of his desire to keep all alarm away from me. He thought I should brood over it if I knew all, and so he was silent."

"How did you know it, then?"

Mrs. Douglas's face lit with a quick smile. "Can a husband ever carry about a secret all his life and a woman who loves him have no suspicion of it? I knew it by his refusal to talk about some episodes in his American life. I knew it by certain precautions he took. I knew it by certain words he let fall. I knew it by the way he looked at unexpected strangers. I was perfectly certain that he had some powerful enemies, that he believed they were on his track, and that he was always on his guard against them. I was so sure of it that for years I have been terrified if ever he came home later than was expected."

"Might I ask," asked Holmes, "what the words were which attracted your attention?"

"The Valley of Fear," the lady answered. "That was an expression he has used when I questioned him. 'I have been in the Valley of Fear. I am not out of it yet.'—'Are we never to get out of the Valley of Fear?' I have asked him when I have seen him more serious than usual. 'Sometimes I think that we never shall,' he has answered."

"Surely you asked him what he meant by the Valley of Fear?"

"I did; but his face would become very grave and he would shake his head. 'It is bad enough that one of us should have been in its shadow,' he said. 'Please God it shall never fall upon you!' It was some real valley in which he had lived and in which something terrible had occurred to him, of that I am certain; but I can tell you no more."

"And he never mentioned any names?"

"Yes, he was delirious with fever once when he had his hunting accident three years ago. Then I remember that there was a name that came continually to his lips. He spoke it with anger and a sort of horror. McGinty was the name—Body master McGinty. I asked him when he recovered who Body master McGinty was, and whose body he was master of. 'Never of mine, thank God!' he answered with a laugh, and that was all I could get from him. But there is a connection between Body master McGinty and the Valley of Fear."

"There is one other point," said Inspector MacDonald. "You met Mr. Douglas in a boarding house in London, did you not, and became engaged to him there? Was there any romance, anything secret or mysterious, about the wedding?"

"There was romance. There is always romance. There was nothing mysterious."

"He had no rival?"

"No, I was quite free."

"You have heard, no doubt, that his wedding ring has been taken. Does that suggest anything to you? Suppose that some enemy of his old life had tracked him down and committed this crime, what possible reason could he have for taking his wedding ring?"

For an instant I could have sworn that the faintest shadow of a smile flickered over the woman's lips.

"I really cannot tell," she answered. "It is certainly a most extraordinary thing."

"Well, we will not detain you any longer, and we are sorry to have put you to this trouble at such a time," said the inspector. "There are some other points, no doubt; but we can refer to you as they arise."

She rose, and I was again conscious of that quick, questioning glance with which she had just surveyed us. "What impression has my evidence made upon you?"

The question might as well have been spoken. Then, with a bow, she swept from the room.

"She's a beautiful woman—a very beautiful woman," said MacDonald thoughtfully, after the door had closed behind her. "This man Barker has certainly been down here a good deal. He is a man who might be attractive to a woman. He admits that the dead man was jealous, and maybe he knew best himself what cause he had for jealousy. Then there's that wedding ring. You can't get past that. The man who tears a wedding ring off a dead man's—What do you say to it, Mr. Holmes?"

My friend had sat with his head upon his hands, sunk in the deepest thought. Now he rose and rang the bell. "Ames," he said, when the butler entered, "where is Mr. Cecil Barker now?"

"I'll see, sir."

He came back in a moment to say that Barker was in the garden.

"Can you remember, Ames, what Mr. Barker had on his feet last night when you joined him in the study?"

"Yes, Mr. Holmes. He had a pair of bedroom slippers. I brought him his boots when he went for the police."

"Where are the slippers now?"

"They are still under the chair in the hall."

"Very good, Ames. It is, of course, important for us to know which tracks may be Mr. Barker's and which from outside."

"Yes, sir. I may say that I noticed that the slippers were stained with blood—so indeed were my own."

"That is natural enough, considering the condition of the room. Very good, Ames. We will ring if we want you."

A few minutes later we were in the study. Holmes had brought with him the carpet slippers from the hall. As Ames had observed, the soles of both were dark with blood.

"Strange!" murmured Holmes, as he stood in the light of the window and examined them minutely. "Very strange indeed!"

Stooping with one of his quick feline pounces, he placed the slipper upon the blood mark on the sill. It exactly corresponded. He smiled in silence at his colleagues.

The inspector was transfigured with excitement. His native accent rattled like a stick upon railings.

"Man," he cried, "there's not a doubt of it! Barker has just marked the window himself. It's a good deal broader than any bootmark. I mind that you said it was a splay-foot, and here's the explanation. But what's the game, Mr. Holmes—what's the game?"

"Ay, what's the game?" my friend repeated thoughtfully.

White Mason chuckled and rubbed his fat hands together in his professional satisfaction. "I said it was a snorter!" he cried. "And a real snorter it is!"

Chapter 6—A Dawning Light

The three detectives had many matters of detail into which to inquire; so I returned alone to our modest quarters at the village inn. But before doing so I took a stroll in the curious old-world garden which flanked the house. Rows of very ancient yew trees cut into strange designs girded it round. Inside was a beautiful stretch of lawn with an old sundial in the middle, the whole effect so soothing and restful that it was welcome to my somewhat jangled nerves.

In that deeply peaceful atmosphere one could forget, or remember only as some fantastic nightmare, that darkened study with the sprawling, bloodstained figure on the floor. And yet, as I strolled round it and tried to steep my soul in its gentle balm, a strange incident occurred, which brought me back to the tragedy and left a sinister impression in my mind.

I have said that a decoration of yew trees circled the garden. At the end farthest from the house they thickened into a continuous hedge. On the other side of this hedge, concealed from the eyes of anyone approaching from the direction of the house, there was a stone seat. As I approached the spot I was aware of voices, some remark in the deep tones of a man, answered by a little ripple of feminine laughter.

An instant later I had come round the end of the hedge and my eyes lit upon Mrs. Douglas and the man Barker before they were aware of my presence. Her appearance gave me a shock. In the dining-room she had been demure and discreet. Now all pretense of grief had passed away from her. Her eyes shone with the joy of living, and her face still quivered with amusement at some remark of her companion. He sat forward, his hands clasped and his forearms on his knees, with an answering smile upon his bold, handsome face. In an instant—but it was just one instant too late—they resumed their solemn masks as my figure came into view. A hurried word or two passed between them, and then Barker rose and came towards me.

"Excuse me, sir," said he, "but am I addressing Dr. Watson?"

I bowed with a coldness which showed, I dare say, very plainly the impression which had been produced upon my mind.

"We thought that it was probably you, as your friendship with Mr. Sherlock Holmes is so well known. Would you mind coming over and speaking to Mrs. Douglas for one instant?"

I followed him with a dour face. Very clearly I could see in my mind's eye that shattered figure on the floor. Here within a few hours of the tragedy were his wife and his nearest friend laughing together behind a bush in the garden which had been his. I greeted the lady with reserve. I had grieved with her grief in the dining room. Now I met her appealing gaze with an unresponsive eye.

"I fear that you think me callous and hard-hearted," said she.

I shrugged my shoulders. "It is no business of mine," said I.

"Perhaps some day you will do me justice. If you only realized—"

"There is no need why Dr. Watson should realize," said Barker quickly. "As he has himself said, it is no possible business of his."

"Exactly," said I, "and so I will beg leave to resume my walk."

"One moment, Dr. Watson," cried the woman in a pleading voice. "There is one question which you can answer with more authority than anyone else in the world, and it may make a very great difference to me. You know Mr. Holmes and his relations with the police better than anyone else can. Supposing that a matter were brought confidentially to his knowledge, is it absolutely necessary that he should pass it on to the detectives?"

"Yes, that's it," said Barker eagerly. "Is he on his own or is he entirely in with them?"

"I really don't know that I should be justified in discussing such a point."

"I beg—I implore that you will, Dr. Watson! I assure you that you will be helping us—helping me greatly if you will guide us on that point."

There was such a ring of sincerity in the woman's voice that for the instant I forgot all about her levity and was moved only to do her will.

"Mr. Holmes is an independent investigator," I said. "He is his own master, and would act as his own judgment directed. At the same time, he would naturally feel loyalty towards the officials who were working on the same case, and he would not conceal from them anything which would help them in bringing a criminal to justice. Beyond this I can say nothing, and I would refer you to Mr. Holmes himself if you wanted fuller information."

So saying I raised my hat and went upon my way, leaving them still seated behind that concealing hedge. I looked back as I rounded the far end of it, and saw that they were still talking very earnestly together, and, as they were gazing after me, it was clear that it was our interview that was the subject of their debate.

"I wish none of their confidences," said Holmes, when I reported to him what had occurred. He had spent the whole afternoon at the Manor House in consultation with his two colleagues, and returned about five with a ravenous appetite for a high tea which I had ordered for him. "No confidences, Watson; for they are mighty awkward if it comes to an arrest for conspiracy and murder."

"You think it will come to that?"

He was in his most cheerful and debonair humour. "My dear Watson, when I have exterminated that fourth egg I shall be ready to put you in touch with the whole situation. I don't say that we have fathomed it—far from it—but when we have traced the missing dumb-bell—"

"The dumb-bell!"

"Dear me, Watson, is it possible that you have not penetrated the fact that the case hangs upon the missing dumb-bell? Well, well, you need not be downcast; for between ourselves I don't think that either Inspector Mac or the excellent local practitioner has grasped the overwhelming importance of this incident. One dumb-bell, Watson! Consider an athlete with one dumb-bell! Picture to yourself the unilateral development, the imminent danger of a spinal curvature. Shocking, Watson, shocking!"

He sat with his mouth full of toast and his eyes sparkling with mischief, watching my intellectual entanglement. The mere sight of his excellent appetite was an assurance of success; for I had very clear recollections of days and nights without a thought of food, when his baffled mind had chafed before some problem while his thin, eager features became more attenuated with the asceticism of complete mental concentration. Finally he lit his pipe, and sitting in the inglenook of the old village inn he talked slowly and at random about his case, rather as one who thinks aloud than as one who makes a considered statement.

"A lie, Watson—a great, big, thumping, obtrusive, uncompromising lie—that's what meets us on the threshold! There is our starting point. The whole story told by Barker is a lie. But Barker's story is corroborated by Mrs. Douglas. Therefore she is lying also. They are both lying, and in a conspiracy. So now we have the clear problem. Why are they lying, and what is the truth which they are trying so hard to conceal? Let us try, Watson, you and I, if we can get behind the lie and reconstruct the truth.

"How do I know that they are lying? Because it is a clumsy fabrication which simply could not be true. Consider! According to the story given to us, the assassin had less than a minute after the murder had been committed to take that ring, which was under another ring, from the dead man's finger, to replace the other ring—a thing which he would surely never have done—and to put that singular card beside his victim. I say that this was obviously impossible.

"You may argue—but I have too much respect for your judgment, Watson, to think that you will do so— that the ring may have been taken before the man was killed. The fact that the candle had been lit only a short time shows that there had been no lengthy interview.

Was Douglas, from what we hear of his fearless character, a man who would be likely to give up his wedding ring at such short notice, or could we conceive of his giving it up at all? No, no, Watson, the assassin was alone with the dead man for some time with the lamp lit. Of that I have no doubt at all.

"But the gunshot was apparently the cause of death. Therefore the shot must have been fired some time earlier than we are told. But there could be no mistake about such a matter as that. We are in the presence, therefore, of a deliberate conspiracy upon the part of the two people who heard the gunshot—of the man Barker and of the woman Douglas. When on the top of this I am able to show that the blood mark on the windowsill was deliberately placed there by Barker, in order to give a false clue to the police, you will admit that the case grows dark against him.

"Now we have to ask ourselves at what hour the murder actually did occur. Up to half-past ten the servants were moving about the house; so it was certainly not before that time. At a quarter to eleven they had all gone to their rooms with the exception of Ames, who was in the pantry. I have been trying some experiments after you left us this afternoon, and I find that no noise which MacDonald can make in the study can penetrate to me in the pantry when the doors are all shut.

"It is otherwise, however, from the housekeeper's room. It is not so far down the corridor, and from it I could vaguely hear a voice when it was very loudly raised. The sound from a shotgun is to some extent muffled when the discharge is at very close range, as it undoubtedly was in this instance. It would not be very loud, and yet in the silence of the night it should have easily penetrated to Mrs. Allen's room. She is, as she has told us, somewhat deaf; but none the less she mentioned in her evidence that she did hear something like a door slamming half an hour before the alarm was given. Half an hour before the alarm was given would be a quarter to eleven. I have no doubt that what she heard was the report of the gun, and that this was the real instant of the murder.

"If this is so, we have now to determine what Barker and Mrs. Douglas, presuming that they are not the actual murderers, could have been doing from quarter to eleven, when the sound of the shot brought them down, until quarter past eleven, when they rang the bell and summoned the servants. What were they doing, and why did they not instantly give the alarm? That is the question which faces us, and when it has been answered we shall surely have gone some way to solve our problem."

"I am convinced myself," said I, "that there is an understanding between those two people. She must be a heartless creature to sit laughing at some jest within a few hours of her husband's murder."

"Exactly. She does not shine as a wife even in her own account of what occurred. I am not a whole-souled admirer of womankind, as you are aware, Watson, but my experience of life has taught me that there are few wives, having any regard for their husbands, who would let any man's spoken word stand between them and that husband's dead body. Should I ever marry, Watson, I should hope to inspire my wife with some feeling which would prevent her from being walked off by a housekeeper when my corpse was lying within a few yards of her. It was badly stage-managed; for even the rawest investigators must be struck by the absence of the usual feminine ululation. If there had been nothing else, this incident alone would have suggested a prearranged conspiracy to my mind."

"You think then, definitely, that Barker and Mrs. Douglas are guilty of the murder?"

"There is an appalling directness about your questions, Watson," said Holmes, shaking his pipe at me. "They come at me like bullets. If you put it that Mrs. Douglas and Barker know the truth about the murder, and are conspiring to conceal it, then I can give you a whole-souled answer. I am sure they do. But your more deadly proposition is not so clear. Let us for a moment consider the difficulties which stand in the way.

"We will suppose that this couple are united by the bonds of a guilty love, and that they have determined to get rid of the man who stands between them. It is a large supposition; for discreet inquiry among servants and others has failed to corroborate it in any way. On the contrary, there is a good deal of evidence that the Douglases were very attached to each other."

"That, I am sure, cannot be true," said I, thinking of the beautiful smiling face in the garden.

"Well at least they gave that impression. However, we will suppose that they are an extraordinarily astute couple, who deceive everyone upon this point, and conspire to murder the husband. He happens to be a man over whose head some danger hangs—"

"We have only their word for that."

Holmes looked thoughtful. "I see, Watson. You are sketching out a theory by which everything they say from the beginning is false. According to your idea, there was never any hidden menace, or secret society, or Valley of Fear, or Boss MacSomebody, or anything else. Well, that is a good sweeping generalization. Let us see what that brings us to. They invent this theory to account for the crime. They then play up to the idea by leaving this bicycle in the park as proof of the existence of some outsider. The stain on the windowsill conveys the same idea. So does the card on the body, which might have been prepared in the house. That all fits into your hypothesis, Watson. But now we come on the nasty, angular, uncompromising bits which won't slip into their places. Why a cut-off shotgun of all weapons—and an American one at that? How could they be so sure that the sound of it would not bring someone on to them? It's a mere chance as it is that Mrs. Allen did not start out to inquire for the slamming door. Why did your guilty couple do all this, Watson?"

"I confess that I can't explain it."

"Then again, if a woman and her lover conspire to murder a husband, are they going to advertise their guilt by ostentatiously removing his wedding ring after his death? Does that strike you as very probable, Watson?"

"No, it does not."

"And once again, if the thought of leaving a bicycle concealed outside had occurred to you, would it really have seemed worth doing when the dullest detective would naturally say this is an obvious blind, as the bicycle is the first thing which the fugitive needed in order to make his escape."

"I can conceive of no explanation."

"And yet there should be no combination of events for which the wit of man cannot conceive an explanation. Simply as a mental exercise, without any assertion that it is true, let me indicate a possible line of thought. It is, I admit, mere imagination; but how often is imagination the mother of truth?

"We will suppose that there was a guilty secret, a really shameful secret in the life of this man Douglas. This leads to his murder by someone who is, we will suppose, an avenger, someone from outside. This avenger, for some reason which I confess I am still at a loss to explain, took the dead man's wedding ring. The vendetta might conceivably date back to the man's first marriage, and the ring be taken for some such reason.

"Before this avenger got away, Barker and the wife had reached the room. The assassin convinced them that any attempt to arrest him would lead to the publication of some hideous scandal. They were converted to this idea, and preferred to let him go. For this purpose they probably lowered the bridge, which can be done quite noiselessly, and then raised it again. He made his escape, and for some reason thought that he could do so more safely on foot than on the bicycle. He therefore left his machine where it would not be discovered until he had got safely away. So far we are within the bounds of possibility, are we not?"

"Well, it is possible, no doubt," said I, with some reserve.

"We have to remember, Watson, that whatever occurred is certainly something very extraordinary. Well, now, to continue our supposititious case, the couple—not necessarily a guilty couple—realize after the murderer is gone that they have placed themselves in a position in which it may be difficult for them to prove that they did not themselves either do the deed or connive at it. They rapidly and rather clumsily met the situation. The mark was put by Barker's bloodstained slipper upon the windowsill to suggest how the fugitive got away. They obviously were the two who must have heard the sound of the gun; so they gave the alarm exactly as they would have done, but a good half hour after the event."

"And how do you propose to prove all this?"

"Well, if there were an outsider, he may be traced and taken. That would be the most effective of all proofs. But if not—well, the resources of science are far from being exhausted. I think that an evening alone in that study would help me much."

"An evening alone!"

"I propose to go up there presently. I have arranged it with the estimable Ames, who is by no means wholehearted about Barker. I shall sit in that room and see if its atmosphere brings me inspiration. I'm a believer in the genius loci. You smile, Friend Watson. Well, we shall see. By the way, you have that big umbrella of yours, have you not?"

"It is here."

"Well, I'll borrow that if I may."

"Certainly—but what a wretched weapon! If there is danger—"

"Nothing serious, my dear Watson, or I should certainly ask for your assistance. But I'll take the umbrella. At present I am only awaiting the return of our colleagues from Tunbridge Wells, where they are at present engaged in trying for a likely owner to the bicycle."

It was nightfall before Inspector MacDonald and White Mason came back from their expedition, and they arrived exultant, reporting a great advance in our investigation.

"Man, I'll admeet that I had my doubts if there was ever an outsider," said MacDonald, "but that's all past now. We've had the bicycle identified, and we have a description of our man; so that's a long step on our journey."

"It sounds to me like the beginning of the end," said Holmes. "I'm sure I congratulate you both with all my heart."

"Well, I started from the fact that Mr. Douglas had seemed disturbed since the day before, when he had been at Tunbridge Wells. It was at Tunbridge Wells then that he had become conscious of some danger. It was clear, therefore, that if a man had come over with a bicycle it was from Tunbridge Wells that he might be expected to have come. We took the bicycle over with us and showed it at the hotels. It was identified at once by the manager of the Eagle Commercial as belonging to a man named Hargrave, who had taken a room there two days before. This bicycle and a small valise were his whole belongings. He had registered his name as coming from London, but had given no address. The valise was London made, and the contents were British; but the man himself was undoubtedly an American."

"Well, well," said Holmes gleefully, "you have indeed done some solid work while I have been sitting spinning theories with my friend! It's a lesson in being practical, Mr. Mac."

"Ay, it's just that, Mr. Holmes," said the inspector with satisfaction.

"But this may all fit in with your theories," I remarked.

"That may or may not be. But let us hear the end, Mr. Mac. Was there nothing to identify this man?"

"So little that it was evident that he had carefully guarded himself against identification. There were no papers or letters, and no marking upon the clothes. A cycle map of the county lay on his bedroom table. He had left the hotel after breakfast yesterday morning on his bicycle, and no more was heard of him until our inquiries."

"That's what puzzles me, Mr. Holmes," said White Mason. "If the fellow did not want the hue and cry raised over him, one would imagine that he would have returned and remained at the hotel as an inoffensive tourist. As it is, he must know that he will be reported to the police by the hotel manager and that his disappearance will be connected with the murder."

"So one would imagine. Still, he has been justified of his wisdom up to date, at any rate, since he has not been taken. But his description—what of that?"

MacDonald referred to his notebook. "Here we have it so far as they could give it. They don't seem to have taken any very particular stock of him; but still the porter, the clerk, and the chambermaid are all agreed that this about covers the points. He was a man about five foot nine in height, fifty or so years of age, his hair slightly grizzled, a grayish moustache, a curved nose, and a face which all of them described as fierce and forbidding."

"Well, bar the expression, that might almost be a description of Douglas himself," said Holmes. "He is just over fifty, with grizzled hair and moustache, and about the same height. Did you get anything else?"

"He was dressed in a heavy gray suit with a reefer jacket, and he wore a short yellow overcoat and a soft cap."

"What about the shotgun?"

"It is less than two feet long. It could very well have fitted into his valise. He could have carried it inside his overcoat without difficulty."

"And how do you consider that all this bears upon the general case?"

"Well, Mr. Holmes," said MacDonald, "when we have got our man—and you may be sure that I had his description on the wires within five minutes of hearing it—we shall be better able to judge. But, even as it stands, we have surely gone a long way. We know that an American calling himself Hargrave came to Tunbridge Wells two days ago with bicycle and valise. In the latter was a sawed-off shotgun; so he came with the deliberate purpose of crime. Yesterday morning he set off for this place on his bicycle, with his gun concealed in his overcoat. No one saw him arrive, so far as we can learn; but he need not pass through the village to reach the park gates, and there are many cyclists upon the road. Presumably he at once concealed his cycle among the laurels where it was found, and possibly lurked there himself, with his eye on the house, waiting for Mr. Douglas to come out. The shotgun is a strange weapon to use inside a house; but he had intended to use it outside, and there it has very obvious advantages, as it would be impossible to miss with it, and the sound of shots is so common in an English sporting neighbourhood that no particular notice would be taken."

"That is all very clear," said Holmes.

"Well, Mr. Douglas did not appear. What was he to do next? He left his bicycle and approached the house in the twilight. He found the bridge down and no one about. He took his chance, intending, no doubt, to make some excuse if he met anyone. He met no one. He slipped into the first room that he saw, and concealed himself behind the curtain. Thence he could see the drawbridge go up, and he knew that his only escape was through the moat. He waited until quarter-past eleven, when Mr. Douglas upon his usual nightly round came into the room. He shot him and escaped, as arranged. He was aware that the bicycle would be described by the hotel people and be a clue against him; so he left it there and made his way by some other means to London or to some safe hiding place which he had already arranged. How is that, Mr. Holmes?"

"Well, Mr. Mac, it is very good and very clear so far as it goes. That is your end of the story. My end is that the crime was committed half an hour earlier than reported; that Mrs. Douglas and Barker are both in a conspiracy to conceal something; that they aided the murderer's escape—or at least that they reached the room before he escaped—and that they fabricated evidence of his escape through the window, whereas in all probability they had themselves let him go by lowering the bridge. That's my reading of the first half."

The two detectives shook their heads.

"Well, Mr. Holmes, if this is true, we only tumble out of one mystery into another," said the London inspector.

"And in some ways a worse one," added White Mason. "The lady has never been in America in all her life. What possible connection could she have with an American assassin which would cause her to shelter him?"

"I freely admit the difficulties," said Holmes. "I propose to make a little investigation of my own to-night, and it is just possible that it may contribute something to the common cause."

"Can we help you, Mr. Holmes?"

"No, no! Darkness and Dr. Watson's umbrella—my wants are simple. And Ames, the faithful Ames, no doubt he will stretch a point for me. All my lines of thought lead me back invariably to the one basic question—why should an athletic man develop his frame upon so unnatural an instrument as a single dumb-bell?"

It was late that night when Holmes returned from his solitary excursion. We slept in a double-bedded room, which was the best that the little country inn could do for us. I was already asleep when I was partly awakened by his entrance.

"Well, Holmes," I murmured, "have you found anything out?"

He stood beside me in silence, his candle in his hand. Then the tall, lean figure inclined towards me. "I say, Watson," he whispered, "would you be afraid to sleep in the same room with a lunatic, a man with softening of the brain, an idiot whose mind has lost its grip?"

"Not in the least," I answered in astonishment.

"Ah, that's lucky," he said, and not another word would he utter that night.

The Valley of Fear Summary and Analysis of Part I Chapters 5 & 6

Summary

Chapter 5

Ames recounts his version of the events of the night time of Douglas's murder. He had labored for Douglas for approximately 5 years and determined him a pleasant enterprise. Douglas by no means appeared much stressed besides for the day of his homicide. That night time Ames did now not listen the shot due to the fact he was in the pantry at the time, but he did pay attention the bell ringing wildly. He saw Mrs. Douglas coming down the stairs and Mr. Barker urging her to move back. She was no longer screaming or crying.

The housekeeper was nearer to the front of the residence but simplest heard the bell ringing. She turned into tough of listening to and may not have heard the shot due to that. She noticed Mr. Barker, faded and anxious, popping out of the have a look at. He instructed Mrs. Allen to stay with Mrs. Douglas, and she did.

Cecil Barker speaks with the guys next. He adds not anything to the account that he'd instructed the other detectives. He sees the bloodstain as conclusive, however does now not recognize how the killer escaped. He speaks of Douglas next, explaining that they met when Cecil became a younger guy in California.

Douglas emigrated there and the 2 became partners at a mining declare. Douglas bought his percentage and moved to England; whilst Barker moved there as nicely, they renewed their friendship.

It seemed to Barker than Douglas had a few sort of chance putting over him, and he puzzled if a few sort of mystery society Douglas belonged to became after him—possibly that become why he moved to England.

Answering the detectives' questions, Barker states that he and Douglas knew each different for five years. The handiest area Douglas had stated changed into Chicago. He turned into not very social on the mining claim, and one time a hard-searching crowd came looking for him. They were Americans however now not miners, which had appeared suspicious. Barker also tells them that Douglas turned into usually armed.

MacDonald asks how near Barker is to Mrs. Douglas. When the detective's questions grow to be a chunk greater probing, Barker grows indignant. Finally he says that Douglas's one fault turned into jealousy. He changed into keen on Barker and his wife, but Douglas continually seemed irritated whenever the two of them could communicate or percentage a look.

MacDonald asks if Barker knew the marriage ring is long gone, and Barker says plainly way. MacDonald fixates on that and asks what he means; Barker explains that sure, the hoop is long past, but he does not recognize why. MacDonald additionally asks approximately when the candle changed into lit; Barker explains that he lit the lamp and blew out the candle whilst he came in.

Not lengthy after this interview, the organization meets Mrs. Douglas, a beautiful and elegant lady of thirty. She asks in the event that they have found something; Watson thinks it sounds like there's extra of an undertone of worry than desire to her query.

She offers her account of listening to the shot and being dispatched lower back to her room. When requested about her historical past she replies that she had been married to Douglas for five years. She admits that she knew there has been some form of chance about him however he always refused to tell her something. Her instinct and listening talents, although, helped her ascertain some of what stricken him. The words 'Valley of Fear' caught out in her mind, and he or she could listen him bemoan the fact that they would in no way get out of this valley. When she might ask him about this, he explained nothing to her, but she found out that the call 'Body master McGinty' has something to do with this terrible place.

MacDonald asks if there is any reason she will be able to think about that a person would take the wedding ring, in particular as she professed to numerous romance among she and her husband, and for a 2nd Watson thinks he sees a grin on her face. She says she has no concept.

The wondering ends and Mrs. Douglas leaves. Holmes muses for a second and asks Ames to come in. He inquires what shoes Barker become carrying the night time of the murder. Ames responds that he was wearing residence slippers. Holmes unearths the slippers and looks on the lowest. They are protected in blood, and the mark of the window matches that of the only of the slipper. The men are all astonished.

Chapter 6

Watson decides to let the detectives talk among themselves and head again to the village hotel. First, although, he decides to wander approximately the lovely and nonviolent gardens round Manor House. As he comes throughout a clump of yew timber with a bench, he sees Barker and Mrs. Douglas. They appear very friendly: Mrs. Douglas's face is lit up in contrast to it was inside the residence, and the 2 lean in toward every different intimately.

Watson turns to leave, however the pair identifies him, and Barker calls him over. Watson is cool and says he cares no longer for their enterprise. He makes to go away but they name him again. Mrs. Douglas asks if Holmes is the form of detective who does things on his own, or if he might inform law enforcement the matters he finds out. Watson is aggravated by way of this and actions to depart again, however the lady cries out and he's struck via the sincerity in her voice. He eventually concedes that Holmes is an impartial investigator, however that he has top notch appreciate for the guys with whom he works. Watson walks away, and sees the two whispering to one another.

Holmes later says he wishes none of their confidence. He then cheerfully says he's making progress so long as they could find the lacking dumbbell, for only one turned into discovered inside the study near the frame. Watson is surprised and wonders what this has to do with the case. Holmes replies that nobody works out with best one dumbbell.

Holmes is the photograph of contentment and highbrow exhilaration. He lights his pipe and starts to ruminate. He notes that Mrs. Douglas and Barker are collaborating at the lie. There turned into no way that the assassin could have killed Douglas and left in the amount of time allocated. The assassin must had been by myself with Douglas for a while earlier than killing him. The gunshot changed into simply the motive of demise, but it maximum possibly passed off in advance than Barker defined. In fact, the housekeeper had mentioned hearing a muffled noise like a door slamming a half of hour earlier than the gunshot become said to have long past off, and this become possibly the real shot. What, he wonders, did Barker and Mrs. Douglas do in that half of hour? It is a badly stage-controlled affair, he observes.

Watson asks if he thinks the 2 of them murdered Douglas; Holmes prefers not to reply that immediately, even though he shows that they have been certainly concerned somehow. Everyone questioned told him that the Douglases regarded very much in love. There is also the problem of the "Valley of Fear," and affiliation of threat with Douglas. Watson is skeptical of this, and Holmes humors him. He says yes, perhaps they made all that up to cowl their tracks, however the preference of the shotgun as weapon makes no sense. It is also absurd that they would take the useless man's wedding ring; this practically advertised their putative affair.

Holmes maintains, suggesting that it seems possibly that an outsider connected to Douglas who become desirous of in search of some kind of vengeance came and killed the person. Barker and Mrs. Douglas arrived, Holmes speculates, and the murderer spoke to them and satisfied them that in the event that they stated something he would screen a scandalous mystery approximately Douglas. The guy then escaped and decided to go walking and left his bicycle. Barker and Mrs. Douglas set up the scene.

Watson is a bit more satisfied, however nonetheless wary. Holmes pronounces he desires a night time by myself in the take a look at to consider this. He says he wishes handiest an umbrella, which Watson factors out is a useless weapon.

That evening, MacDonald and Mason return. MacDonald is thrilled due to the fact he turned into capable of hint the bicycle to a person named Hargrave. This man, certainly an American however wearing a British suitcase and the bicycle, checked into a resort days ago. There is no greater records approximately his heritage, and no understanding of what he did after he left the day gone by along with his bicycle. MacDonald reads the outline of the person that is quite curious because it seems like Douglas, the murdered guy.

MacDonald gives a theory as to what took place. Hargrave carried the shotgun in his valise and prompt for Manor House. He concealed his bicycle and waited for Douglas. He supposed to apply the gun out of doors in which it might have attracted no undue word. Douglas by no means got here outside, so Hargrave snuck into the house, shot Douglas, and escaped.

Holmes nods in appreciation, and tells them bluntly Barker and Mrs. Douglas are in a conspiracy collectively. Mason sighs and says that the girl has in no way been to America, and therefore this is all very abnormal. Holmes tells them his plan to live in the study and determine out why there is only one dumbbell.

Watson retires to mattress. Holmes wakes him in the middle of the night and asks if Watson could be afraid to sleep inside the identical room as a lunatic or an idiot. Watson is surprised and says no, and Holmes replies that that may be an excellent factor.

Analysis

The thriller deepens in these few chapters, with the suspicions concerning Cecil Barker and Mrs. Douglas apparently higher based than earlier than. Douglas's historical past also gives fodder for notion. The phrases "Valley of Fear" and "Body master McGinty" will loom big within the story for the time, as they may be instead inscrutable and trace at something extraordinarily ominous.

One of the maximum salient characteristics of the Holmes testimonies narrated by means of Watson is the very truth that readers are saved at arm's duration from the detective and his mind. We are best able to see what Watson sees; we cannot pay attention Holmes's thoughts or observe to wherein the ones thoughts are main. When Holmes muses, vanishes, and alludes without explanation, we are left ready and thinking just like Watson and, on this tale, Mason and MacDonald. MacDonald's frustration resonates due to the fact it's miles indeed difficult to assume that Holmes is aware of the answer to the mystery however isn't always yet inclined to percentage with the officials at the case. A cynical take in this posits that Holmes does no longer need to be tested wrong and hence holds off till his accuracy is demonstrated, however it's far much more likely that Holmes is aware of that involving greater humans in his hypothesis could make it more likely that something would pass wrong.

Another feature of Watson's narration is that readers definitely discover little or no about Watson himself. He comes throughout as enthusiastic, supportive, laudatory of Holmes, and possessive of a sturdy moral compass and mined himself. He is referred to as a historian, and is likewise an able participant inside the fixing of the mystery, however occasionally extracts himself from the work of the detectives understanding he isn't always truly one in every of them. He possesses appropriate intuition and a potential to discover sincerity and authenticity inside people. He has his own speculations and feels loose to challenge Holmes inside the detective's conclusions, however in the end he permits rationality, opportunity, common sense, and evidence to rule the day. He does not zealously guard positions once they no longer seem tenable.

These wonderful characteristics absolute confidence stem from and strengthen the reality that Watson is a widespread practitioner. As a scientific man, he no question wishes to own a clearheaded, logical, and pragmatic mentality. He became as honest as he turned into devoted, and if he did not spend his complete working years solidly at the back of a GP's table it changed into best due to the fact he didn't permit his one profession dominate his life. We his readers could not have acknowledged Holmes within the manner we do, had no longer his zealotry been viewed thru Watson's balance, his cold analysis thru Watson's empathy, and his specialization thru Watson's nicely-rounded comprehensively."

Some readers may additionally need to understand greater about Dr. John Watson, especially if this is one among their first forays into the arena of Sherlock Holmes. To begin, there were many speculations as to whom Watson changed into primarily based on (if he was certainly based on an actual character). In 2014 a BBC article explained the same old attributions, and also posed a brand new speculation. A guy named Cuthbert Smith said in 1938 that his father, William Smith, who had an exercise in Dundee in the early twentieth century, was the person on whom Watson turned into based totally. Members of the Scottish Osteopathy Society who have been searching at vintage newspapers located this newspaper article penned with the aid of Cuthbert Smith. Dr. Smith met Dr. Joseph Bell even as he changed into analyzing in Edinburgh; Bell become the muse for Sherlock Holmes. Cuthbert Smith wrote that Doyle and his father marveled at Dr. Bell, and that Doyle requested to create a character based on him. Other hints for Watson's concept encompass Dr. James Watson, a South sea medical doctor and acquaintance of Doyle's, and Surgeon-Major Alexander Francis Preston, who served inside the Afghan battle.

Chapter 7—The Solution

Next morning, after breakfast, we found Inspector MacDonald and White Mason seated in close consultation in the small parlour of the local police sergeant. On the table in front of them were piled a number of letters and telegrams, which they were carefully sorting and docketing. Three had been placed on one side.

"Still on the track of the elusive bicyclist?" Holmes asked cheerfully. "What is the latest news of the ruffian?"

MacDonald pointed ruefully to his heap of correspondence.

"He is at present reported from Leicester, Nottingham, Southampton, Derby, East Ham, Richmond, and fourteen other places. In three of them—East Ham, Leicester, and Liverpool—there is a clear case against him, and he has actually been arrested. The country seems to be full of the fugitives with yellow coats."

"Dear me!" said Holmes sympathetically. "Now, Mr. Mac and you, Mr. White Mason, I wish to give you a very earnest piece of advice. When I went into this case with you I bargained, as you will no doubt remember, that I should not present you with half-proved theories, but that I should retain and work out my own ideas until I had satisfied myself that they were correct. For this reason I am not at the present moment telling you all that is in my mind. On the other hand, I said that I would play the game fairly by you, and I do not think it is a fair game to allow you for one unnecessary moment to waste your energies upon a profitless task. Therefore I am here to advise you this morning, and my advice to you is summed up in three words—abandon the case."

MacDonald and White Mason stared in amazement at their celebrated colleague.

"You consider it hopeless!" cried the inspector.

"I consider your case to be hopeless. I do not consider that it is hopeless to arrive at the truth."

"But this cyclist. He is not an invention. We have his description, his valise, his bicycle. The fellow must be somewhere. Why should we not get him?"

"Yes, yes, no doubt he is somewhere, and no doubt we shall get him; but I would not have you waste your energies in East Ham or Liverpool. I am sure that we can find some shorter cut to a result."

"You are holding something back. It's hardly fair of you, Mr. Holmes." The inspector was annoyed.

"You know my methods of work, Mr. Mac. But I will hold it back for the shortest time possible. I only wish to verify my details in one way, which can very readily be done, and then I make my bow and return to London, leaving my results entirely at your service. I owe you too much to act otherwise; for in all my experience I cannot recall any more singular and interesting study."

"This is clean beyond me, Mr. Holmes. We saw you when we returned from Tunbridge Wells last night, and you were in general agreement with our results. What has happened since then to give you a completely new idea of the case?"

"Well, since you ask me, I spent, as I told you that I would, some hours last night at the Manor House."

"Well, what happened?"

"Ah, I can only give you a very general answer to that for the moment. By the way, I have been reading a short but clear and interesting account of the old building, purchasable at the modest sum of one penny from the local tobacconist."

Here Holmes drew a small tract, embellished with a rude engraving of the ancient Manor House, from his waistcoat pocket.

"It immensely adds to the zest of an investigation, my dear Mr. Mac, when one is in conscious sympathy with the historical atmosphere of one's surroundings. Don't look so impatient; for I assure you that even so bald an account as this raises some sort of picture of the past in one's mind. Permit me to give you a sample. 'Erected in the fifth year of the reign of James I, and standing upon the site of a much older building, the Manor House of Birlstone presents one of the finest surviving examples of the moated Jacobean residence—'"

"You are making fools of us, Mr. Holmes!"

"Tut, tut, Mr. Mac!—the first sign of temper I have detected in you. Well, I won't read it verbatim, since you feel so strongly upon the subject. But when I tell you that there is some account of the taking of the place by a parliamentary colonel in 1644, of the concealment of Charles for several days in the course of the Civil War, and finally of a visit there by the second George, you will admit that there are various associations of interest connected with this ancient house."

"I don't doubt it, Mr. Holmes; but that is no business of ours."

"Is it not? Is it not? Breadth of view, my dear Mr. Mac, is one of the essentials of our profession. The interplay of ideas and the oblique uses of knowledge are often of extraordinary interest. You will excuse these remarks from one who, though a mere connoisseur of crime, is still rather older and perhaps more experienced than yourself."

"I'm the first to admit that," said the detective heartily. "You get to your point, I admit; but you have such a deuced round-the-corner way of doing it."

"Well, well, I'll drop past history and get down to present-day facts. I called last night, as I have already said, at the Manor House. I did not see either Barker or Mrs. Douglas. I saw no necessity to disturb them; but I was pleased to hear that the lady was not visibly pining and that she had partaken of an excellent dinner. My visit was specially made to the good Mr. Ames, with whom I exchanged some amiabilities, which culminated in his allowing me, without reference to anyone else, to sit alone for a time in the study."

"What! With that?" I ejaculated.

"No, no, everything is now in order. You gave permission for that, Mr. Mac, as I am informed. The room was in its normal state, and in it I passed an instructive quarter of an hour."

"What were you doing?"

"Well, not to make a mystery of so simple a matter, I was looking for the missing dumb-bell. It has always bulked rather large in my estimate of the case. I ended by finding it."

"Where?"

"Ah, there we come to the edge of the unexplored. Let me go a little further, a very little further, and I will promise that you shall share everything that I know."

"Well, we're bound to take you on your own terms," said the inspector; "but when it comes to telling us to abandon the case—why in the name of goodness should we abandon the case?"

"For the simple reason, my dear Mr. Mac, that you have not got the first idea what it is that you are investigating."

"We are investigating the murder of Mr. John Douglas of Birlstone Manor."

"Yes, yes, so you are. But don't trouble to trace the mysterious gentleman upon the bicycle. I assure you that it won't help you."

"Then what do you suggest that we do?"

"I will tell you exactly what to do, if you will do it."

"Well, I'm bound to say I've always found you had reason behind all your queer ways. I'll do what you advise."

"And you, Mr. White Mason?"

The country detective looked helplessly from one to the other. Holmes and his methods were new to him. "Well, if it is good enough for the inspector, it is good enough for me," he said at last.

"Capital!" said Holmes. "Well, then, I should recommend a nice, cheery country walk for both of you. They tell me that the views from Birlstone Ridge over the Weald are very remarkable. No doubt lunch could be got at some suitable hostelry; though my ignorance of the country prevents me from recommending one. In the evening, tired but happy—"

"Man, this is getting past a joke!" cried MacDonald, rising angrily from his chair.

"Well, well, spend the day as you like," said Holmes, patting him cheerfully upon the shoulder. "Do what you like and go where you will, but meet me here before dusk without fail—without fail, Mr. Mac."

"That sounds more like sanity."

"All of it was excellent advice; but I don't insist, so long as you are here when I need you. But now, before we part, I want you to write a note to Mr. Barker."

"Well?"

"I'll dictate it, if you like. Ready?

"Dear Sir:

"It has struck me that it is our duty to drain the moat, in the hope that we may find some—"

"It's impossible," said the inspector. "I've made inquiry."

"Tut, tut! My dear sir, please do what I ask you."

"Well, go on."

"—in the hope that we may find something which may bear upon our investigation. I have made arrangements, and the workmen will be at work early to-morrow morning diverting the stream—"

"Impossible!"

"—diverting the stream; so I thought it best to explain matters beforehand.

"Now sign that, and send it by hand about four o'clock. At that hour we shall meet again in this room. Until then we may each do what we like; for I can assure you that this inquiry has come to a definite pause."

Evening was drawing in when we reassembled. Holmes was very serious in his manner, myself curious, and the detectives obviously critical and annoyed.

"Well, gentlemen," said my friend gravely, "I am asking you now to put everything to the test with me, and you will judge for yourselves whether the observations I have made justify the conclusions to which I have come. It is a chill evening, and I do not know how long our expedition may last; so I beg that you will wear your warmest coats. It is of the first importance that we should be in our places before it grows dark; so with your permission we shall get started at once."

We passed along the outer bounds of the Manor House park until we came to a place where there was a gap in the rails which fenced it. Through this we slipped, and then in the gathering gloom we followed Holmes until we had reached a shrubbery which lies nearly opposite to the main door and the drawbridge. The latter had not been raised. Holmes crouched down behind the screen of laurels, and we all three followed his example.

"Well, what are we to do now?" asked MacDonald with some gruffness.

"Possess our souls in patience and make as little noise as possible," Holmes answered.

"What are we here for at all? I really think that you might treat us with more frankness."

Holmes laughed. "Watson insists that I am the dramatist in real life," said he. "Some touch of the artist wells up within me, and calls insistently for a well-staged performance. Surely our profession, Mr. Mac, would be a drab and sordid one if we did not sometimes set the scene so as to glorify our results. The blunt accusation, the brutal tap upon the shoulder—what can one make of such a denouement? But the quick inference, the subtle trap, the clever forecast of coming events, the triumphant vindication of bold theories—

are these not the pride and the justification of our life's work? At the present moment you thrill with the glamour of the situation and the anticipation of the hunt. Where would be that thrill if I had been as definite as a timetable? I only ask a little patience, Mr. Mac, and all will be clear to you."

"Well, I hope the pride and justification and the rest of it will come before we all get our death of cold," said the London detective with comic resignation.

We all had good reason to join in the aspiration; for our vigil was a long and bitter one. Slowly the shadows darkened over the long, sombre face of the old house. A cold, damp reek from the moat chilled us to the bones and set our teeth chattering. There was a single lamp over the gateway and a steady globe of light in the fatal study. Everything else was dark and still.

"How long is this to last?" asked the inspector finally. "And what is it we are watching for?"

"I have no more notion than you how long it is to last," Holmes answered with some asperity. "If criminals would always schedule their movements like railway trains, it would certainly be more convenient for all of us. As to what it is we—Well, THAT'S what we are watching for!"

As he spoke the bright, yellow light in the study was obscured by somebody passing to and fro before it. The laurels among which we lay were immediately opposite the window and not more than a hundred feet from it. Presently it was thrown open with a whining of hinges, and we could dimly see the dark outline of a man's head and shoulders looking out into the gloom. For some minutes he peered forth in furtive, stealthy fashion, as one who wishes to be assured that he is unobserved.

Then he leaned forward, and in the intense silence we were aware of the soft lapping of agitated water. He seemed to be stirring up the moat with something which he held in his hand. Then suddenly he hauled something in as a fisherman lands a fish—some large, round object which obscured the light as it was dragged through the open casement.

"Now!" cried Holmes. "Now!"

We were all upon our feet, staggering after him with our stiffened limbs, while he ran swiftly across the bridge and rang violently at the bell. There was the rasping of bolts from the other side, and the amazed Ames stood in the entrance. Holmes brushed him aside without a word and, followed by all of us, rushed into the room which had been occupied by the man whom we had been watching.

The oil lamp on the table represented the glow which we had seen from outside. It was now in the hand of Cecil Barker, who held it towards us as we entered. Its light shone upon his strong, resolute, clean-shaved face and his menacing eyes.

"What the devil is the meaning of all this?" he cried. "What are you after, anyhow?"

Holmes took a swift glance round, and then pounced upon a sodden bundle tied together with cord which lay where it had been thrust under the writing table.

"This is what we are after, Mr. Barker—this bundle, weighted with a dumb-bell, which you have just raised from the bottom of the moat."

Barker stared at Holmes with amazement in his face. "How in thunder came you to know anything about it?" he asked.

"Simply that I put it there."

"You put it there! You!"

"Perhaps I should have said 'replaced it there,'" said Holmes. "You will remember, Inspector MacDonald, that I was somewhat struck by the absence of a dumb-bell. I drew your attention to it; but with the pressure of other events you had hardly the time to give it the consideration which would have enabled you to draw deductions from it. When water is near and a weight is missing it is not a very far-fetched supposition that something has been sunk in the water. The idea was at least worth testing; so with the help of Ames, who admitted me to the room, and the crook of Dr. Watson's umbrella, I was able last night to fish up and inspect this bundle.

"It was of the first importance, however, that we should be able to prove who placed it there. This we accomplished by the very obvious device of announcing that the moat would be dried to-morrow, which had, of course, the effect that whoever had hidden the bundle would most certainly withdraw it the moment that darkness enabled him to do so. We have no less than four witnesses as to who it was who took advantage of the opportunity, and so, Mr. Barker, I think the word lies now with you."

Sherlock Holmes put the sopping bundle upon the table beside the lamp and undid the cord which bound it. From within he extracted a dumb-bell, which he tossed down to its fellow in the corner. Next he drew forth a pair of boots. "American, as you perceive," he remarked, pointing to the toes. Then he laid upon the table a long, deadly, sheathed knife. Finally he unravelled a bundle of clothing, comprising a complete set of underclothes, socks, a gray tweed suit, and a short yellow overcoat.

"The clothes are commonplace," remarked Holmes, "save only the overcoat, which is full of suggestive touches." He held it tenderly towards the light. "Here, as you perceive, is the inner pocket prolonged into the lining in such fashion as to give ample space for the truncated fowling piece. The tailor's tab is on the neck— 'Neal, Outfitter, Vermissa, U.S.A.' I have spent an instructive afternoon in the rector's library, and have enlarged my knowledge by adding the fact that Vermissa is a flourishing little town at the head of one of the best known coal and iron valleys in the United States. I have some recollection, Mr. Barker, that you associated the coal districts with Mr. Douglas's first wife, and it would surely not be too far-fetched an inference that the V.V. upon the card by the dead body might stand for Vermissa Valley, or that this very valley which sends forth emissaries of murder may be that Valley of Fear of which we have heard. So much is fairly clear. And now, Mr. Barker, I seem to be standing rather in the way of your explanation."

It was a sight to see Cecil Barker's expressive face during this exposition of the great detective. Anger, amazement, consternation, and indecision swept over it in turn. Finally he took refuge in a somewhat acrid irony.

"You know such a lot, Mr. Holmes, perhaps you had better tell us some more," he sneered.

"I have no doubt that I could tell you a great deal more, Mr. Barker; but it would come with a better grace from you."

"Oh, you think so, do you? Well, all I can say is that if there's any secret here it is not my secret, and I am not the man to give it away."

"Well, if you take that line, Mr. Barker," said the inspector quietly, "we must just keep you in sight until we have the warrant and can hold you."

"You can do what you damn please about that," said Barker defiantly.

The proceedings seemed to have come to a definite end so far as he was concerned; for one had only to look at that granite face to realize that no peine forte et dure would ever force him to plead against his will. The deadlock was broken, however, by a woman's voice. Mrs. Douglas had been standing listening at the half opened door, and now she entered the room.

"You have done enough for now, Cecil," said she. "Whatever comes of it in the future, you have done enough."

"Enough and more than enough," remarked Sherlock Holmes gravely. "I have every sympathy with you, madam, and should strongly urge you to have some confidence in the common sense of our jurisdiction and to take the police voluntarily into your complete confidence. It may be that I am myself at fault for not following up the hint which you conveyed to me through my friend, Dr. Watson; but, at that time I had every reason to believe that you were directly concerned in the crime. Now I am assured that this is not so. At the same time, there is much that is unexplained, and I should strongly recommend that you ask Mr. Douglas to tell us his own story."

Mrs. Douglas gave a cry of astonishment at Holmes's words. The detectives and I must have echoed it, when we were aware of a man who seemed to have emerged from the wall, who advanced now from the gloom of the corner in which he had appeared. Mrs. Douglas turned, and in an instant her arms were round him. Barker had seized his outstretched hand.

"It's best this way, Jack," his wife repeated; "I am sure that it is best."

"Indeed, yes, Mr. Douglas," said Sherlock Holmes, "I am sure that you will find it best."

The man stood blinking at us with the dazed look of one who comes from the dark into the light. It was a remarkable face, bold gray eyes, a strong, short-clipped, grizzled moustache, a square, projecting chin, and a humorous mouth. He took a good look at us all, and then to my amazement he advanced to me and handed me a bundle of paper.

"I've heard of you," said he in a voice which was not quite English and not quite American, but was altogether mellow and pleasing. "You are the historian of this bunch. Well, Dr. Watson, you've never had such a story as that pass through your hands before, and I'll lay my last dollar on that. Tell it your own way; but there are the facts, and you can't miss the public so long as you have those. I've been cooped up two days, and I've spent the daylight hours—as much daylight as I could get in that rat trap—in putting the thing into words. You're welcome to them—you and your public. There's the story of the Valley of Fear."

"That's the past, Mr. Douglas," said Sherlock Holmes quietly. "What we desire now is to hear your story of the present."

"You'll have it, sir," said Douglas. "May I smoke as I talk? Well, thank you, Mr. Holmes. You're a smoker yourself, if I remember right, and you'll guess what it is to be sitting for two days with tobacco in your pocket and afraid that the smell will give you away." He leaned against the mantelpiece and sucked at the cigar which Holmes had handed him. "I've heard of you, Mr. Holmes. I never guessed that I should meet you. But before you are through with that," he nodded at my papers, "you will say I've brought you something fresh."

Inspector MacDonald had been staring at the newcomer with the greatest amazement. "Well, this fairly beats me!" he cried at last. "If you are Mr. John Douglas of Birlstone Manor, then whose death have we been investigating for these two days, and where in the world have you sprung from now? You seemed to me to come out of the floor like a jack-in-a-box."

"Ah, Mr. Mac," said Holmes, shaking a reproving forefinger, "you would not read that excellent local compilation which described the concealment of King Charles. People did not hide in those days without excellent hiding places, and the hiding place that has once been used may be again. I had persuaded myself that we should find Mr. Douglas under this roof."

"And how long have you been playing this trick upon us, Mr. Holmes?" said the inspector angrily. "How long have you allowed us to waste ourselves upon a search that you knew to be an absurd one?"

"Not one instant, my dear Mr. Mac. Only last night did I form my views of the case. As they could not be put to the proof until this evening, I invited you and your colleague to take a holiday for the day. Pray what more could I do? When I found the suit of clothes in the moat, it at once became apparent to me that the body we had found could not have been the body of Mr. John Douglas at all, but must be that of the bicyclist from Tunbridge Wells. No other conclusion was possible. Therefore I had to determine where Mr. John Douglas himself could be, and the balance of probability was that with the connivance of his wife and his friend he was concealed in a house which had such conveniences for a fugitive, and awaiting quieter times when he could make his final escape."

"Well, you figured it out about right," said Douglas approvingly. "I thought I'd dodge your British law; for I was not sure how I stood under it, and also I saw my chance to throw these hounds once for all off my track. Mind you, from first to last I have done nothing to be ashamed of, and nothing that I would not do again; but you'll judge that for yourselves when I tell you my story. Never mind warning me, Inspector: I'm ready to stand pat upon the truth.

"I'm not going to begin at the beginning. That's all there," he indicated my bundle of papers, "and a mighty queer yarn you'll find it. It all comes down to this: That there are some men that have good cause to hate me and would give their last dollar to know that they had got me. So long as I am alive and they are alive, there is no safety in this world for me. They hunted me from Chicago to California, then they chased me out of America; but when I married and settled down in this quiet spot I thought my last years were going to be peaceable.

"I never explained to my wife how things were. Why should I pull her into it? She would never have a quiet moment again; but would always be imagining trouble. I fancy she knew something, for I may have dropped a word here or a word there; but until yesterday, after you gentlemen had seen her, she never knew the rights of the matter. She told you all she knew, and so did Barker here; for on the night when this thing happened there was mighty little time for explanations. She knows everything now, and I would have been a wiser man if I had told her sooner. But it was a hard question, dear," he took her hand for an instant in his own, "and I acted for the best.

"Well, gentlemen, the day before these happenings I was over in Tunbridge Wells, and I got a glimpse of a man in the street. It was only a glimpse; but I have a quick eye for these things, and I never doubted who it was. It was the worst enemy I had among them all—one who has been after me like a hungry wolf after a caribou all these years. I knew there was trouble coming, and I came home and made ready for it. I guessed I'd fight through it all right on my own, my luck was a proverb in the States about '76. I never doubted that it would be with me still.

"I was on my guard all that next day, and never went out into the park. It's as well, or he'd have had the drop on me with that buckshot gun of his before ever I could draw on him. After the bridge was up—my mind was always more restful when that bridge was up in the evenings—I put the thing clear out of my head. I never dreamed of his getting into the house and waiting for me. But when I made my round in my dressing gown, as was my habit, I had no sooner entered the study than I scented danger. I guess when a man has had dangers in his life—and I've had more than most in my time— there is a kind of sixth sense that waves the red flag. I saw the signal clear enough, and yet I couldn't tell you why. Next instant I spotted a boot under the window curtain, and then I saw why plain enough.

"I'd just the one candle that was in my hand; but there was a good light from the hall lamp through the open door. I put down the candle and jumped for a hammer that I'd left on the mantel. At the same moment he sprang at me. I saw the glint of a knife, and I lashed at him with the hammer. I got him somewhere; for the knife tinkled down on the floor. He dodged round the table as quick as an eel, and a moment later he'd got his gun from under his coat. I heard him cock it; but I had got hold of it before he could fire. I had it by the barrel, and we wrestled for it all ends up for a minute or more. It was death to the man that lost his grip.

"He never lost his grip; but he got it butt downward for a moment too long. Maybe it was I that pulled the trigger. Maybe we just jolted it off between us. Anyhow, he got both barrels in the face, and there I was, staring down at all that was left of Ted Baldwin. I'd recognized him in the township, and again when he sprang for me; but his own mother wouldn't recognize him as I saw him then. I'm used to rough work; but I fairly turned sick at the sight of him.

"I was hanging on the side of the table when Barker came hurrying down. I heard my wife coming, and I ran to the door and stopped her. It was no sight for a woman. I promised I'd come to her soon. I said a word or two to Barker—he took it all in at a glance—and we waited for the rest to come along. But there was no sign of them. Then we understood that they could hear nothing, and that all that had happened was known only to ourselves.

"It was at that instant that the idea came to me. I was fairly dazzled by the brilliance of it. The man's sleeve had slipped up and there was the branded mark of the lodge upon his forearm. See here!"

The man whom we had known as Douglas turned up his own coat and cuff to show a brown triangle within a circle exactly like that which we had seen upon the dead man.

"It was the sight of that which started me on it. I seemed to see it all clear at a glance. There were his height and hair and figure, about the same as my own. No one could swear to his face, poor devil! I brought down this suit of clothes, and in a quarter of an hour Barker and I had put my dressing gown on him and he lay as you found him. We tied all his things into a bundle, and I weighted them with the only weight I could find and put them through the window. The card he had meant to lay upon my body was lying beside his own.

"My rings were put on his finger; but when it came to the wedding ring," he held out his muscular hand, "you can see for yourselves that I had struck the limit. I have not moved it since the day I was married, and it would have taken a file to get it off. I don't know, anyhow, that I should have cared to part with it; but if I had wanted to I couldn't. So we just had to leave that detail to take care of itself. On the other hand, I brought a bit of plaster down and put it where I am wearing one myself at this instant. You slipped up there, Mr. Holmes, clever as you are; for if you had chanced to take off that plaster you would have found no cut underneath it.

"Well, that was the situation. If I could lie low for a while and then get away where I could be joined by my 'widow' we should have a chance at last of living in peace for the rest of our lives. These devils would give me no rest so long as I was above ground; but if they saw in the papers that Baldwin had got his man, there would be an end of all my troubles. I hadn't much time to make it all clear to Barker and to my wife; but they understood enough to be able to help me. I knew all about this hiding place, so did Ames; but it never entered his head to connect it with the matter. I retired into it, and it was up to Barker to do the rest.

"I guess you can fill in for yourselves what he did. He opened the window and made the mark on the sill to give an idea of how the murderer escaped. It was a tall order, that; but as the bridge was up there was no other way. Then, when everything was fixed, he rang the bell for all he was worth. What happened afterward you know. And so, gentlemen, you can do what you please; but I've told you the truth and the whole truth, so help me God! What I ask you now is how do I stand by the English law?"

There was a silence which was broken by Sherlock Holmes.

"The English law is in the main a just law. You will get no worse than your deserts from that, Mr. Douglas. But I would ask you how did this man know that you lived here, or how to get into your house, or where to hide to get you?"

"I know nothing of this."

Holmes's face was very white and grave. "The story is not over yet, I fear," said he. "You may find worse dangers than the English law, or even than your enemies from America. I see trouble before you, Mr. Douglas. You'll take my advice and still be on your guard."

And now, my long-suffering readers, I will ask you to come away with me for a time, far from the Sussex Manor House of Birlstone, and far also from the year of grace in which we made our eventful journey which ended with the strange story of the man who had been known as John Douglas. I wish you to journey back some twenty years in time, and westward some thousands of miles in space, that I may lay before you a singular and terrible narrative—so singular and so terrible that you may find it hard to believe that even as I tell it, even so did it occur.

Do not think that I intrude one story before another is finished. As you read on you will find that this is not so. And when I have detailed those distant events and you have solved this mystery of the past, we shall meet once more in those rooms on Baker Street, where this, like so many other wonderful happenings, will find its end.

PART 2—The Scowrers

Chapter 1—The Man

It was the fourth of February in the year 1875. It had been a severe winter, and the snow lay deep in the gorges of the Gilmerton Mountains. The steam ploughs had, however, kept the railroad open, and the evening train which connects the long line of coal-mining and iron-working settlements was slowly groaning its way up the steep gradients which lead from Stagville on the plain to Vermissa, the central township which lies at the head of Vermissa Valley. From this point the track sweeps downward to Bartons Crossing, Helmdale, and the purely agricultural county of Merton. It was a single track railroad; but at every siding—and they were numerous—long lines of trucks piled with coal and iron ore told of the hidden wealth which had brought a rude population and a bustling life to this most desolate corner of the United States of America.

For desolate it was! Little could the first pioneer who had traversed it have ever imagined that the fairest prairies and the most lush water pastures were valueless compared to this gloomy land of black crag and tangled forest. Above the dark and often scarcely penetrable woods upon their flanks, the high, bare crowns of the mountains, white snow, and jagged rock towered upon each flank, leaving a long, winding, tortuous valley in the center. Up this the little train was slowly crawling.

The oil lamps had just been lit in the leading passenger car, a long, bare carriage in which some twenty or thirty people were seated. The greater number of these were workmen returning from their day's toil in the lower part of the valley. At least a dozen, by their grimed faces and the safety lanterns which they carried, proclaimed themselves miners. These sat smoking in a group and conversed in low voices, glancing occasionally at two men on the opposite side of the car, whose uniforms and badges showed them to be policemen.

Several women of the labouring class and one or two travellers who might have been small local storekeepers made up the rest of the company, with the exception of one young man in a corner by himself. It is with this man that we are concerned. Take a good look at him; for he is worth it.

He is a fresh-complexioned, middle-sized young man, not far, one would guess, from his thirtieth year. He has large, shrewd, humorous gray eyes which twinkle inquiringly from time to time as he looks round through his spectacles at the people about him. It is easy to see that he is of a sociable and possibly simple disposition, anxious to be friendly to all men. Anyone could pick him at once as gregarious in his habits and communicative in his nature, with a quick wit and a ready smile. And yet the man who studied him more closely might discern a certain firmness of jaw and grim tightness about the lips which would warn him that there were depths beyond, and that this pleasant, brown-haired young Irishman might conceivably leave his mark for good or evil upon any society to which he was introduced.

Having made one or two tentative remarks to the nearest miner, and receiving only short, gruff replies, the traveller resigned himself to uncongenial silence, staring moodily out of the window at the fading landscape.

It was not a cheering prospect. Through the growing gloom there pulsed the red glow of the furnaces on the sides of the hills. Great heaps of slag and dumps of cinders loomed up on each side, with the high shafts of the collieries towering above them. Huddled groups of mean, wooden houses, the windows of which were beginning to outline themselves in light, were scattered here and there along the line, and the frequent halting places were crowded with their swarthy inhabitants.

The iron and coal valleys of the Vermissa district were no resorts for the leisured or the cultured. Everywhere there were stern signs of the crudest battle of life, the rude work to be done, and the rude, strong workers who did it.

The young traveller gazed out into this dismal country with a face of mingled repulsion and interest, which showed that the scene was new to him. At intervals he drew from his pocket a bulky letter to which he referred, and on the margins of which he scribbled some notes. Once from the back of his waist he produced something which one would hardly have expected to find in the possession of so mild-mannered a man. It was a navy revolver of the largest size. As he turned it slantwise to the light, the glint upon the rims of the copper shells within the drum showed that it was fully loaded. He quickly restored it to his secret pocket, but not before it had been observed by a working man who had seated himself upon the adjoining bench.

"Hullo, mate!" said he. "You seem heeled and ready."

The young man smiled with an air of embarrassment.

"Yes," said he, "we need them sometimes in the place I come from."

"And where may that be?"

"I'm last from Chicago."

"A stranger in these parts?"

"Yes."

"You may find you need it here," said the workman.

"Ah! is that so?" The young man seemed interested.

"Have you heard nothing of doings hereabouts?"

"Nothing out of the way."

"Why, I thought the country was full of it. You'll hear quick enough. What made you come here?"

"I heard there was always work for a willing man."

"Are you a member of the union?"

"Sure."

"Then you'll get your job, I guess. Have you any friends?"

"Not yet; but I have the means of making them."

"How's that, then?"

"I am one of the Eminent Order of Freemen. There's no town without a lodge, and where there is a lodge I'll find my friends."

The remark had a singular effect upon his companion. He glanced round suspiciously at the others in the car. The miners were still whispering among themselves. The two police officers were dozing. He came across, seated himself close to the young traveller, and held out his hand.

"Put it there," he said.

A hand-grip passed between the two.

"I see you speak the truth," said the workman. "But it's well to make certain." He raised his right hand to his right eyebrow. The traveller at once raised his left hand to his left eyebrow.

"Dark nights are unpleasant," said the workman.

"Yes, for strangers to travel," the other answered.

"That's good enough. I'm Brother Scanlan, Lodge 341, Vermissa Valley. Glad to see you in these parts."

"Thank you. I'm Brother John McMurdo, Lodge 29, Chicago. Body master J.H. Scott. But I am in luck to meet a brother so early."

"Well, there are plenty of us about. You won't find the order more flourishing anywhere in the States than right here in Vermissa Valley. But we could do with some lads like you. I can't understand a spry man of the union finding no work to do in Chicago."

"I found plenty of work to do," said McMurdo.

"Then why did you leave?"

McMurdo nodded towards the policemen and smiled. "I guess those chaps would be glad to know," he said.

Scanlan groaned sympathetically. "In trouble?" he asked in a whisper.

"Deep."

"A penitentiary job?"

"And the rest."

"Not a killing!"

"It's early days to talk of such things," said McMurdo with the air of a man who had been surprised into saying more than he intended. "I've my own good reasons for leaving Chicago, and let that be enough for you. Who are you that you should take it on yourself to ask such things?" His gray eyes gleamed with sudden and dangerous anger from behind his glasses.

"All right, mate, no offense meant. The boys will think none the worse of you, whatever you may have done. Where are you bound for now?"

"Vermissa."

"That's the third halt down the line. Where are you staying?"

McMurdo took out an envelope and held it close to the murky oil lamp. "Here is the address—Jacob Shafter, Sheridan Street. It's a boarding house that was recommended by a man I knew in Chicago."

"Well, I don't know it; but Vermissa is out of my beat. I live at Hobson's Patch, and that's here where we are drawing up. But, say, there's one bit of advice I'll give you before we part: If you're in trouble in Vermissa, go straight to the Union House and see Boss McGinty. He is the Body master of Vermissa Lodge, and nothing can happen in these parts unless Black Jack McGinty wants it. So long, mate! Maybe we'll meet in lodge one of these evenings. But mind my words: If you are in trouble, go to Boss McGinty."

Scanlan descended, and McMurdo was left once again to his thoughts. Night had now fallen, and the flames of the frequent furnaces were roaring and leaping in the darkness. Against their lurid background dark figures were bending and straining, twisting and turning, with the motion of winch or of windlass, to the rhythm of an eternal clank and roar.

"I guess hell must look something like that," said a voice.

McMurdo turned and saw that one of the policemen had shifted in his seat and was staring out into the fiery waste.

"For that matter," said the other policeman, "I allow that hell must BE something like that. If there are worse devils down yonder than some we could name, it's more than I'd expect. I guess you are new to this part, young man?"

"Well, what if I am?" McMurdo answered in a surly voice.

"Just this, mister, that I should advise you to be careful in choosing your friends. I don't think I'd begin with Mike Scanlan or his gang if I were you."

"What the hell is it to you who are my friends?" roared McMurdo in a voice which brought every head in the carriage round to witness the altercation. "Did I ask you for your advice, or did you think me such a sucker that I couldn't move without it? You speak when you are spoken to, and by the Lord you'd have to wait a long time if it was me!" He thrust out his face and grinned at the patrolmen like a snarling dog.

The two policemen, heavy, good-natured men, were taken aback by the extraordinary vehemence with which their friendly advances had been rejected.

"No offense, stranger," said one. "It was a warning for your own good, seeing that you are, by your own showing, new to the place."

"I'm new to the place; but I'm not new to you and your kind!" cried McMurdo in cold fury. "I guess you're the same in all places, shoving your advice in when nobody asks for it."

"Maybe we'll see more of you before very long," said one of the patrolmen with a grin. "You're a real hand-picked one, if I am a judge."

"I was thinking the same," remarked the other. "I guess we may meet again."

"I'm not afraid of you, and don't you think it!" cried McMurdo. "My name's Jack McMurdo—see? If you want me, you'll find me at Jacob Shafter's on Sheridan Street,

Vermissa; so I'm not hiding from you, am I? Day or night I dare to look the like of you in the face—don't make any mistake about that!"

There was a murmur of sympathy and admiration from the miners at the dauntless demeanour of the newcomer, while the two policemen shrugged their shoulders and renewed a conversation between themselves.

A few minutes later the train ran into the ill-lit station, and there was a general clearing; for Vermissa was by far the largest town on the line. McMurdo picked up his leather gripsack and was about to start off into the darkness, when one of the miners accosted him.

"By Gar, mate! you know how to speak to the cops," he said in a voice of awe. "It was grand to hear you. Let me carry your grip and show you the road. I'm passing Shafter's on the way to my own shack."

There was a chorus of friendly "Good-nights" from the other miners as they passed from the platform. Before ever he had set foot in it, McMurdo the turbulent had become a character in Vermissa.

The country had been a place of terror; but the town was in its way even more depressing. Down that long valley there was at least a certain gloomy grandeur in the huge fires and the clouds of drifting smoke, while the strength and industry of man found fitting monuments in the hills which he had spilled by the side of his monstrous excavations. But the town showed a dead level of mean ugliness and squalor. The broad street was churned up by the traffic into a horrible rutted paste of muddy snow. The sidewalks were narrow and uneven. The numerous gas-lamps served only to show more clearly a long line of wooden houses, each with its veranda facing the street, unkempt and dirty.

As they approached the center of the town the scene was brightened by a row of well-lit stores, and even more by a cluster of saloons and gaming houses, in which the miners spent their hard-earned but generous wages.

"That's the Union House," said the guide, pointing to one saloon which rose almost to the dignity of being a hotel. "Jack McGinty is the boss there."

"What sort of a man is he?" McMurdo asked.

"What! have you never heard of the boss?"

"How could I have heard of him when you know that I am a stranger in these parts?"

"Well, I thought his name was known clear across the country. It's been in the papers often enough."

"What for?"

"Well," the miner lowered his voice—"over the affairs."

"What affairs?"

"Good Lord, mister! you are queer, if I must say it without offense. There's only one set of affairs that you'll hear of in these parts, and that's the affairs of the Scowrers."

"Why, I seem to have read of the Scowrers in Chicago. A gang of murderers, are they not?"

"Hush, on your life!" cried the miner, standing still in alarm, and gazing in amazement at his companion. "Man, you won't live long in these parts if you speak in the open street like that. Many a man has had the life beaten out of him for less."

"Well, I know nothing about them. It's only what I have read."

"And I'm not saying that you have not read the truth." The man looked nervously round him as he spoke, peering into the shadows as if he feared to see some lurking danger. "If killing is murder, then God knows there is murder and to spare. But don't you dare to breathe the name of Jack McGinty in connection with it, stranger; for every whisper goes back to him, and he is not one that is likely to let it pass. Now, that's the house you're after, that one standing back from the street. You'll find old Jacob Shafter that runs it as honest a man as lives in this township."

"I thank you," said McMurdo, and shaking hands with his new acquaintance he plodded, gripsack in hand, up the path which led to the dwelling house, at the door of which he gave a resounding knock.

It was opened at once by someone very different from what he had expected. It was a woman, young and singularly beautiful. She was of the German type, blonde and fair-haired, with the piquant contrast of a pair of beautiful dark eyes with which she surveyed the stranger with surprise and a pleasing embarrassment which brought a wave of colour over her pale face. Framed in the bright light of the open doorway, it seemed to McMurdo that he had never seen a more beautiful picture; the more attractive for its contrast with the sordid and gloomy surroundings. A lovely violet growing upon one of those black slag-heaps of the mines would not have seemed more surprising. So entranced was he that he stood staring without a word, and it was she who broke the silence.

"I thought it was father," said she with a pleasing little touch of a German accent. "Did you come to see him? He is down town. I expect him back every minute."

McMurdo continued to gaze at her in open admiration until her eyes dropped in confusion before this masterful visitor.

"No, miss," he said at last, "I'm in no hurry to see him. But your house was recommended to me for board. I thought it might suit me—and now I know it will."

"You are quick to make up your mind," said she with a smile.

"Anyone but a blind man could do as much," the other answered.

She laughed at the compliment. "Come right in, sir," she said. "I'm Miss Ettie Shafter, Mr. Shafter's daughter. My mother's dead, and I run the house. You can sit down by the stove in the front room until father comes along—Ah, here he is! So you can fix things with him right away."

A heavy, elderly man came plodding up the path. In a few words McMurdo explained his business. A man of the name of Murphy had given him the address in Chicago. He in turn had had it from someone else. Old Shafter was quite ready. The stranger made no bones about terms, agreed at once to every condition, and was apparently fairly flush of money. For seven dollars a week paid in advance he was to have board and lodging.

So it was that McMurdo, the self-confessed fugitive from justice, took up his abode under the roof of the Shafters, the first step which was to lead to so long and dark a train of events, ending in a far distant land.

Chapter 2—The Body master

McMurdo was a man who made his mark quickly. Wherever he was the folk around soon knew it. Within a week he had become infinitely the most important person at Shafter's. There were ten or a dozen boarders there; but they were honest foremen or commonplace clerks from the stores, of a very different calibre from the young Irishman. Of an evening when they gathered together his joke was always the readiest, his conversation the brightest, and his song the best. He was a born boon companion, with a magnetism which drew good humour from all around him.

And yet he showed again and again, as he had shown in the railway carriage, a capacity for sudden, fierce anger, which compelled the respect and even the fear of those who met him. For the law, too, and all who were connected with it, he exhibited a bitter contempt which delighted some and alarmed others of his fellow boarders.

From the first he made it evident, by his open admiration, that the daughter of the house had won his heart from the instant that he had set eyes upon her beauty and her grace. He was no backward suitor. On the second day he told her that he loved her, and from then onward he repeated the same story with an absolute disregard of what she might say to discourage him.

"Someone else?" he would cry. "Well, the worse luck for someone else! Let him look out for himself! Am I to lose my life's chance and all my heart's desire for someone else? You can keep on saying no, Ettie: the day will come when you will say yes, and I'm young enough to wait."

He was a dangerous suitor, with his glib Irish tongue, and his pretty, coaxing ways. There was about him also that glamour of experience and of mystery which attracts a woman's interest, and finally her love. He could talk of the sweet valleys of County Monaghan from which he came, of the lovely, distant island, the low hills and green meadows of which seemed the more beautiful when imagination viewed them from this place of grime and snow.

Then he was versed in the life of the cities of the North, of Detroit, and the lumber camps of Michigan, and finally of Chicago, where he had worked in a planing mill. And afterwards came the hint of romance, the feeling that strange things had happened to him in that great city, so strange and so intimate that they might not be spoken of. He spoke wistfully of a sudden leaving, a breaking of old ties, a flight into a strange world, ending in this dreary valley, and Ettie listened, her dark eyes gleaming with pity and with sympathy—those two qualities which may turn so rapidly and so naturally to love.

McMurdo had obtained a temporary job as bookkeeper for he was a well-educated man. This kept him out most of the day, and he had not found occasion yet to report himself to the head of the lodge of the Eminent Order of Freemen. He was reminded of his omission, however, by a visit one evening from Mike Scanlan, the fellow member whom he had met in the train. Scanlan, the small, sharp-faced, nervous, black-eyed man, seemed glad to see him once more. After a glass or two of whisky he broached the object of his visit.

"Say, McMurdo," said he, "I remembered your address, so I made bold to call. I'm surprised that you've not reported to the Body master. Why haven't you seen Boss McGinty yet?"

"Well, I had to find a job. I have been busy."

"You must find time for him if you have none for anything else. Good Lord, man! you're a fool not to have been down to the Union House and registered your name the first morning after you came here! If you run against him—well, you mustn't, that's all!"

McMurdo showed mild surprise. "I've been a member of the lodge for over two years, Scanlan, but I never heard that duties were so pressing as all that."

"Maybe not in Chicago."

"Well, it's the same society here."

"Is it?"

Scanlan looked at him long and fixedly. There was something sinister in his eyes.

"Isn't it?"

"You'll tell me that in a month's time. I hear you had a talk with the patrolmen after I left the train."

"How did you know that?"

"Oh, it got about—things do get about for good and for bad in this district."

"Well, yes. I told the hounds what I thought of them."

"By the Lord, you'll be a man after McGinty's heart!"

"What, does he hate the police too?"

Scanlan burst out laughing. "You go and see him, my lad," said he as he took his leave. "It's not the police but you that he'll hate if you don't! Now, take a friend's advice and go at once!"

It chanced that on the same evening McMurdo had another more pressing interview which urged him in the same direction. It may have been that his attentions to Ettie had been more evident than before, or that they had gradually obtruded themselves into the slow mind of his good German host; but, whatever the cause, the boarding-house keeper beckoned the young man into his private room and started on the subject without any circumlocution.

"It seems to me, mister," said he, "that you are gettin' set on my Ettie. Ain't that so, or am I wrong?"

"Yes, that is so," the young man answered.

"Vell, I vant to tell you right now that it ain't no manner of use. There's someone slipped in afore you."

"She told me so."

"Vell, you can lay that she told you truth. But did she tell you who it vas?"

"No, I asked her; but she wouldn't tell."

"I dare say not, the leetle baggage! Perhaps she did not vish to frighten you avay."

"Frighten!" McMurdo was on fire in a moment.

"Ah, yes, my friend! You need not be ashamed to be frightened of him. It is Teddy Baldwin."

"And who the devil is he?"

"He is a boss of Scowrers."

"Scowrers! I've heard of them before. It's Scowrers here and Scowrers there, and always in a whisper! What are you all afraid of? Who are the Scowrers?"

The boarding-house keeper instinctively sank his voice, as everyone did who talked about that terrible society. "The Scowrers," said he, "are the Eminent Order of Freemen!"

The young man stared. "Why, I am a member of that order myself."

"You! I vould never have had you in my house if I had known it—not if you vere to pay me a hundred dollar a veek."

"What's wrong with the order? It's for charity and good fellowship. The rules say so."

"Maybe in some places. Not here!"

"What is it here?"

"It's a murder society, that's vat it is."

McMurdo laughed incredulously. "How can you prove that?" he asked.

"Prove it! Are there not fifty murders to prove it? Vat about Milman and Van Shorst, and the Nicholson family, and old Mr. Hyam, and little Billy James, and the others? Prove it! Is there a man or a voman in this valley vat does not know it?"

"See here!" said McMurdo earnestly. "I want you to take back what you've said, or else make it good. One or the other you must do before I quit this room. Put yourself in my place. Here am I, a stranger in the town. I belong to a society that I know only as an innocent one. You'll find it through the length and breadth of the States, but always as an innocent one. Now, when I am counting upon joining it here, you tell me that it is the same as a murder society called the Scowrers. I guess you owe me either an apology or else an explanation, Mr. Shafter."

"I can but tell you vat the whole vorld knows, mister. The bosses of the one are the bosses of the other. If you offend the one, it is the other vat vill strike you. We have proved it too often."

"That's just gossip—I want proof!" said McMurdo.

"If you live here long you vill get your proof. But I forget that you are yourself one of them. You vill soon be as bad as the rest. But you vill find other lodgings, mister. I cannot have you here. Is it not bad enough that one of these people come courting my Ettie, and that I dare not turn him down, but that I should have another for my boarder? Yes, indeed, you shall not sleep here after to-night!"

McMurdo found himself under sentence of banishment both from his comfortable quarters and from the girl whom he loved. He found her alone in the sitting-room that same evening, and he poured his troubles into her ear.

"Sure, your father is after giving me notice," he said. "It's little I would care if it was just my room, but indeed, Ettie, though it's only a week that I've known you, you are the very breath of life to me, and I can't live without you!"

"Oh, hush, Mr. McMurdo, don't speak so!" said the girl. "I have told you, have I not, that you are too late? There is another, and if I have not promised to marry him at once, at least I can promise no one else."

"Suppose I had been first, Ettie, would I have had a chance?"

The girl sank her face into her hands. "I wish to heaven that you had been first!" she sobbed.

McMurdo was down on his knees before her in an instant. "For God's sake, Ettie, let it stand at that!" he cried. "Will you ruin your life and my own for the sake of this promise? Follow your heart, acushla! 'Tis a safer guide than any promise before you knew what it was that you were saying."

He had seized Ettie's white hand between his own strong brown ones.

"Say that you will be mine, and we will face it out together!"

"Not here?"

"Yes, here."

"No, no, Jack!" His arms were round her now. "It could not be here. Could you take me away?"

A struggle passed for a moment over McMurdo's face; but it ended by setting like granite. "No, here," he said. "I'll hold you against the world, Ettie, right here where we are!"

"Why should we not leave together?"

"No, Ettie, I can't leave here."

"But why?"

"I'd never hold my head up again if I felt that I had been driven out. Besides, what is there to be afraid of? Are we not free folks in a free country? If you love me, and I you, who will dare to come between?"

"You don't know, Jack. You've been here too short a time. You don't know this Baldwin. You don't know McGinty and his Scowrers."

"No, I don't know them, and I don't fear them, and I don't believe in them!" said McMurdo. "I've lived among rough men, my darling, and instead of fearing them it has always ended that they have feared me—always, Ettie. It's mad on the face of it! If these men, as your father says, have done crime after crime in the valley, and if everyone knows them by name, how comes it that none are brought to justice? You answer me that, Ettie!"

"Because no witness dares to appear against them. He would not live a month if he did. Also because they have always their own men to swear that the accused one was far from the scene of the crime. But surely, Jack, you must have read all this. I had understood that every paper in the United States was writing about it."

"Well, I have read something, it is true; but I had thought it was a story. Maybe these men have some reason in what they do. Maybe they are wronged and have no other way to help themselves."

"Oh, Jack, don't let me hear you speak so! That is how he speaks—the other one!"

"Baldwin—he speaks like that, does he?"

"And that is why I loathe him so. Oh, Jack, now I can tell you the truth. I loathe him with all my heart; but I fear him also. I fear him for myself; but above all I fear him for father. I know that some great sorrow would come upon us if I dared to say what I really felt. That is why I have put him off with half-promises. It was in real truth our only hope. But if you would fly with me, Jack, we could take father with us and live forever far from the power of these wicked men."

Again there was the struggle upon McMurdo's face, and again it set like granite. "No harm shall come to you, Ettie—nor to your father either. As to wicked men, I expect you may find that I am as bad as the worst of them before we're through."

"No, no, Jack! I would trust you anywhere."

McMurdo laughed bitterly. "Good Lord! how little you know of me! Your innocent soul, my darling, could not even guess what is passing in mine. But, hullo, who's the visitor?"

The door had opened suddenly, and a young fellow came swaggering in with the air of one who is the master. He was a handsome, dashing young man of about the same age and build as McMurdo himself. Under his broad-brimmed black felt hat, which he had not troubled to remove, a handsome face with fierce, domineering eyes and a curved hawk-bill of a nose looked savagely at the pair who sat by the stove.

Ettie had jumped to her feet full of confusion and alarm. "I'm glad to see you, Mr. Baldwin," said she. "You're earlier than I had thought. Come and sit down."

Baldwin stood with his hands on his hips looking at McMurdo. "Who is this?" he asked curtly.

"It's a friend of mine, Mr. Baldwin, a new boarder here. Mr. McMurdo, may I introduce you to Mr. Baldwin?"

The young men nodded in surly fashion to each other.

"Maybe Miss Ettie has told you how it is with us?" said Baldwin.

"I didn't understand that there was any relation between you."

"Didn't you? Well, you can understand it now. You can take it from me that this young lady is mine, and you'll find it a very fine evening for a walk."

"Thank you, I am in no humour for a walk."

"Aren't you?" The man's savage eyes were blazing with anger. "Maybe you are in a humour for a fight, Mr. Boarder!"

"That I am!" cried McMurdo, springing to his feet. "You never said a more welcome word."

"For God's sake, Jack! Oh, for God's sake!" cried poor, distracted Ettie. "Oh, Jack, Jack, he will hurt you!"

"Oh, it's Jack, is it?" said Baldwin with an oath. "You've come to that already, have you?"

"Oh, Ted, be reasonable—be kind! For my sake, Ted, if ever you loved me, be big-hearted and forgiving!"

"I think, Ettie, that if you were to leave us alone we could get this thing settled," said McMurdo quietly. "Or maybe, Mr. Baldwin, you will take a turn down the street with me. It's a fine evening, and there's some open ground beyond the next block."

"I'll get even with you without needing to dirty my hands," said his enemy. "You'll wish you had never set foot in this house before I am through with you!"

"No time like the present," cried McMurdo.

"I'll choose my own time, mister. You can leave the time to me. See here!" He suddenly rolled up his sleeve and showed upon his forearm a peculiar sign which appeared to have been branded there. It was a circle with a triangle within it. "D'you know what that means?"

"I neither know nor care!"

"Well, you will know, I'll promise you that. You won't be much older, either. Perhaps Miss Ettie can tell you something about it. As to you, Ettie, you'll come back to me on your knees—d'ye hear, girl?—on your knees—and then I'll tell you what your punishment may be. You've sowed—and by the Lord, I'll see that you reap!" He glanced at them both in fury. Then he turned upon his heel, and an instant later the outer door had banged behind him.

For a few moments McMurdo and the girl stood in silence. Then she threw her arms around him.

"Oh, Jack, how brave you were! But it is no use, you must fly! To-night—Jack—to-night! It's your only hope. He will have your life. I read it in his horrible eyes. What chance have you against a dozen of them, with Boss McGinty and all the power of the lodge behind them?"

McMurdo disengaged her hands, kissed her, and gently pushed her back into a chair. "There, acushla, there! Don't be disturbed or fear for me. I'm a Freeman myself. I'm after telling your father about it. Maybe I am no better than the others; so don't make a saint of me. Perhaps you hate me too, now that I've told you as much?"

"Hate you, Jack? While life lasts I could never do that! I've heard that there is no harm in being a Freeman anywhere but here; so why should I think the worse of you for that? But if you are a Freeman, Jack, why should you not go down and make a friend of Boss McGinty? Oh, hurry, Jack, hurry! Get your word in first, or the hounds will be on your trail."

"I was thinking the same thing," said McMurdo. "I'll go right now and fix it. You can tell your father that I'll sleep here to-night and find some other quarters in the morning."

The bar of McGinty's saloon was crowded as usual; for it was the favourite loafing place of all the rougher elements of the town. The man was popular; for he had a rough, jovial disposition which formed a mask, covering a great deal which lay behind it. But apart from this popularity, the fear in which he was held throughout the township, and indeed down the whole thirty miles of the valley and past the mountains on each side of it, was enough in itself to fill his bar; for none could afford to neglect his good will.

Besides those secret powers which it was universally believed that he exercised in so pitiless a fashion, he was a high public official, a municipal councillor, and a commissioner of roads, elected to the office through the votes of the ruffians who in turn expected to receive favours at his hands. Assessments and taxes were enormous; the public works were notoriously neglected, the accounts were slurred over by bribed auditors, and the decent citizen was terrorized into paying public blackmail, and holding his tongue lest some worse thing befall him.

Thus it was that, year by year, Boss McGinty's diamond pins became more obtrusive, his gold chains more weighty across a more gorgeous vest, and his saloon stretched farther and farther, until it threatened to absorb one whole side of the Market Square.

McMurdo pushed open the swinging door of the saloon and made his way amid the crowd of men within, through an atmosphere blurred with tobacco smoke and heavy with the smell of spirits. The place was brilliantly lighted, and the huge, heavily gilt mirrors upon every wall reflected and multiplied the garish illumination. There were several bartenders in their shirt sleeves, hard at work mixing drinks for the loungers who fringed the broad, brass-trimmed counter.

At the far end, with his body resting upon the bar and a cigar stuck at an acute angle from the corner of his mouth, stood a tall, strong, heavily built man who could be none other than the famous McGinty himself. He was a black-maned giant, bearded to the cheek-bones, and with a shock of raven hair which fell to his collar. His complexion was as swarthy as that of an Italian, and his eyes were of a strange dead black, which, combined with a slight squint, gave them a particularly sinister appearance.

All else in the man—his noble proportions, his fine features, and his frank bearing—fitted in with that jovial, man-to-man manner which he affected. Here, one would say, is a bluff, honest fellow, whose heart would be sound however rude his outspoken words might seem. It was only when those dead, dark eyes, deep and remorseless, were turned upon a man that he shrank within himself, feeling that he was face to face with an infinite possibility of latent evil, with a strength and courage and cunning behind it which made it a thousand times more deadly.

Having had a good look at his man, McMurdo elbowed his way forward with his usual careless audacity, and pushed himself through the little group of courtiers who were fawning upon the powerful boss, laughing uproariously at the smallest of his jokes. The young stranger's bold gray eyes looked back fearlessly through their glasses at the deadly black ones which turned sharply upon him.

"Well, young man, I can't call your face to mind."

"I'm new here, Mr. McGinty."

"You are not so new that you can't give a gentleman his proper title."

"He's Councillor McGinty, young man," said a voice from the group.

"I'm sorry, Councillor. I'm strange to the ways of the place. But I was advised to see you."

"Well, you see me. This is all there is. What d'you think of me?"

"Well, it's early days. If your heart is as big as your body, and your soul as fine as your face, then I'd ask for nothing better," said McMurdo.

"By Gar! you've got an Irish tongue in your head anyhow," cried the saloon-keeper, not quite certain whether to humour this audacious visitor or to stand upon his dignity.

"So you are good enough to pass my appearance?"

"Sure," said McMurdo.

"And you were told to see me?"

"I was."

"And who told you?"

"Brother Scanlan of Lodge 341, Vermissa. I drink your health Councillor, and to our better acquaintance." He raised a glass with which he had been served to his lips and elevated his little finger as he drank it.

McGinty, who had been watching him narrowly, raised his thick black eyebrows. "Oh, it's like that, is it?" said he. "I'll have to look a bit closer into this, Mister—"

"McMurdo."

"A bit closer, Mr. McMurdo; for we don't take folk on trust in these parts, nor believe all we're told neither. Come in here for a moment, behind the bar."

There was a small room there, lined with barrels. McGinty carefully closed the door, and then seated himself on one of them, biting thoughtfully on his cigar and surveying his companion with those disquieting eyes. For a couple of minutes he sat in complete silence. McMurdo bore the inspection cheerfully, one hand in his coat pocket, the other twisting his brown moustache. Suddenly McGinty stooped and produced a wicked-looking revolver.

"See here, my joker," said he, "if I thought you were playing any game on us, it would be short work for you."

"This is a strange welcome," McMurdo answered with some dignity, "for the Body master of a lodge of Freemen to give to a stranger brother."

"Ay, but it's just that same that you have to prove," said McGinty, "and God help you if you fail! Where were you made?"

"Lodge 29, Chicago."

"When?"

"June 24, 1872."

"What Body master?"

"James H. Scott."

"Who is your district ruler?"

"Bartholomew Wilson."

"Hum! You seem glib enough in your tests. What are you doing here?"

"Working, the same as you—but a poorer job."

"You have your back answer quick enough."

"Yes, I was always quick of speech."

"Are you quick of action?"

"I have had that name among those that knew me best."

"Well, we may try you sooner than you think. Have you heard anything of the lodge in these parts?"

"I've heard that it takes a man to be a brother."

"True for you, Mr. McMurdo. Why did you leave Chicago?"

"I'm damned if I tell you that!"

McGinty opened his eyes. He was not used to being answered in such fashion, and it amused him. "Why won't you tell me?"

"Because no brother may tell another a lie."

"Then the truth is too bad to tell?"

"You can put it that way if you like."

"See here, mister, you can't expect me, as Body master, to pass into the lodge a man for whose past he can't answer."

McMurdo looked puzzled. Then he took a worn newspaper cutting from an inner pocket.

"You wouldn't squeal on a fellow?" said he.

"I'll wipe my hand across your face if you say such words to me!" cried McGinty hotly.

"You are right, Councillor," said McMurdo meekly. "I should apologize. I spoke without thought. Well, I know that I am safe in your hands. Look at that clipping."

McGinty glanced his eyes over the account of the shooting of one Jonas Pinto, in the Lake Saloon, Market Street, Chicago, in the New Year week of 1874.

"Your work?" he asked, as he handed back the paper.

McMurdo nodded.

"Why did you shoot him?"

"I was helping Uncle Sam to make dollars. Maybe mine were not as good gold as his, but they looked as well and were cheaper to make. This man Pinto helped me to shove the queer—"

"To do what?"

"Well, it means to pass the dollars out into circulation. Then he said he would split. Maybe he did split. I didn't wait to see. I just killed him and lighted out for the coal country."

"Why the coal country?"

"'Cause I'd read in the papers that they weren't too particular in those parts."

McGinty laughed. "You were first a coiner and then a murderer, and you came to these parts because you thought you'd be welcome."

"That's about the size of it," McMurdo answered.

"Well, I guess you'll go far. Say, can you make those dollars yet?"

McMurdo took half a dozen from his pocket. "Those never passed the Philadelphia mint," said he.

"You don't say!" McGinty held them to the light in his enormous hand, which was hairy as a gorilla's. "I can see no difference. Gar! you'll be a mighty useful brother, I'm thinking! We can do with a bad man or two among us, Friend McMurdo: for there are times when we have to take our own part. We'd soon be against the wall if we didn't shove back at those that were pushing us."

"Well, I guess I'll do my share of shoving with the rest of the boys."

"You seem to have a good nerve. You didn't squirm when I shoved this gun at you."

"It was not me that was in danger."

"Who then?"

"It was you, Councillor." McMurdo drew a cocked pistol from the side pocket of his peajacket. "I was covering you all the time. I guess my shot would have been as quick as yours."

"By Gar!" McGinty flushed an angry red and then burst into a roar of laughter. "Say, we've had no such holy terror come to hand this many a year. I reckon the lodge will learn to be proud of you.... Well, what the hell do you want? And can't I speak alone with a gentleman for five minutes but you must butt in on us?"

The bartender stood abashed. "I'm sorry, Councillor, but it's Ted Baldwin. He says he must see you this very minute."

The message was unnecessary; for the set, cruel face of the man himself was looking over the servant's shoulder. He pushed the bartender out and closed the door on him.

"So," said he with a furious glance at McMurdo, "you got here first, did you? I've a word to say to you, Councillor, about this man."

"Then say it here and now before my face," cried McMurdo.

"I'll say it at my own time, in my own way."

"Tut! Tut!" said McGinty, getting off his barrel. "This will never do. We have a new brother here, Baldwin, and it's not for us to greet him in such fashion. Hold out your hand, man, and make it up!"

"Never!" cried Baldwin in a fury.

"I've offered to fight him if he thinks I have wronged him," said McMurdo. "I'll fight him with fists, or, if that won't satisfy him, I'll fight him any other way he chooses. Now, I'll leave it to you, Councillor, to judge between us as a Body master should."

"What is it, then?"

"A young lady. She's free to choose for herself."

"Is she?" cried Baldwin.

"As between two brothers of the lodge I should say that she was," said the Boss.

"Oh, that's your ruling, is it?"

"Yes, it is, Ted Baldwin," said McGinty, with a wicked stare. "Is it you that would dispute it?"

"You would throw over one that has stood by you this five years in favour of a man that you never saw before in your life? You're not Body master for life, Jack McGinty, and by God! when next it comes to a vote—"

The Councillor sprang at him like a tiger. His hand closed round the other's neck, and he hurled him back across one of the barrels. In his mad fury he would have squeezed the life out of him if McMurdo had not interfered.

"Easy, Councillor! For heaven's sake, go easy!" he cried, as he dragged him back.

McGinty released his hold, and Baldwin, cowed and shaken gasping for breath, and shivering in every limb, as one who has looked over the very edge of death, sat up on the barrel over which he had been hurled.

"You've been asking for it this many a day, Ted Baldwin—now you've got it!" cried McGinty, his huge chest rising and falling. "Maybe you think if I was voted down from Body master you would find yourself in my shoes. It's for the lodge to say that. But so long as I am the chief I'll have no man lift his voice against me or my rulings."

"I have nothing against you," mumbled Baldwin, feeling his throat.

"Well, then," cried the other, relapsing in a moment into a bluff joviality, "we are all good friends again and there's an end of the matter."

He took a bottle of champagne down from the shelf and twisted out the cork.

"See now," he continued, as he filled three high glasses. "Let us drink the quarrelling toast of the lodge.

After that, as you know, there can be no bad blood between us. Now, then the left hand on the apple of my throat. I say to you, Ted Baldwin, what is the offense, sir?"

"The clouds are heavy," answered Baldwin

"But they will forever brighten."

"And this I swear!"

The men drank their glasses, and the same ceremony was performed between Baldwin and McMurdo

"There!" cried McGinty, rubbing his hands. "That's the end of the black blood. You come under lodge discipline if it goes further, and that's a heavy hand in these parts, as Brother Baldwin knows—and as you will damn soon find out, Brother McMurdo, if you ask for trouble!"

"Faith, I'd be slow to do that," said McMurdo. He held out his hand to Baldwin. "I'm quick to quarrel and quick to forgive. It's my hot Irish blood, they tell me. But it's over for me, and I bear no grudge."

Baldwin had to take the proffered hand; for the baleful eye of the terrible Boss was upon him. But his sullen face showed how little the words of the other had moved him.

McGinty clapped them both on the shoulders. "Tut! These girls! These girls!" he cried. "To think that the same petticoats should come between two of my boys! It's the devil's own luck! Well, it's the colleen inside of them that must settle the question; for it's outside the jurisdiction of a Body master—and the Lord be praised for that! We have enough on us, without the women as well. You'll have to be affiliated to Lodge 341, Brother McMurdo. We have our own ways and methods, different from Chicago. Saturday night is our meeting, and if you come then, we'll make you free forever of the Vermissa Valley."

The Valley of Fear Summary and Analysis of Part I Chapter 7 and Part II Chapters 1 & 2

Summary

Chapter 7

In the morning Holmes and Watson join Mason and MacDonald on the police station, wherein Holmes proceeds to inform them they ought to not waste their time at the bicyclist. Astonished, MacDonald asks why. Holmes says he cannot tell them pretty yet, after which speaks of the history of Manor House. MacDonald grows aggravated and Holmes courteously begs forgiveness.

Holmes then tells the men that he spent time within the study the previous night and discovered the lacking dumbbell. They are at the edge of the unexplored and shortly, he says, he'll percentage the entirety he knows. Holmes asks them to all meet once more at dusk. Although Mason and MacDonald locate it a bit difficult to go with the plan without understanding extra information, they ultimately agree.

Confused, MacDonald replies that they cannot try this, but Holmes insists the note be sent.

In the evening, the four guys reassemble. Holmes thanks them for going on this little excursion, and warns them it could be bloodless and take a while. They walk to Manor House, wait close to the shrubbery that lies in view of the drawbridge, and observe the window.

The shadows darken and the night time grows bitterly bloodless. Everything within the residence is dark except for a mild burning within the take a look at. Finally MacDonald asks what they're looking ahead to, and Holmes suddenly points to the window. A figure is within the study. He actions about stealthily and leans out the window, apparently stirring the moat beneath him. He hauls up something. At this second Holmes indicators; the organization runs forward across the bridge and rings the bell. Ames lets them in and Holmes rushes past him to look Cecil Barker standing inside the take a look at. Barker is aghast and indignant, but Holmes factors to a bundle hurriedly thrust underneath the desk. He proclaims that that is what they had been after.

Barker is taken aback and wonders how Holmes knew approximately this. Holmes explains that he became searching out the lacking dumbbell and deduced that, for the reason that there was water nearby, the dumbbell—likely used as a weight for something—would be there.

He undoes the package deal and unearths the dumbbell, boots, a knife, and garb. Holding up the clothes he reads the label: 'Neal, Outfitter, Vermissa, U.S.A.' This was Vermissa Valley, a coal mining locale that Barker had instructed them in one in every of his earlier interviews changed into related to Douglas's first spouse. This can also be the Valley of Fear.

Barker's face is going through "anger, amazement, consternation, and indecision" (231). He says acridly that he's going to tell them nothing, to which the inspector says he'll should be kept in sight until they get a warrant.

Suddenly Mrs. Douglas's voice breaks the impasse. She implores Barker to prevent, and Holmes advises him to believe inside the law. He then provides that perhaps Mr. Douglas have to inform his personal story.

To everyone's shock, a man emerges from the wall. Mrs. Douglas embraces this guy, and Barker grasps his hand. The man blinks within the light and turns to Watson. He tells him he's heard he is the historian of the bunch, and has papers for him on the Valley of Fear.

Amid the amazement of all those accumulated, Holmes asks for the story. First, even though, Holmes explains that when he discovered the garments inside the moat he'd deduced that the frame turned into no longer Mr. Douglas's, but rather the bicyclist's.

Mr. Douglas starts by staying there are many men who want to hurt him, and as long as he is alive they may not prevent pursuing him. He turned into chased from Chicago to California, then out of America, but his idea he turned into subsequently secure. He by no means advised his wife because he did no longer need to burden her.

The day before the murder, Douglas had glimpsed a man whom he knew for his worst enemy. He became on guard all day, however felt secure as soon as the drawbridge become up. He by no means dreamed the man could get in, but while he entered the study that night time he saw a boot below the curtain. The guys fought to the death, and Douglas fired the shot that killed Ted Stanley Baldwin. Barker and his wife came down, saw the frame, and found out that no one else had heard. They decided to set the scene, knowing that the person's face become so unrecognizable because of the gunshot that nobody will be the wiser. The wedding ring couldn't come off his very own determine, however he turned into capable of positioned the other jewelry on the man. He knew of a hiding vicinity within the house and retired there; Barker did the rest.

Douglas stops talking for a second. Holmes asks how the man got in, and Douglas admits he has no idea. Holmes then tells Douglas that he has worse enemies to stand than the English regulation or even enemies in America, and tells him to be on his protect.

Watson now says the tale must cross returned two decades and thousands of miles away.

Part II: The Scowrers

Chapter 1

It turned into February 1875 inside the cold, wintry ironworking and coalmining land of Pennsylvania. This became a desolate area packed with dark and craggy wooded area and rock. Most men on it are workmen, but there may be another. This guy is young and good-looking; he is likewise gregarious and witty but has an aspect to him. He sits alone after attempting futilely to talk to others.

The iron and coal valleys of Vermissa have symptoms of "the crudest conflict of existence" (240). The young guy looks out the window, repulsed and intrigued. Sometimes he appears at letters he holds, as well as a massive revolver.

Another man notices the gun and conversationally says that the younger man would possibly need it right here someday. The young guy says he from time to time wanted it in which he got here from—Chicago. The workman asks why he came to Pennsylvania, and the younger man says he came for paintings; he does no longer assume he can have trouble finding it due to the fact he's within the union and is likewise a member of the Eminent Order of Freemen. The different guy pauses in recognition and appears around the car, then shakes the young guy's hand. They change coded words and sooner or later slip into less difficult members of the family. The younger guy is John McMurdo, and the workman is Scanlan.

Scanlan asks why McMurdo left Chicago if there has been paintings for him there. McMurdo cagily says that he left due to problem, however he grows a touch indignant at Scanlan's questions. Scanlan says he met no offense. He recommends a boarding house and then tells him he have to go see Boss McGinty, the Body master of Vermissa.

After Scanlan walks off, the 2 policemen who had been casually talking in a corner inform McMurdo to avoid guys like Scanlan. McMurdo grows irate and yells loudly that he did now not ask for their recommendation, is not a sucker, and is neither fearful of them nor of their kind. The policemen are bemused and warn him to be careful.

The relaxation of the workmen on the educate specific their admiration of McMurdo and say goodnight to him. The younger man's recognition accordingly became made earlier than he even stepped into the town. As for that city, it's miles horribly squalid and dirty. Someone on the street factors out Union House because the homestead of Jack McGinty. When McMurdo says he did no longer understand McGinty, the person is surprised. He asks if McMurdo has heard of the Scowrers. McMurdo says that he has: he heard that they're a gang of murderers. The man is taken aback and hushes him, caution him now not to be loud like that.

After they component, McMurdo walks to the house of Jacob Shafter to searching for room and board. A noticeably stunning younger lady opens the door, and McMurdo is dumbstruck. She invitations him in and introduces herself as Ettie, saying her father could be returned quickly. Old Jacob Shafter returns and accepts McMurdo's request for lodging.

Chapter 2

McMurdo turns into very famous and liked in Shafter's and beyond. He is good-humored but occasionally has flashes of anger. He is in love with Ettie, and he or she eventually returns the sentiment, entranced with the aid of his testimonies of Ireland and different American towns.

McMurdo will become a bookkeeper due to the fact he's well-knowledgeable. He has not pronounced to the inn of the Freemen, and at some point Scanlan, the person he'd met in the train, asks why he has not met McGinty yet. McMurdo is amazed and says he has been busy. Scanlan suggests he now not run afoul of the body master, and anticipates that they will surely have lots in commonplace. McMurdo asks if McGinty hates the police too, and Scanlan laughs.

That equal night Shafter calls McMurdo apart and asks if he has designs on Ettie. The young man admits he loves her, but Shafter says she is already spoken for by means of Teddy Baldwin, an md of the Scowrers. McMurdo has heard this call before, however wonders why everybody is afraid. Shafter says they're the Eminent Order of the Freedmen. McMurdo is taken aback and says he is a member of that. Shafter recoils and says he would no longer have allowed McMurdo to board there if he had recognized that, and says that the Scowrers are a murder society. McMurdo is annoyed; he demands an apology and evidence of the Scowrers' bad deeds. Shafter warns him that if he stays right here long enough he will get his proof; he tells him he have to locate other accommodations and leave Ettie alone.

McMurdo speaks with Ettie and she bursts into tears pronouncing she does not love Teddy and wishes she could be with him. She wishes them to flee the vicinity, however McMurdo says he is not afraid and could not go away. Ettie loathes Baldwin, however fears what's going to occur to her father if she says something. McMurdo pronounces he's going to take care of factors.

At that second a younger man is available in. Teddy Baldwin is handsome and fierce, and he looks suspiciously at McMurdo. Ettie introduces him as a brand new boarder and 1st Earl Baldwin of Bewdley responds by way of asking if he is aware of the expertise among him and Ettie. McMurdo fires returned that he does not. Tensions start to flare, and the 2 guys almost combat. 1st earl baldwin of bewdley suggests McMurdo a mark on his arm and tells him to heed it. He furiously tells Ettie she had higher come back to him on her knees. With that, he departs.

Ettie cries that McMurdo become so courageous but they have to leave. When McMurdo refuses, she tells him to head see McGinty. McMurdo is of the same opinion.

The saloon, opulent and shiny, is crowded. McGinty is well-appreciated, however human beings also fear him and realize his strength in the course of the whole valley. He held many municipal positions, gave out favors, and became particularly wealthy.

McMurdo spies the man who can handiest be McGinty. He is big, robust, and has long dark hair with a swarthy complexion. His noble capabilities are matched by way of the jovial manners he possesses; he gives the impression of being honest, but his eyes endorse his true malice and threat.

Having found his man, McMurdo moves audaciously ahead and greets him. McGinty appraises him and tells him that he should use his real title. McMurdo apologizes as he's new, and gives complimentary words. He says Scanlan told him to come back by means of. McMurdo calls him over privately, indicates him his revolver to warn him in opposition to rash behavior, and tests him on in which he turned into made in Chicago, who his body master become, and so on. McGinty admires McMurdo's brief speech and tells him he may additionally need quick motion too. McMurdo will now not tell him why he left Chicago, which angers McGinty, however McMurdo says he can't mislead a brother. Finally, although, he makes a decision to inform him the truth: he was partners with a person making faux foreign money and killed the man after he stated he'd cut up. He then came here, thinking he could suit in here. McGinty is impressed and thinks he can have use for him right here.

At that moment Teddy Baldwin comes up, impassioned and indignant. He bursts out that McMurdo wronged him, however McMurdo coolly replies that whom Ettie loves is her choice. McGinty concurs due to the fact she is choosing among two freemen. This does no longer appease 1st Earl Baldwin of Bewdley, who starts to rise up towards McGinty for selecting this new man over him. He even shows McGinty is probably voted out of his function. This infuriates McGinty, and he slams Baldwin kind of to the floor.

Finally, sputtering, 1st Earl Baldwin of Bewdley apologizes and says he did no longer imply to offend. McGinty jovially releases him and procures champagne. He makes the two young men comply with halt the bad blood. McMurdo gives out his hand to 1st Earl Baldwin of Bewdley, alongside an apology. 1st Earl Baldwin of Bewdley accepts reluctantly.

McGinty laughs approximately how ladies can come between guys. He then tells McMurdo he ought to come to their motel meeting Saturday night time.

Analysis

The structure of this novel is truly rather unconventional: Doyle wraps up the main mystery of the supposed killing of John Douglas after which jumps backward in time and area to provide the prolonged account of why Douglas needed to fake his personal homicide. To Doyle's credit score, the various revelations are legitimately unexpected. While readers ought to guess that something was strange approximately Mrs. Douglas and Cecil's courting, most likely they might not wager that the characters have been overlaying up Douglas's faked demise. It is also sudden that Douglas is still alive, that he's hiding inside his own domestic, and that Barker and Mrs. Douglas were able to assist him in putting in place the scene. What is perhaps now not so sudden for enthusiasts of the Holmes books and movie adaptations is that Holmes is capable of take one of the unnoticed portions of evidence—the dumbbell—and figure that it's far that very issue with a view to yield the most in terms of fixing the case. Holmes's mind, eager observational and deductive abilities, and tenacity are on complete display right here.

The novel's second part introduces a new protagonist (that term is used loosely!), McMurdo, and a new placing in the 1870s coalmines of Pennsylvania. Although Holmes and Watson are nowhere to be located, this story is compelling however. McMurdo's past is ambiguous and for that reason mysterious; the Scowrers are a society to be reckoned with, and McGinty is a captivating villain. Teddy Baldwin and Ettie Shafter are greater prosaic and one-dimensional, but upload properly to the drama of the story.

That drama is essentially based on an actual-life situation: the Molly Maguires, a secret-society-inside-a-union of Irish-American murderers in the coal mines of Pennsylvania, who had been infiltrated by a Pinkerton detective and subsequently put on trial for his or her misdeeds (see "Other" in this Classic Note). This is the handiest tale of Doyle's that explicitly deals with Irish problem rely, even though different tales of his introduced in a few Irish political motifs.

A bit of historical past on this count number can also light up the motives why Doyle chose this topic for one in all his 4 Holmes novels. In 1815 Doyle's grandfather emigrated from Ireland to London because of the persecution of Catholics below the Penal Laws. In Edinburgh Doyle located it difficult to come to terms together with his Irish Catholic identification, but he located it even more tough to include a Scottish identification.

Doyle would have recognized of the name of the game society of the Fenian Brotherhood, or the Irish Republican Brotherhood because it became recognized in Ireland, and their purpose of separatism from Britain. The Fenians engaged in numerous violent incidents inside the 1860s, and anti-Irish sentiment swept the United Kingdom. Though submit-famine Ireland noticed erosion inside the agrarian secret societies, those societies migrated with immigrants to America. In the Pennsylvania coal fields, critic Catherine Wynne explains, "The Irish...determined little change of their situations. Absentee landlords were replaced by means of absentee mine-owners; wages were equally low; and people were frequently pressured to save within the organization keep wherein fees had been exorbitantly high. Mining was for the majority of the Irish an alien enterprise. The unskilled Irish had been pressured to enroll in the low-fame laboring ranks, while their English and Welsh fellow employees occupied the better paid and extra socially prestigious mining positions. Ethnic divisions therefore ensued." Many joined the Ancient Order of the Hibernians, and their accommodations became fronts for the greater violent Molly Maguires.

Although Doyle turned into a Unionist for the early years of the 1900s, through 1911 he had come to support Irish home rule. Critic Catherine Wynne explains, "Fundamentally, [this view] abrades the unitary idea of Doyle as an essential Englishman, patriotically devoted to Crown, empire's defender and empire's apologist. That Doyle become of Irish Catholic parents and born in Scotland complicates his mindset to Irish political needs; as Pierre Nordon proposes." When it came time for Doyle to write his 1915 novel, he had a whole lot to navigate—a topic to which we shall go back later inside the evaluation.

Chapter 3—Lodge 341, Vermissa

On the day following the evening which had contained so many exciting events, McMurdo moved his lodgings from old Jacob Shafter's and took up his quarters at the Widow MacNamara's on the extreme outskirts of the town. Scanlan, his original acquaintance aboard the train, had occasion shortly afterwards to move into Vermissa, and the two lodged together. There was no other boarder, and the hostess was an easy-going old Irishwoman who left them to themselves; so that they had a freedom for speech and action welcome to men who had secrets in common.

Shafter had relented to the extent of letting McMurdo come to his meals there when he liked; so that his intercourse with Ettie was by no means broken. On the contrary, it drew closer and more intimate as the weeks went by.

In his bedroom at his new abode McMurdo felt it safe to take out the coining moulds, and under many a pledge of secrecy a number of brothers from the lodge were allowed to come in and see them, each carrying away in his pocket some examples of the false money, so cunningly struck that there was never the slightest difficulty or danger in passing it. Why, with such a wonderful art at his command, McMurdo should condescend to work at all was a perpetual mystery to his companions; though he made it clear to anyone who asked him that if he lived without any visible means it would very quickly bring the police upon his track.

One policeman was indeed after him already; but the incident, as luck would have it, did the adventurer a great deal more good than harm. After the first introduction there were few evenings when he did not find his way to McGinty's saloon, there to make closer acquaintance with "the boys," which was the jovial title by which the dangerous gang who infested the place were known to one another. His dashing manner and fearlessness of speech made him a favourite with them all; while the rapid and scientific way in which he polished off his antagonist in an "all in" bar-room scrap earned the respect of that rough community. Another incident, however, raised him even higher in their estimation.

Just at the crowded hour one night, the door opened and a man entered with the quiet blue uniform and peaked cap of the mine police. This was a special body raised by the railways and colliery owners to supplement the efforts of the ordinary civil police, who were perfectly helpless in the face of the organized ruffianism which terrorized the district. There was a hush as he entered, and many a curious glance was cast at him; but the relations between policemen and criminals are peculiar in some parts of the States, and McGinty himself, standing behind his counter, showed no surprise when the policeman enrolled himself among his customers.

"A straight whisky; for the night is bitter," said the police officer. "I don't think we have met before, Councillor?"

"You'll be the new captain?" said McGinty.

"That's so. We're looking to you, Councillor, and to the other leading citizens, to help us in upholding law and order in this township. Captain Marvin is my name."

"We'd do better without you, Captain Marvin," said McGinty coldly; "for we have our own police of the township, and no need for any imported goods. What are you but the paid tool of the capitalists, hired by them to club or shoot your poorer fellow citizen?"

"Well, well, we won't argue about that," said the police officer good-humouredly. "I expect we all do our duty same as we see it; but we can't all see it the same." He had drunk off his glass and had turned to go, when his eyes fell upon the face of Jack McMurdo, who was scowling at his elbow. "Hullo! Hullo!" he cried, looking him up and down. "Here's an old acquaintance!"

McMurdo shrank away from him. "I was never a friend to you nor any other cursed copper in my life," said he.

"An acquaintance isn't always a friend," said the police captain, grinning. "You're Jack McMurdo of Chicago, right enough, and don't you deny it!"

McMurdo shrugged his shoulders. "I'm not denying it," said he. "D'ye think I'm ashamed of my own name?"

"You've got good cause to be, anyhow."

"What the devil d'you mean by that?" he roared with his fists clenched.

"No, no, Jack, bluster won't do with me. I was an officer in Chicago before ever I came to this darned coal bunker, and I know a Chicago crook when I see one."

McMurdo's face fell. "Don't tell me that you're Marvin of the Chicago Central!" he cried.

"Just the same old Teddy Marvin, at your service. We haven't forgotten the shooting of Jonas Pinto up there."

"I never shot him."

"Did you not? That's good impartial evidence, ain't it? Well, his death came in uncommon handy for you, or they would have had you for shoving the queer. Well, we can let that be bygones; for, between you and me—and perhaps I'm going further than my duty in saying it—they could get no clear case against you, and Chicago's open to you to-morrow."

"I'm very well where I am."

"Well, I've given you the pointer, and you're a sulky dog not to thank me for it."

"Well, I suppose you mean well, and I do thank you," said McMurdo in no very gracious manner.

"It's mum with me so long as I see you living on the straight," said the captain. "But, by the Lord! if you get off after this, it's another story! So good-night to you—and good-night, Councillor."

He left the bar-room; but not before he had created a local hero. McMurdo's deeds in far Chicago had been whispered before. He had put off all questions with a smile, as one who did not wish to have greatness thrust upon him. But now the thing was officially confirmed. The bar loafers crowded round him and shook him heartily by the hand. He was free of the community from that time on. He could drink hard and show little trace of it; but that evening, had his mate Scanlan not been at hand to lead him home, the feted hero would surely have spent his night under the bar.

On a Saturday night McMurdo was introduced to the lodge. He had thought to pass in without ceremony as being an initiate of Chicago; but there were particular rites in Vermissa of which they were proud, and these had to be undergone by every postulant. The assembly met in a large room reserved for such purposes at the

Union House. Some sixty members assembled at Vermissa; but that by no means represented the full strength of the organization, for there were several other lodges in the valley, and others across the mountains on each side, who exchanged members when any serious business was afoot, so that a crime might be done by men who were strangers to the locality. Altogether there were not less than five hundred scattered over the coal district.

In the bare assembly room the men were gathered round a long table. At the side was a second one laden with bottles and glasses, on which some members of the company were already turning their eyes. McGinty sat at the head with a flat black velvet cap upon his shock of tangled black hair, and a coloured purple stole round his neck, so that he seemed to be a priest presiding over some diabolical ritual. To right and left of him were the higher lodge officials, the cruel, handsome face of Ted Baldwin among them. Each of these wore some scarf or medallion as emblem of his office.

They were, for the most part, men of mature age; but the rest of the company consisted of young fellows from eighteen to twenty-five, the ready and capable agents who carried out the commands of their seniors. Among the older men were many whose features showed the tigerish, lawless souls within; but looking at the rank and file it was difficult to believe that these eager and open-faced young fellows were in very truth a dangerous gang of murderers, whose minds had suffered such complete moral perversion that they took a horrible pride in their proficiency at the business, and looked with deepest respect at the man who had the reputation of making what they called "a clean job."

To their contorted natures it had become a spirited and chivalrous thing to volunteer for service against some man who had never injured them, and whom in many cases they had never seen in their lives. The crime committed, they quarrelled as to who had actually struck the fatal blow, and amused one another and the company by describing the cries and contortions of the murdered man.

At first they had shown some secrecy in their arrangements; but at the time which this narrative describes their proceedings were extraordinarily open, for the repeated failure of the law had proved to them that, on the one hand, no one would dare to witness against them, and on the other they had an unlimited number of stanch witnesses upon whom they could call, and a well-filled treasure chest from which they could draw the funds to engage the best legal talent in the state. In ten long years of outrage there had been no single conviction, and the only danger that ever threatened the Scowrers lay in the victim himself—who, however outnumbered and taken by surprise, might and occasionally did leave his mark upon his assailants.

McMurdo had been warned that some ordeal lay before him; but no one would tell him in what it consisted. He was led now into an outer room by two solemn brothers. Through the plank partition he could hear the murmur of many voices from the assembly within. Once or twice he caught the sound of his own name, and he knew that they were discussing his candidacy. Then there entered an inner guard with a green and gold sash across his chest.

"The Body master orders that he shall be trussed, blinded, and entered," said he.

The three of them removed his coat, turned up the sleeve of his right arm, and finally passed a rope round above the elbows and made it fast. They next placed a thick black cap right over his head and the upper part of his face, so that he could see nothing. He was then led into the assembly hall.

It was pitch dark and very oppressive under his hood. He heard the rustle and murmur of the people round him, and then the voice of McGinty sounded dull and distant through the covering of his ears.

"John McMurdo," said the voice, "are you already a member of the Ancient Order of Freemen?"

He bowed in assent.

"Is your lodge No. 29, Chicago?"

He bowed again.

"Dark nights are unpleasant," said the voice.

"Yes, for strangers to travel," he answered.

"The clouds are heavy."

"Yes, a storm is approaching."

"Are the brethren satisfied?" asked the Body master.

There was a general murmur of assent.

"We know, Brother, by your sign and by your countersign that you are indeed one of us," said McGinty. "We would have you know, however, that in this county and in other counties of these parts we have certain rites, and also certain duties of our own which call for good men. Are you ready to be tested?"

"I am."

"Are you of stout heart?"

"I am."

"Take a stride forward to prove it."

As the words were said he felt two hard points in front of his eyes, pressing upon them so that it appeared as if he could not move forward without a danger of losing them. None the less, he nerved himself to step resolutely out, and as he did so the pressure melted away. There was a low murmur of applause.

"He is of stout heart," said the voice. "Can you bear pain?"

"As well as another," he answered.

"Test him!"

It was all he could do to keep himself from screaming out, for an agonizing pain shot through his forearm. He nearly fainted at the sudden shock of it; but he bit his lip and clenched his hands to hide his agony.

"I can take more than that," said he.

This time there was loud applause. A finer first appearance had never been made in the lodge. Hands clapped him on the back, and the hood was plucked from his head. He stood blinking and smiling amid the congratulations of the brothers.

"One last word, Brother McMurdo," said McGinty. "You have already sworn the oath of secrecy and fidelity, and you are aware that the punishment for any breach of it is instant and inevitable death?"

"I am," said McMurdo.

"And you accept the rule of the Body master for the time being under all circumstances?"

"I do."

"Then in the name of Lodge 341, Vermissa, I welcome you to its privileges and debates. You will put the liquor on the table, Brother Scanlan, and we will drink to our worthy brother."

McMurdo's coat had been brought to him; but before putting it on he examined his right arm, which still smarted heavily. There on the flesh of the forearm was a circle with a triangle within it, deep and red, as the branding iron had left it. One or two of his neighbours pulled up their sleeves and showed their own lodge marks.

"We've all had it," said one; "but not all as brave as you over it."

"Tut! It was nothing," said he; but it burned and ached all the same.

When the drinks which followed the ceremony of initiation had all been disposed of, the business of the lodge proceeded. McMurdo, accustomed only to the prosaic performances of Chicago, listened with open ears and more surprise than he ventured to show to what followed.

"The first business on the agenda paper," said McGinty, "is to read the following letter from Division Master Windle of Merton County Lodge 249. He says:

"Dear Sir:

"There is a job to be done on Andrew Rae of Rae & Sturmash, coal owners near this place. You will remember that your lodge owes us a return, having had the service of two brethren in the matter of the patrolman last fall. You will send two good men, they will be taken charge of by Treasurer Higgins of this lodge, whose address you know. He will show them when to act and where. Yours in freedom,

"J.W. WINDLE D.M.A.O.F."

"Windle has never refused us when we have had occasion to ask for the loan of a man or two, and it is not for us to refuse him." McGinty paused and looked round the room with his dull, malevolent eyes. "Who will volunteer for the job?"

Several young fellows held up their hands. The Body master looked at them with an approving smile.

"You'll do, Tiger Cormac. If you handle it as well as you did the last, you won't be wrong. And you, Wilson."

"I've no pistol," said the volunteer, a mere boy in his teens.

"It's your first, is it not? Well, you have to be blooded some time. It will be a great start for you. As to the pistol, you'll find it waiting for you, or I'm mistaken. If you report yourselves on Monday, it will be time enough. You'll get a great welcome when you return."

"Any reward this time?" asked Cormac, a thick-set, dark-faced, brutal-looking young man, whose ferocity had earned him the nickname of "Tiger."

"Never mind the reward. You just do it for the honour of the thing. Maybe when it is done there will be a few odd dollars at the bottom of the box."

"What has the man done?" asked young Wilson.

"Sure, it's not for the likes of you to ask what the man has done. He has been judged over there. That's no business of ours. All we have to do is to carry it out for them, same as they would for us. Speaking of that, two brothers from the Merton lodge are coming over to us next week to do some business in this quarter."

"Who are they?" asked someone.

"Faith, it is wiser not to ask. If you know nothing, you can testify nothing, and no trouble can come of it. But they are men who will make a clean job when they are about it."

"And time, too!" cried Ted Baldwin. "Folk are gettin' out of hand in these parts. It was only last week that three of our men were turned off by Foreman Blaker. It's been owing him a long time, and he'll get it full and proper."

"Get what?" McMurdo whispered to his neighbour.

"The business end of a buckshot cartridge!" cried the man with a loud laugh. "What think you of our ways, Brother?"

McMurdo's criminal soul seemed to have already absorbed the spirit of the vile association of which he was now a member. "I like it well," said he. "'Tis a proper place for a lad of mettle."

Several of those who sat around heard his words and applauded them.

"What's that?" cried the black-maned Body master from the end of the table.

"'Tis our new brother, sir, who finds our ways to his taste."

McMurdo rose to his feet for an instant. "I would say, Eminent Body master, that if a man should be wanted I should take it as an honour to be chosen to help the lodge."

There was great applause at this. It was felt that a new sun was pushing its rim above the horizon. To some of the elders it seemed that the progress was a little too rapid.

"I would move," said the secretary, Harraway, a vulture-faced old graybeard who sat near the chairman, "that Brother McMurdo should wait until it is the good pleasure of the lodge to employ him."

"Sure, that was what I meant; I'm in your hands," said McMurdo.

"Your time will come, Brother," said the chairman. "We have marked you down as a willing man, and we believe that you will do good work in these parts. There is a small matter to-night in which you may take a hand if it so please you."

"I will wait for something that is worth while."

"You can come to-night, anyhow, and it will help you to know what we stand for in this community. I will make the announcement later. Meanwhile," he glanced at his agenda paper, "I have one or two more points to bring before the meeting. First of all, I will ask the treasurer as to our bank balance. There is the pension to Jim Carnaway's widow. He was struck down doing the work of the lodge, and it is for us to see that she is not the loser."

"Jim was shot last month when they tried to kill Chester Wilcox of Marley Creek," McMurdo's neighbour informed him.

"The funds are good at the moment," said the treasurer, with the bankbook in front of him. "The firms have been generous of late. Max Linder & Co. paid five hundred to be left alone. Walker Brothers sent in a hundred; but I took it on myself to return it and ask for five. If I do not hear by Wednesday, their winding gear may get out of order. We had to burn their breaker last year before they became reasonable. Then the West Section Coaling Company has paid its annual contribution. We have enough on hand to meet any obligations."

"What about Archie Swindon?" asked a brother.

"He has sold out and left the district. The old devil left a note for us to say that he had rather be a free crossing sweeper in New York than a large mine owner under the power of a ring of blackmailers. By Gar! it was as well that he made a break for it before the note reached us! I guess he won't show his face in this valley again."

An elderly, clean-shaved man with a kindly face and a good brow rose from the end of the table which faced the chairman. "Mr. Treasurer," he asked, "may I ask who has bought the property of this man that we have driven out of the district?"

"Yes, Brother Morris. It has been bought by the State & Merton County Railroad Company."

"And who bought the mines of Todman and of Lee that came into the market in the same way last year?"

"The same company, Brother Morris."

"And who bought the ironworks of Manson and of Shuman and of Van Deher and of Atwood, which have all been given up of late?"

"They were all bought by the West Gilmerton General Mining Company."

"I don't see, Brother Morris," said the chairman, "that it matters to us who buys them, since they can't carry them out of the district."

"With all respect to you, Eminent Body master, I think it may matter very much to us. This process has been going on now for ten long years. We are gradually driving all the small men out of trade. What is the result? We find in their places great companies like the Railroad or the General Iron, who have their directors in New York or Philadelphia, and care nothing for our threats. We can take it out of their local bosses; but it only means that others will be sent in their stead. And we are making it dangerous for ourselves. The small men could not harm us. They had not the money nor the power. So long as we did not squeeze them too dry, they would stay on under our power. But if these big companies find that we stand between them and their profits, they will spare no pains and no expense to hunt us down and bring us to court."

There was a hush at these ominous words, and every face darkened as gloomy looks were exchanged. So omnipotent and unchallenged had they been that the very thought that there was possible retribution in the background had been banished from their minds. And yet the idea struck a chill to the most reckless of them.

"It is my advice," the speaker continued, "that we go easier upon the small men. On the day that they have all been driven out the power of this society will have been broken."

Unwelcome truths are not popular. There were angry cries as the speaker resumed his seat. McGinty rose with gloom upon his brow.

"Brother Morris," said he, "you were always a croaker. So long as the members of this lodge stand together there is no power in the United States that can touch them. Sure, have we not tried it often enough in the lawcourts? I expect the big companies will find it easier to pay than to fight, same as the little companies do. And now, Brethren," McGinty took off his black velvet cap and his stole as he spoke, "this lodge has finished its business for the evening, save for one small matter which may be mentioned when we are parting. The time has now come for fraternal refreshment and for harmony."

Strange indeed is human nature. Here were these men, to whom murder was familiar, who again and again had struck down the father of the family, some man against whom they had no personal feeling, without one thought of compunction or of compassion for his weeping wife or helpless children, and yet the tender or pathetic in music could move them to tears. McMurdo had a fine tenor voice, and if he had failed to gain the good will of the lodge before, it could no longer have been withheld after he had thrilled them with "I'm Sitting on the Stile, Mary," and "On the Banks of Allan Water."

In his very first night the new recruit had made himself one of the most popular of the brethren, marked already for advancement and high office. There were other qualities needed, however, besides those of good fellowship, to make a worthy Freeman, and of these he was given an example before the evening was over. The whisky bottle had passed round many times, and the men were flushed and ripe for mischief when their Body master rose once more to address them.

"Boys," said he, "there's one man in this town that wants trimming up, and it's for you to see that he gets it. I'm speaking of James Stanger of the Herald. You've seen how he's been opening his mouth against us again?"

There was a murmur of assent, with many a muttered oath. McGinty took a slip of paper from his waistcoat pocket.

"LAW AND ORDER!"

That's how he heads it.

"REIGN OF TERROR IN THE COAL AND IRON DISTRICT

"Twelve years have now elapsed since the first assassinations which proved the existence of a criminal organization in our midst. From that day these outrages have never ceased, until now they have reached a pitch which makes us the opprobrium of the civilized world. Is it for such results as this that our great country welcomes to its bosom the alien who flies from the despotisms of Europe? Is it that they shall themselves become tyrants over the very men who have given them shelter, and that a state of terrorism and lawlessness should be established under the very shadow of the sacred folds of the starry Flag of Freedom which would raise horror in our minds if we read of it as existing under the most effete monarchy of the East? The men are known. The organization is patent and public. How long are we to endure it? Can we forever live—

"Sure, I've read enough of the slush!" cried the chairman, tossing the paper down upon the table. "That's what he says of us. The question I'm asking you is what shall we say to him?"

"Kill him!" cried a dozen fierce voices.

"I protest against that," said Brother Morris, the man of the good brow and shaved face. "I tell you, Brethren, that our hand is too heavy in this valley, and that there will come a point where in self-defense every man will unite to crush us out. James Stanger is an old man. He is respected in the township and the district. His paper stands for all that is solid in the valley. If that man is struck down, there will be a stir through this state that will only end with our destruction."

"And how would they bring about our destruction, Mr. Standback?" cried McGinty. "Is it by the police? Sure, half of them are in our pay and half of them afraid of us.

Or is it by the law courts and the judge? Haven't we tried that before now, and what ever came of it?"

"There is a Judge Lynch that might try the case," said Brother Morris.

A general shout of anger greeted the suggestion.

"I have but to raise my finger," cried McGinty, "and I could put two hundred men into this town that would clear it out from end to end." Then suddenly raising his voice and bending his huge black brows into a terrible frown, "See here, Brother Morris, I have my eye on you, and have had for some time! You've no heart yourself, and you try to take the heart out of others. It will be an ill day for you, Brother Morris, when your own name comes on our agenda paper, and I'm thinking that it's just there that I ought to place it."

Morris had turned deadly pale, and his knees seemed to give way under him as he fell back into his chair. He raised his glass in his trembling hand and drank before he could answer. "I apologize, Eminent Body master, to you and to every brother in this lodge if I have said more than I should. I am a faithful member—you all know that—and it is my fear lest evil come to the lodge which makes me speak in anxious words. But I have greater trust in your judgment than in my own, Eminent Body master, and I promise you that I will not offend again."

The Bodymaster's scowl relaxed as he listened to the humble words. "Very good, Brother Morris. It's myself that would be sorry if it were needful to give you a lesson. But so long as I am in this chair we shall be a united lodge in word and in deed. And now, boys," he continued, looking round at the company, "I'll say this much, that if Stanger got his full deserts there would be more trouble than we need ask for. These editors hang together, and every journal in the state would be crying out for police and troops. But I guess you can give him a pretty severe warning. Will you fix it, Brother Baldwin?"

"Sure!" said the young man eagerly.

"How many will you take?"

"Half a dozen, and two to guard the door. You'll come, Gower, and you, Mansel, and you, Scanlan, and the two Willabys."

"I promised the new brother he should go," said the chairman.

Ted Baldwin looked at McMurdo with eyes which showed that he had not forgotten nor forgiven. "Well, he can come if he wants," he said in a surly voice. "That's enough. The sooner we get to work the better."

The company broke up with shouts and yells and snatches of drunken song. The bar was still crowded with revellers, and many of the brethren remained there. The little band who had been told off for duty passed out into the street, proceeding in twos and threes along the sidewalk so as not to provoke attention. It was a bitterly cold night, with a half-moon shining brilliantly in a frosty, star-spangled sky. The men stopped and gathered in a yard which faced a high building. The words, "Vermissa Herald" were printed in gold lettering between the brightly lit windows. From within came the clanking of the printing press.

"Here, you," said Baldwin to McMurdo, "you can stand below at the door and see that the road is kept open for us. Arthur Willaby can stay with you. You others come with me. Have no fears, boys; for we have a dozen witnesses that we are in the Union Bar at this very moment."

It was nearly midnight, and the street was deserted save for one or two revellers upon their way home. The party crossed the road, and, pushing open the door of the newspaper office, Baldwin and his men rushed in and up the stair which faced them. McMurdo and another remained below. From the room above came a shout, a cry for help, and then the sound of trampling feet and of falling chairs. An instant later a gray-haired man rushed out on the landing.

He was seized before he could get farther, and his spectacles came tinkling down to McMurdo's feet. There was a thud and a groan. He was on his face, and half a dozen sticks were clattering together as they fell upon him. He writhed, and his long, thin limbs quivered under the blows. The others ceased at last; but Baldwin, his cruel face set in an infernal smile, was hacking at the man's head, which he vainly endeavoured to defend with his arms. His white hair was dabbled with patches of blood. Baldwin was still stooping over his victim, putting in a short, vicious blow whenever he could see a part exposed, when McMurdo dashed up the stair and pushed him back.

"You'll kill the man," said he. "Drop it!"

Baldwin looked at him in amazement. "Curse you!" he cried. "Who are you to interfere—you that are new to the lodge? Stand back!" He raised his stick; but McMurdo had whipped his pistol out of his pocket.

"Stand back yourself!" he cried. "I'll blow your face in if you lay a hand on me. As to the lodge, wasn't it the order of the Body master that the man was not to be killed—and what are you doing but killing him?"

"It's truth he says," remarked one of the men.

"By Gar! you'd best hurry yourselves!" cried the man below. "The windows are all lighting up, and you'll have the whole town here inside of five minutes."

There was indeed the sound of shouting in the street, and a little group of compositors and pressmen was forming in the hall below and nerving itself to action. Leaving the limp and motionless body of the editor at the head of the stair, the criminals rushed down and made their way swiftly along the street. Having reached the Union House, some of them mixed with the crowd in McGinty's saloon, whispering across the bar to the Boss that the job had been well carried through. Others, and among them McMurdo, broke away into side streets, and so by devious paths to their own homes.

Chapter 4—The Valley of Fear

When McMurdo awoke next morning he had good reason to remember his initiation into the lodge. His head ached with the effect of the drink, and his arm, where he had been branded, was hot and swollen. Having his own peculiar source of income, he was irregular in his attendance at his work; so he had a late breakfast, and remained at home for the morning writing a long letter to a friend. Afterwards he read the Daily Herald. In a special column put in at the last moment he read:

OUTRAGE AT THE HERALD OFFICE—EDITOR SERIOUSLY INJURED.

It was a short account of the facts with which he was himself more familiar than the writer could have been. It ended with the statement:

The matter is now in the hands of the police; but it can hardly be hoped that their exertions will be attended by any better results than in the past. Some of the men were recognized, and there is hope that a conviction may be obtained. The source of the outrage was, it need hardly be said, that infamous society which has held this community in bondage for so long a period, and against which the Herald has taken so uncompromising a stand. Mr. Stanger's many friends will rejoice to hear that, though he has been cruelly and brutally beaten, and though he has sustained severe injuries about the head, there is no immediate danger to his life.

Below it stated that a guard of police, armed with Winchester rifles, had been requisitioned for the defense of the office.

McMurdo had laid down the paper, and was lighting his pipe with a hand which was shaky from the excesses of the previous evening, when there was a knock outside, and his landlady brought to him a note which had just been handed in by a lad. It was unsigned, and ran thus:

I should wish to speak to you, but would rather not do so in your house. You will find me beside the flagstaff upon Miller Hill. If you will come there now, I have something which it is important for you to hear and for me to say.

McMurdo read the note twice with the utmost surprise; for he could not imagine what it meant or who was the author of it. Had it been in a feminine hand, he might have imagined that it was the beginning of one of those adventures which had been familiar enough in his past life. But it was the writing of a man, and of a well educated one, too. Finally, after some hesitation, he determined to see the matter through.

Miller Hill is an ill-kept public park in the very center of the town. In summer it is a favourite resort of the people, but in winter it is desolate enough. From the top of it one has a view not only of the whole straggling, grimy town, but of the winding valley beneath, with its scattered mines and factories blackening the snow on each side of it, and of the wooded and white-capped ranges flanking it.

McMurdo strolled up the winding path hedged in with evergreens until he reached the deserted restaurant which forms the center of summer gaiety.

Beside it was a bare flagstaff, and underneath it a man, his hat drawn down and the collar of his overcoat turned up. When he turned his face McMurdo saw that it was Brother Morris, he who had incurred the anger of the Body master the night before. The lodge sign was given and exchanged as they met.

"I wanted to have a word with you, Mr. McMurdo," said the older man, speaking with a hesitation which showed that he was on delicate ground. "It was kind of you to come."

"Why did you not put your name to the note?"

"One has to be cautious, mister. One never knows in times like these how a thing may come back to one. One never knows either who to trust or who not to trust."

"Surely one may trust brothers of the lodge."

"No, no, not always," cried Morris with vehemence. "Whatever we say, even what we think, seems to go back to that man McGinty."

"Look here!" said McMurdo sternly. "It was only last night, as you know well, that I swore good faith to our Body master. Would you be asking me to break my oath?"

"If that is the view you take," said Morris sadly, "I can only say that I am sorry I gave you the trouble to come and meet me. Things have come to a bad pass when two free citizens cannot speak their thoughts to each other."

McMurdo, who had been watching his companion very narrowly, relaxed somewhat in his bearing. "Sure I spoke for myself only," said he. "I am a newcomer, as you know, and I am strange to it all. It is not for me to open my mouth, Mr. Morris, and if you think well to say anything to me I am here to hear it."

"And to take it back to Boss McGinty!" said Morris bitterly.

"Indeed, then, you do me injustice there," cried McMurdo. "For myself I am loyal to the lodge, and so I tell you straight; but I would be a poor creature if I were to repeat to any other what you might say to me in confidence. It will go no further than me; though I warn you that you may get neither help nor sympathy."

"I have given up looking for either the one or the other," said Morris. "I may be putting my very life in your hands by what I say; but, bad as you are—and it seemed to me last night that you were shaping to be as bad as the worst—still you are new to it, and your conscience cannot yet be as hardened as theirs. That was why I thought to speak with you."

"Well, what have you to say?"

"If you give me away, may a curse be on you!"

"Sure, I said I would not."

"I would ask you, then, when you joined the Freeman's society in Chicago and swore vows of charity and fidelity, did ever it cross your mind that you might find it would lead you to crime?"

"If you call it crime," McMurdo answered.

"Call it crime!" cried Morris, his voice vibrating with passion. "You have seen little of it if you can call it anything else. Was it crime last night when a man old enough to be your father was beaten till the blood dripped from his white hairs? Was that crime—or what else would you call it?"

"There are some would say it was war," said McMurdo, "a war of two classes with all in, so that each struck as best it could."

"Well, did you think of such a thing when you joined the Freeman's society at Chicago?"

"No, I'm bound to say I did not."

"Nor did I when I joined it at Philadelphia. It was just a benefit club and a meeting place for one's fellows. Then I heard of this place—curse the hour that the name first fell upon my ears!—and I came to better myself! My God! to better myself! My wife and three children came with me. I started a drygoods store on Market Square, and I prospered well. The word had gone round that I was a Freeman, and I was forced to join the local lodge, same as you did last night. I've the badge of shame on my forearm and something worse branded on my heart. I found that I was under the orders of a black villain and caught in a meshwork of crime. What could I do? Every word I said to make things better was taken as treason, same as it was last night. I can't get away; for all I have in the world is in my store. If I leave the society, I know well that it means murder to me, and God knows what to my wife and children. Oh, man, it is awful—awful!" He put his hands to his face, and his body shook with convulsive sobs.

McMurdo shrugged his shoulders. "You were too soft for the job," said he. "You are the wrong sort for such work."

"I had a conscience and a religion; but they made me a criminal among them. I was chosen for a job. If I backed down I knew well what would come to me. Maybe I'm a coward. Maybe it's the thought of my poor little woman and the children that makes me one. Anyhow I went. I guess it will haunt me forever.

"It was a lonely house, twenty miles from here, over the range yonder. I was told off for the door, same as you were last night. They could not trust me with the job. The others went in. When they came out their hands were crimson to the wrists. As we turned away a child was screaming out of the house behind us. It was a boy of five who had seen his father murdered. I nearly fainted with the horror of it, and yet I had to keep a bold and smiling face; for well I knew that if I did not it would be out of my house that they would come next with their bloody hands and it would be my little Fred that would be screaming for his father.

"But I was a criminal then, part sharer in a murder, lost forever in this world, and lost also in the next. I am a good Catholic; but the priest would have no word with me when he heard I was a Scowrer, and I am excommunicated from my faith. That's how it stands with me. And I see you going down the same road, and I ask you what the end is to be. Are you ready to be a cold-blooded murderer also, or can we do anything to stop it?"

"What would you do?" asked McMurdo abruptly. "You would not inform?"

"God forbid!" cried Morris. "Sure, the very thought would cost me my life."

"That's well," said McMurdo. "I'm thinking that you are a weak man and that you make too much of the matter."

"Too much! Wait till you have lived here longer. Look down the valley! See the cloud of a hundred chimneys that overshadows it! I tell you that the cloud of murder hangs thicker and lower than that over the heads of the people. It is the Valley of Fear, the Valley of Death. The terror is in the hearts of the people from the dusk to the dawn. Wait, young man, and you will learn for yourself."

"Well, I'll let you know what I think when I have seen more," said McMurdo carelessly. "What is very clear is that you are not the man for the place, and that the sooner you sell out—if you only get a dime a dollar for what the business is worth—the better it will be for you. What you have said is safe with me; but, by Gar! if I thought you were an informer—"

"No, no!" cried Morris piteously.

"Well, let it rest at that. I'll bear what you have said in mind, and maybe some day I'll come back to it. I expect you meant kindly by speaking to me like this. Now I'll be getting home."

"One word before you go," said Morris. "We may have been seen together. They may want to know what we have spoken about."

"Ah! that's well thought of."

"I offer you a clerkship in my store."

"And I refuse it. That's our business. Well, so long, Brother Morris, and may you find things go better with you in the future."

That same afternoon, as McMurdo sat smoking, lost in thought beside the stove of his sitting-room, the door swung open and its framework was filled with the huge figure of Boss McGinty. He passed the sign, and then seating himself opposite to the young man he looked at him steadily for some time, a look which was as steadily returned.

"I'm not much of a visitor, Brother McMurdo," he said at last. "I guess I am too busy over the folk that visit me. But I thought I'd stretch a point and drop down to see you in your own house."

"I'm proud to see you here, Councillor," McMurdo answered heartily, bringing his whisky bottle out of the cupboard. "It's an honour that I had not expected."

"How's the arm?" asked the Boss.

McMurdo made a wry face. "Well, I'm not forgetting it," he said; "but it's worth it."

"Yes, it's worth it," the other answered, "to those that are loyal and go through with it and are a help to the lodge. What were you speaking to Brother Morris about on Miller Hill this morning?"

The question came so suddenly that it was well that he had his answer prepared. He burst into a hearty laugh. "Morris didn't know I could earn a living here at home. He shan't know either; for he has got too much conscience for the likes of me. But he's a good-hearted old chap. It was his idea that I was at a loose end, and that he would do me a good turn by offering me a clerkship in a drygoods store."

"Oh, that was it?"

"Yes, that was it."

"And you refused it?"

"Sure. Couldn't I earn ten times as much in my own bedroom with four hours' work?"

"That's so. But I wouldn't get about too much with Morris."

"Why not?"

"Well, I guess because I tell you not. That's enough for most folk in these parts."

"It may be enough for most folk; but it ain't enough for me, Councillor," said McMurdo boldly. "If you are a judge of men, you'll know that."

The swarthy giant glared at him, and his hairy paw closed for an instant round the glass as though he would hurl it at the head of his companion. Then he laughed in his loud, boisterous, insincere fashion.

"You're a queer card, for sure," said he. "Well, if you want reasons, I'll give them. Did Morris say nothing to you against the lodge?"

"No."

"Nor against me?"

"No."

"Well, that's because he daren't trust you. But in his heart he is not a loyal brother. We know that well. So we watch him and we wait for the time to admonish him. I'm thinking that the time is drawing near. There's no room for scabby sheep in our pen. But if you keep company with a disloyal man, we might think that you were disloyal, too. See?"

"There's no chance of my keeping company with him; for I dislike the man," McMurdo answered. "As to being disloyal, if it was any man but you he would not use the word to me twice."

"Well, that's enough," said McGinty, draining off his glass. "I came down to give you a word in season, and you've had it."

"I'd like to know," said McMurdo, "how you ever came to learn that I had spoken with Morris at all?"

McGinty laughed. "It's my business to know what goes on in this township," said he. "I guess you'd best reckon on my hearing all that passes. Well, time's up, and I'll just say—"

But his leavetaking was cut short in a very unexpected fashion. With a sudden crash the door flew open, and three frowning, intent faces glared in at them from under the peaks of police caps. McMurdo sprang to his feet and half drew his revolver; but his arm stopped midway as he became conscious that two Winchester rifles were levelled at his head. A man in uniform advanced into the room, a six-shooter in his hand. It was Captain Marvin, once of Chicago, and now of the Mine Constabulary. He shook his head with a half-smile at McMurdo.

"I thought you'd be getting into trouble, Mr. Crooked McMurdo of Chicago," said he. "Can't keep out of it, can you? Take your hat and come along with us."

"I guess you'll pay for this, Captain Marvin," said McGinty. "Who are you, I'd like to know, to break into a house in this fashion and molest honest, law-abiding men?"

"You're standing out in this deal, Councillor McGinty," said the police captain. "We are not out after you, but after this man McMurdo. It is for you to help, not to hinder us in our duty."

"He is a friend of mine, and I'll answer for his conduct," said the Boss.

"By all accounts, Mr. McGinty, you may have to answer for your own conduct some of these days," the captain answered. "This man McMurdo was a crook before ever he came here, and he's a crook still. Cover him, Patrolman, while I disarm him."

"There's my pistol," said McMurdo coolly. "Maybe, Captain Marvin, if you and I were alone and face to face you would not take me so easily."

"Where's your warrant?" asked McGinty. "By Gar! a man might as well live in Russia as in Vermissa while folk like you are running the police. It's a capitalist outrage, and you'll hear more of it, I reckon."

"You do what you think is your duty the best way you can, Councillor. We'll look after ours."

"What am I accused of?" asked McMurdo.

"Of being concerned in the beating of old Editor Stanger at the Herald office. It wasn't your fault that it isn't a murder charge."

"Well, if that's all you have against him," cried McGinty with a laugh, "you can save yourself a deal of trouble by dropping it right now. This man was with me in my saloon playing poker up to midnight, and I can bring a dozen to prove it."

"That's your affair, and I guess you can settle it in court to-morrow. Meanwhile, come on, McMurdo, and come quietly if you don't want a gun across your head. You stand wide, Mr. McGinty; for I warn you I will stand no resistance when I am on duty!"

So determined was the appearance of the captain that both McMurdo and his boss were forced to accept the situation. The latter managed to have a few whispered words with the prisoner before they parted.

"What about—" he jerked his thumb upward to signify the coining plant.

"All right," whispered McMurdo, who had devised a safe hiding place under the floor.

"I'll bid you good-bye," said the Boss, shaking hands. "I'll see Reilly the lawyer and take the defense upon myself. Take my word for it that they won't be able to hold you."

"I wouldn't bet on that. Guard the prisoner, you two, and shoot him if he tries any games. I'll search the house before I leave."

He did so; but apparently found no trace of the concealed plant. When he had descended he and his men escorted McMurdo to headquarters. Darkness had fallen, and a keen blizzard was blowing so that the streets were nearly deserted; but a few loiterers followed the group, and emboldened by invisibility shouted imprecations at the prisoner.

"Lynch the cursed Scowrer!" they cried. "Lynch him!" They laughed and jeered as he was pushed into the police station. After a short, formal examination from the inspector in charge he was put into the common cell. Here he found Baldwin and three other criminals of the night before, all arrested that afternoon and waiting their trial next morning.

But even within this inner fortress of the law the long arm of the Freemen was able to extend. Late at night there came a jailer with a straw bundle for their bedding, out of which he extracted two bottles of whisky, some glasses, and a pack of cards. They spent a hilarious night, without an anxious thought as to the ordeal of the morning.

Nor had they cause, as the result was to show. The magistrate could not possibly, on the evidence, have held them for a higher court. On the one hand the compositors and pressmen were forced to admit that the light was uncertain, that they were themselves much perturbed, and that it was difficult for them to swear to the identity of the assailants; although they believed that the accused were among them. Cross examined by the clever attorney who had been engaged by McGinty, they were even more nebulous in their evidence.

The injured man had already deposed that he was so taken by surprise by the suddenness of the attack that he could state nothing beyond the fact that the first man who struck him wore a moustache. He added that he knew them to be Scowrers, since no one else in the community could possibly have any enmity to him, and he had long been threatened on account of his outspoken editorials. On the other hand, it was clearly shown by the united and unfaltering evidence of six citizens, including that high municipal official, Councillor McGinty, that the men had been at a card party at the Union House until an hour very much later than the commission of the outrage.

Needless to say that they were discharged with something very near to an apology from the bench for the inconvenience to which they had been put, together with an implied censure of Captain Marvin and the police for their officious zeal.

The verdict was greeted with loud applause by a court in which McMurdo saw many familiar faces. Brothers of the lodge smiled and waved. But there were others who sat with compressed lips and brooding eyes as the men filed out of the dock. One of them, a little, dark-bearded, resolute fellow, put the thoughts of himself and comrades into words as the ex-prisoners passed him.

"You damned murderers!" he said. "We'll fix you yet!"

Chapter 5—The Darkest Hour

If anything had been needed to give an impetus to Jack McMurdo's popularity among his fellows it would have been his arrest and acquittal. That a man on the very night of joining the lodge should have done something which brought him before the magistrate was a new record in the annals of the society. Already he had earned the reputation of a good boon companion, a cheery reveller, and withal a man of high temper, who would not take an insult even from the all-powerful Boss himself. But in addition to this he impressed his comrades with the idea that among them all there was not one whose brain was so ready to devise a bloodthirsty scheme, or whose hand would be more capable of carrying it out. "He'll be the boy for the clean job," said the oldsters to one another, and waited their time until they could set him to his work.

McGinty had instruments enough already; but he recognized that this was a supremely able one. He felt like a man holding a fierce bloodhound in leash. There were curs to do the smaller work; but some day he would slip this creature upon its prey. A few members of the lodge, Ted Baldwin among them, resented the rapid rise of the stranger and hated him for it; but they kept clear of him, for he was as ready to fight as to laugh.

But if he gained favour with his fellows, there was another quarter, one which had become even more vital to him, in which he lost it. Ettie Shafter's father would have nothing more to do with him, nor would he allow him to enter the house. Ettie herself was too deeply in love to give him up altogether, and yet her own good sense warned her of what would come from a marriage with a man who was regarded as a criminal.

One morning after a sleepless night she determined to see him, possibly for the last time, and make one strong endeavour to draw him from those evil influences which were sucking him down. She went to his house, as he had often begged her to do, and made her way into the room which he used as his sitting-room. He was seated at a table, with his back turned and a letter in front of him. A sudden spirit of girlish mischief came over her—she was still only nineteen. He had not heard her when she pushed open the door. Now she tiptoed forward and laid her hand lightly upon his bended shoulders.

If she had expected to startle him, she certainly succeeded; but only in turn to be startled herself. With a tiger spring he turned on her, and his right hand was feeling for her throat. At the same instant with the other hand he crumpled up the paper that lay before him. For an instant he stood glaring. Then astonishment and joy took the place of the ferocity which had convulsed his features—a ferocity which had sent her shrinking back in horror as from something which had never before intruded into her gentle life.

"It's you!" said he, mopping his brow. "And to think that you should come to me, heart of my heart, and I should find nothing better to do than to want to strangle you! Come then, darling," and he held out his arms, "let me make it up to you."

But she had not recovered from that sudden glimpse of guilty fear which she had read in the man's face. All her woman's instinct told her that it was not the mere fright of a man who is startled. Guilt—that was it—guilt and fear!

"What's come over you, Jack?" she cried. "Why were you so scared of me? Oh, Jack, if your conscience was at ease, you would not have looked at me like that!"

"Sure, I was thinking of other things, and when you came tripping so lightly on those fairy feet of yours—"

"No, no, it was more than that, Jack." Then a sudden suspicion seized her. "Let me see that letter you were writing."

"Ah, Ettie, I couldn't do that."

Her suspicions became certainties. "It's to another woman," she cried. "I know it! Why else should you hold it from me? Was it to your wife that you were writing? How am I to know that you are not a married man— you, a stranger, that nobody knows?"

"I am not married, Ettie. See now, I swear it! You're the only one woman on earth to me. By the cross of Christ I swear it!"

He was so white with passionate earnestness that she could not but believe him.

"Well, then," she cried, "why will you not show me the letter?"

"I'll tell you, acushla," said he. "I'm under oath not to show it, and just as I wouldn't break my word to you so I would keep it to those who hold my promise. It's the business of the lodge, and even to you it's secret. And if I was scared when a hand fell on me, can't you understand it when it might have been the hand of a detective?"

She felt that he was telling the truth. He gathered her into his arms and kissed away her fears and doubts.

"Sit here by me, then. It's a queer throne for such a queen; but it's the best your poor lover can find. He'll do better for you some of these days, I'm thinking. Now your mind is easy once again, is it not?"

"How can it ever be at ease, Jack, when I know that you are a criminal among criminals, when I never know the day that I may hear you are in court for murder? 'McMurdo the Scowrer,' that's what one of our boarders called you yesterday. It went through my heart like a knife."

"Sure, hard words break no bones."

"But they were true."

"Well, dear, it's not so bad as you think. We are but poor men that are trying in our own way to get our rights."

Ettie threw her arms round her lover's neck. "Give it up, Jack! For my sake, for God's sake, give it up! It was to ask you that I came here to-day. Oh, Jack, see—I beg it of you on my bended knees! Kneeling here before you I implore you to give it up!"

He raised her and soothed her with her head against his breast.

"Sure, my darlin', you don't know what it is you are asking. How could I give it up when it would be to break my oath and to desert my comrades? If you could see how things stand with me you could never ask it of me. Besides, if I wanted to, how could I do it? You don't suppose that the lodge would let a man go free with all its secrets?"

"I've thought of that, Jack. I've planned it all. Father has saved some money. He is weary of this place where the fear of these people darkens our lives. He is ready to go. We would fly together to Philadelphia or New York, where we would be safe from them."

McMurdo laughed. "The lodge has a long arm. Do you think it could not stretch from here to Philadelphia or New York?"

"Well, then, to the West, or to England, or to Germany, where father came from—anywhere to get away from this Valley of Fear!"

McMurdo thought of old Brother Morris. "Sure, it is the second time I have heard the valley so named," said he. "The shadow does indeed seem to lie heavy on some of you."

"It darkens every moment of our lives. Do you suppose that Ted Baldwin has ever forgiven us? If it were not that he fears you, what do you suppose our chances would be? If you saw the look in those dark, hungry eyes of his when they fall on me!"

"By Gar! I'd teach him better manners if I caught him at it! But see here, little girl. I can't leave here. I can't—take that from me once and for all. But if you will leave me to find my own way, I will try to prepare a way of getting honourably out of it."

"There is no honour in such a matter."

"Well, well, it's just how you look at it. But if you'll give me six months, I'll work it so that I can leave without being ashamed to look others in the face."

The girl laughed with joy. "Six months!" she cried. "Is it a promise?"

"Well, it may be seven or eight. But within a year at the furthest we will leave the valley behind us."

It was the most that Ettie could obtain, and yet it was something. There was this distant light to illuminate the gloom of the immediate future. She returned to her father's house more light-hearted than she had ever been since Jack McMurdo had come into her life.

It might be thought that as a member, all the doings of the society would be told to him; but he was soon to discover that the organization was wider and more complex than the simple lodge. Even Boss McGinty was ignorant as to many things; for there was an official named the County Delegate, living at Hobson's Patch farther down the line, who had power over several different lodges which he wielded in a sudden and arbitrary way. Only once did McMurdo see him, a sly, little gray-haired rat of a man, with a slinking gait and a sidelong glance which was charged with malice. Evans Pott was his name, and even the great Boss of Vermissa felt towards him something of the repulsion and fear which the huge Danton may have felt for the puny but dangerous Robespierre.

One day Scanlan, who was McMurdo's fellow boarder, received a note from McGinty inclosing one from Evans Pott, which informed him that he was sending over two good men, Lawler and Andrews, who had instructions to act in the neighbourhood; though it was best for the cause that no particulars as to their objects should be given. Would the Body master see to it that suitable arrangements be made for their lodgings and comfort until the time for action should arrive? McGinty added that it was impossible for anyone to remain secret at the Union House, and that, therefore, he would be obliged if McMurdo and Scanlan would put the strangers up for a few days in their boarding house.

The same evening the two men arrived, each carrying his gripsack. Lawler was an elderly man, shrewd, silent, and self-contained, clad in an old black frock coat, which with his soft felt hat and ragged, grizzled beard gave him a general resemblance to an itinerant preacher. His companion Andrews was little more than a boy, frank-faced and cheerful, with the breezy manner of one who is out for a holiday and means to enjoy every minute of it. Both men were total abstainers, and behaved in all ways as exemplary members of the society, with the one simple exception that they were assassins who had often proved themselves to be most capable instruments for this association of murder. Lawler had already carried out fourteen commissions of the kind, and Andrews three.

They were, as McMurdo found, quite ready to converse about their deeds in the past, which they recounted with the half-bashful pride of men who had done good and unselfish service for the community. They were reticent, however, as to the immediate job in hand.

"They chose us because neither I nor the boy here drink," Lawler explained. "They can count on us saying no more than we should. You must not take it amiss, but it is the orders of the County Delegate that we obey."

"Sure, we are all in it together," said Scanlan, McMurdo's mate, as the four sat together at supper.

"That's true enough, and we'll talk till the cows come home of the killing of Charlie Williams or of Simon Bird, or any other job in the past. But till the work is done we say nothing."

"There are half a dozen about here that I have a word to say to," said McMurdo, with an oath. "I suppose it isn't Jack Knox of Ironhill that you are after. I'd go some way to see him get his deserts."

"No, it's not him yet."

"Or Herman Strauss?"

"No, nor him either."

"Well, if you won't tell us we can't make you; but I'd be glad to know."

Lawler smiled and shook his head. He was not to be drawn.

In spite of the reticence of their guests, Scanlan and McMurdo were quite determined to be present at what they called "the fun." When, therefore, at an early hour one morning McMurdo heard them creeping down the stairs he awakened Scanlan, and the two hurried on their clothes. When they were dressed they found that the others had stolen out, leaving the door open behind them. It was not yet dawn, and by the light of the lamps they could see the two men some distance down the street. They followed them warily, treading noiselessly in the deep snow.

The boarding house was near the edge of the town, and soon they were at the crossroads which is beyond its boundary. Here three men were waiting, with whom Lawler and Andrews held a short, eager conversation. Then they all moved on together. It was clearly some notable job which needed numbers. At this point there are several trails which lead to various mines. The strangers took that which led to the Crow Hill, a huge business which was in strong hands which had been able, thanks to their energetic and fearless New England manager, Josiah H. Dunn, to keep some order and discipline during the long reign of terror.

Day was breaking now, and a line of workmen were slowly making their way, singly and in groups, along the blackened path.

McMurdo and Scanlan strolled on with the others, keeping in sight of the men whom they followed. A thick mist lay over them, and from the heart of it there came the sudden scream of a steam whistle. It was the ten-minute signal before the cages descended and the day's labour began.

When they reached the open space round the mine shaft there were a hundred miners waiting, stamping their feet and blowing on their fingers; for it was bitterly cold. The strangers stood in a little group under the shadow of the engine house. Scanlan and McMurdo climbed a heap of slag from which the whole scene lay before them. They saw the mine engineer, a great bearded Scotchman named Menzies, come out of the engine house and blow his whistle for the cages to be lowered.

At the same instant a tall, loose-framed young man with a clean-shaved, earnest face advanced eagerly towards the pit head. As he came forward his eyes fell upon the group, silent and motionless, under the engine house. The men had drawn down their hats and turned up their collars to screen their faces. For a moment the presentiment of Death laid its cold hand upon the manager's heart. At the next he had shaken it off and saw only his duty towards intrusive strangers.

"Who are you?" he asked as he advanced. "What are you loitering there for?"

There was no answer; but the lad Andrews stepped forward and shot him in the stomach. The hundred waiting miners stood as motionless and helpless as if they were paralyzed. The manager clapped his two hands to the wound and doubled himself up. Then he staggered away; but another of the assassins fired, and he went down sidewise, kicking and clawing among a heap of clinkers. Menzies, the Scotchman, gave a roar of rage at the sight and rushed with an iron spanner at the murderers; but was met by two balls in the face which dropped him dead at their very feet.

There was a surge forward of some of the miners, and an inarticulate cry of pity and of anger; but a couple of the strangers emptied their six-shooters over the heads of the crowd, and they broke and scattered, some of them rushing wildly back to their homes in Vermissa.

When a few of the bravest had rallied, and there was a return to the mine, the murderous gang had vanished in the mists of morning, without a single witness being able to swear to the identity of these men who in front of a hundred spectators had wrought this double crime.

Scanlan and McMurdo made their way back; Scanlan somewhat subdued, for it was the first murder job that he had seen with his own eyes, and it appeared less funny than he had been led to believe. The horrible screams of the dead manager's wife pursued them as they hurried to the town. McMurdo was absorbed and silent; but he showed no sympathy for the weakening of his companion.

"Sure, it is like a war," he repeated. "What is it but a war between us and them, and we hit back where we best can."

There was high revel in the lodge room at the Union House that night, not only over the killing of the manager and engineer of the Crow Hill mine, which would bring this organization into line with the other blackmailed and terror-stricken companies of the district, but also over a distant triumph which had been wrought by the hands of the lodge itself.

It would appear that when the County Delegate had sent over five good men to strike a blow in Vermissa, he had demanded that in return three Vermissa men should be secretly selected and sent across to kill William Hales of Stake Royal, one of the best known and most popular mine owners in the Gilmerton district, a man who was believed not to have an enemy in the world; for he was in all ways a model employer. He had insisted, however, upon efficiency in the work, and had, therefore, paid off certain drunken and idle employees who were members of the all-powerful society. Coffin notices hung outside his door had not weakened his resolution, and so in a free, civilized country he found himself condemned to death.

The execution had now been duly carried out. Ted Baldwin, who sprawled now in the seat of honour beside the Body master, had been chief of the party. His flushed face and glazed, bloodshot eyes told of sleeplessness and drink. He and his two comrades had spent the night before among the mountains. They were unkempt and weather-stained. But no heroes, returning from a forlorn hope, could have had a warmer welcome from their comrades.

The story was told and retold amid cries of delight and shouts of laughter. They had waited for their man as he drove home at nightfall, taking their station at the top of a steep hill, where his horse must be at a walk. He was so furred to keep out the cold that he could not lay his hand on his pistol. They had pulled him out and shot him again and again. He had screamed for mercy. The screams were repeated for the amusement of the lodge.

"Let's hear again how he squealed," they cried.

None of them knew the man; but there is eternal drama in a killing, and they had shown the Scowrers of

Gilmerton that the Vermissa men were to be relied upon.

There had been one contretemps; for a man and his wife had driven up while they were still emptying their revolvers into the silent body. It had been suggested that they should shoot them both; but they were harmless folk who were not connected with the mines, so they were sternly bidden to drive on and keep silent, lest a worse thing befall them. And so the blood-mottled figure had been left as a warning to all such hard-hearted employers, and the three noble avengers had hurried off into the mountains where unbroken nature comes down to the very edge of the furnaces and the slag heaps. Here they were, safe and sound, their work well done, and the plaudits of their companions in their ears.

It had been a great day for the Scowrers. The shadow had fallen even darker over the valley. But as the wise general chooses the moment of victory in which to redouble his efforts, so that his foes may have no time to steady themselves after disaster, so Boss McGinty, looking out upon the scene of his operations with his brooding and malicious eyes, had devised a new attack upon those who opposed him. That very night, as the half-drunken company broke up, he touched McMurdo on the arm and led him aside into that inner room where they had their first interview.

"See here, my lad," said he, "I've got a job that's worthy of you at last. You'll have the doing of it in your own hands."

"Proud I am to hear it," McMurdo answered.

"You can take two men with you—Manders and Reilly. They have been warned for service. We'll never be right in this district until Chester Wilcox has been settled, and you'll have the thanks of every lodge in the coal fields if you can down him."

"I'll do my best, anyhow. Who is he, and where shall I find him?"

McGinty took his eternal half-chewed, half-smoked cigar from the corner of his mouth, and proceeded to draw a rough diagram on a page torn from his notebook.

"He's the chief foreman of the Iron Dike Company. He's a hard citizen, an old colour sergeant of the war, all scars and grizzle. We've had two tries at him; but had no luck, and Jim Carnaway lost his life over it. Now it's for you to take it over. That's the house—all alone at the Iron Dike crossroad, same as you see here on the map— without another within earshot. It's no good by day. He's armed and shoots quick and straight, with no questions asked. But at night—well, there he is with his wife, three children, and a hired help. You can't pick or choose. It's all or none. If you could get a bag of blasting powder at the front door with a slow match to it—"

"What's the man done?"

"Didn't I tell you he shot Jim Carnaway?"

"Why did he shoot him?"

"What in thunder has that to do with you? Carnaway was about his house at night, and he shot him. That's enough for me and you. You've got to settle the thing right."

"There's these two women and the children. Do they go up too?"

"They have to—else how can we get him?"

"It seems hard on them; for they've done nothing."

"What sort of fool's talk is this? Do you back out?"

"Easy, Councillor, easy! What have I ever said or done that you should think I would be after standing back from an order of the Body master of my own lodge? If it's right or if it's wrong, it's for you to decide."

"You'll do it, then?"

"Of course I will do it."

"When?"

"Well, you had best give me a night or two that I may see the house and make my plans. Then—"

"Very good," said McGinty, shaking him by the hand. "I leave it with you. It will be a great day when you bring us the news. It's just the last stroke that will bring them all to their knees."

McMurdo thought long and deeply over the commission which had been so suddenly placed in his hands. The isolated house in which Chester Wilcox lived was about five miles off in an adjacent valley. That very night he started off all alone to prepare for the attempt. It was daylight before he returned from his reconnaissance. Next day he interviewed his two subordinates, Manders and Reilly, reckless youngsters who were as elated as if it were a deer-hunt.

Two nights later they met outside the town, all three armed, and one of them carrying a sack stuffed with the powder which was used in the quarries. It was two in the morning before they came to the lonely house. The night was a windy one, with broken clouds drifting swiftly across the face of a three-quarter moon. They had been warned to be on their guard against bloodhounds; so they moved forward cautiously, with their pistols cocked in their hands. But there was no sound save the howling of the wind, and no movement but the swaying branches above them.

McMurdo listened at the door of the lonely house; but all was still within. Then he leaned the powder bag against it, ripped a hole in it with his knife, and attached the fuse. When it was well alight he and his two companions took to their heels, and were some distance off, safe and snug in a sheltering ditch, before the shattering roar of the explosion, with the low, deep rumble of the collapsing building, told them that their work was done. No cleaner job had ever been carried out in the bloodstained annals of the society.

But alas that work so well organized and boldly carried out should all have gone for nothing! Warned by the fate of the various victims, and knowing that he was marked down for destruction, Chester Wilcox had moved himself and his family only the day before to some safer and less known quarters, where a guard of police should watch over them. It was an empty house which had been torn down by the gunpowder, and the grim old colour sergeant of the war was still teaching discipline to the miners of Iron Dike.

"Leave him to me," said McMurdo. "He's my man, and I'll get him sure if I have to wait a year for him."

A vote of thanks and confidence was passed in full lodge, and so for the time the matter ended. When a few weeks later it was reported in the papers that Wilcox had been shot at from an ambuscade, it was an open secret that McMurdo was still at work upon his unfinished job.

Such were the methods of the Society of Freemen, and such were the deeds of the Scowrers by which they spread their rule of fear over the great and rich district which was for so long a period haunted by their terrible presence. Why should these pages be stained by further crimes? Have I not said enough to show the men and their methods?

These deeds are written in history, and there are records wherein one may read the details of them. There one may learn of the shooting of Policemen Hunt and Evans because they had ventured to arrest two members of the society—a double outrage planned at the Vermissa lodge and carried out in cold blood upon two helpless and disarmed men. There also one may read of the shooting of Mrs. Larbey when she was nursing her husband, who had been beaten almost to death by orders of Boss McGinty. The killing of the elder Jenkins, shortly followed by that of his brother, the mutilation of James Murdoch, the blowing up of the Staphouse family, and the murder of the Stendals all followed hard upon one another in the same terrible winter.

Darkly the shadow lay upon the Valley of Fear. The spring had come with running brooks and blossoming trees. There was hope for all Nature bound so long in an iron grip; but nowhere was there any hope for the men and women who lived under the yoke of the terror. Never had the cloud above them been so dark and hopeless as in the early summer of the year 1875.

The Valley of Fear Summary and Analysis of Part II Chapters 3-5

Summary

Chapter 3

McMurdo moves to the Widow MacNamara's at the outskirts of city; Scanlan movements there as nicely. Shafter nevertheless shall we McMurdo devour his food on the boarding residence, and as a result his dating with Ettie continues. McMurdo shows off his coining molds to his traffic; he says that he might do this complete-time if the police weren't after him.

One day at the saloon a brand new member of the mine police comes in for a drink. McGinty greets him amiably but tells the person, Captain Marvin, that they do now not need his services within the city. Marvin stays properly-humored, however abruptly he sees McMurdo and calls him out as a crook from Chicago. McMurdo is rude to him; however, Marvin says his call is now clear in Chicago, and that he's going to simplest get in problem if he does something wrong here. The tale of McMurdo's exploits makes him even more of a hero in the miners' eyes. On Saturday night, McMurdo attends the motel meeting for his initiation. McGinty sits at front like some type of priest. Old guys and enthusiastic younger men talk; the young men boast of murderous deeds. The complaints of those conferences are very open; they was once secret, however they no longer ought to be due to the fact no authority can stop them from doing as they please.

McMurdo is aware of there will be some form of ordeal for his initiation, however does now not know what it is going to be like. McGinty orders him certain and blindfolded, asks him inquiries to show he is aware of the code, asks him to prove his bravery by using strolling ahead blindly, and to prove he can resist ache by means of branding him with the image. Though the ache is excessive, he handles himself nicely, and all the men are impressed. He accepts the guidelines of the Body master and is officially welcomed in.

After this official commercial enterprise ensues. One guy is to be killed for you to satisfy a pledge to any other inn. Two young guys are given the assignment, and McMurdo says he would love to do this as well. Many people approve of his audacity, but others think things are shifting speedy. McGinty says that his time will come, however he can come hear every other count number that night. They then talk a pension for Jim Carnaway's widow; Jim become killed when the raid to kill Chester Wilcox failed.

An aged man with a kind face rises and asks who's taking up all of the small mining groups. The answer is State & Merton County Railroad Company, which appears to be making large inroads within the place. Morris suggests they not force out all the small bosses because as soon as the massive agencies are absolutely in charge they will have the assets to harm the union and convey them to courtroom. People are hushed and grumble. Morris says they need to cross clean at the small men; McGinty considers this in brief and says there's nothing to fear approximately.

It is then time for refreshments and making a song, and McMurdo's exceptional tenor distinguishes him. The Body master rises once more and reads a passage from the newspaper editor, James Stanger. It may be very essential of the union, and the men come to be angry. They need to do something about it, however Morris speaks once more and says they cannot: Stanger is reputable in the township and will bring about their destruction. McGinty taunts after which will become irritated with Morris. Morris backs down and apologizes.

Baldwin and a few other young men get the task to harm (but now not kill) Stanger, and McMurdo is such a guys. They head to the workplace that evening after organizing an alibi at the bar. The street is abandoned and darkish. McMurdo guards the door, and the alternative men pass inside and beat up Stanger. Stanger attempts to escape, however McMurdo stops him. The guys almost kill the editor, but McMurdo stops them, reminding them that McGinty didn't want him killed.

Lights come on after humans nearby pay attention the commotion. The men flee.

Chapter 4

The subsequent morning McMurdo sees a newspaper record detailing the assault; it appears Mr. Stanger survived and diagnosed a number of the guys.

A word arrives from the landlady. It is unsigned and asks McMurdo to fulfill Stanger up on Mason Hill. McMurdo has no idea who wrote it, but he walks to the hill out of interest. In the isolated location he reveals Brother Morris.

Morris asks the amazed McMurdo if he can communicate to him in confidence. McMurdo is clear that he is loyal to McGinty however will listen to his brother and now not squeal on him. Morris is going into an anguished account of the violence he has needed to perpetrate; he says that he wants to go away but fears for his spouse and kids. He never knew the union turned into like this, and feels his judgment of right and wrong and faith threatened; he has even been excommunicated. He says the union brings terror to the valley and McMurdo need to be privy to that.

McMurdo arrogantly says that he is fine, however that he may additionally don't forget Morris' warning a few day. Morris says that earlier than they disband they need to don't forget what they may say when requested why they talked; they agree to mention that Morris offered McMurdo a clerkship and the young guy refused.

Later that day McGinty can pay McMurdo a visit. They alternate pleasantries and McGinty unexpectedly asks what he changed into talking to Morris approximately. McMurdo laughs, repeats the lie, and sets McGinty's mind relaxed while the Body master asks in addition questions regarding Morris criticizing the union.

As they speak the door all of sudden bursts open. Captain Marvin and other guys enter forcefully and arrest McMurdo. Despite McGinty's threats, McMurdo is taken away for his involvement in the beating of Stanger.

Amazingly, though, not anything comes of the trial. There is no evidence, the witnesses admit the light changed into uncertain and that they noticed no one definitively, and even Stanger says he saw little. The alibis stand, McMurdo and the others are acquitted, and the police are even implicitly censured. However, the humans seem irritated with the murderers getting off, and that they shake their fists on the Brothers.

Chapter 5

McMurdo's reputation skyrockets even extra. He is considered an excellent accomplice, a cheery fellow, a bloodthirsty and clever schemer, and magnificent for buying out of trouble with the law.

However, even as things are going properly in a few regions of McMurdo's lifestyles, Shafter has forbidden him from coming to look Ettie. Ettie nonetheless loves McMurdo, however matters are hard for them.

One night Ettie is going to surprise McMurdo. She creeps up at the back of him, however, to her horror, he reacts fiercely and comes for her throat. He then recognizes her and apologizes, but she is unnerved by using the look she noticed in his eyes. She cries and begs him to stay away from these violent men. She proposes leaving the Valley of Fear. McMurdo says he can't do that proper now, however subsequently says that he's going to work to make it possible for them to get out of the valley inside six-to-eight months. Ettie is elated.

It isn't lengthy earlier than McMurdo starts to look just how substantial this organization surely is. McGinty himself solutions to Evans Potts, the County Delegate and a man of huge electricity.

Scanlan and McMurdo analyze that guys in Potts' hire need a place to live while they're on the town on commercial enterprise and consequently could be staying on the boarding residence. Lawler, an elderly guy, and Andrews, a cheerful younger boy, arrive. They are each friendly however will not inform any details of why they were dispatched. The handiest component they point out is that they're assassins and abstainers from drink.

That night time, when Lawler and Andrews quietly depart to carry out their business, Scanlan and McMurdo follow them. They stroll through the snow, watch the men choose up others to assist the task, and then head to Crow Hill, a large mining operation run with the aid of Josiah H. Dunn. McMurdo and Scanlan cover themselves and watch the group of fellows stand off to the facet near the miners.

The morning whistle sounds the 10-minute alarm. The mine engineer, a Scotsman named Menzies, orders the cages diminished. A younger guy additionally walks out and notices the organization of fellows collected. He asks who they're; Andrews steps forward and shoots him dead. When Menzies protests, he too is killed. The different miners scatter.

Scanlan and McMurdo retreat, both surprised. Scanlan feels poorly about what befell, but McMurdo does not appear sympathetic to the dead men.

The brothers celebrate at Union House that night. The killing of the mine supervisor, together with every other killing accomplished via 1st earl baldwin of bewdley, contributes to the revelry. McGinty is aware of the time is right to hold his enemies volatile; he makes a decision every other killing need to occur, so he calls McMurdo over and tells him he has a process for him and two different men.

McGinty explains that the district will never be right until the businessman Chester Wilcox is useless. McMurdo wonders what the person did and why his wife and youngsters also should be killed. McGinty gruffly asks if he has a hassle with wearing out his orders, and McMurdo says he does not. He takes a night time to do reconnaissance, and receives his other younger men ready.

Two nights later, McMurdo and the 2 different guys meet and travel to Wilcox's residence, which they blow up with a powder bag. Unfortunately for the murderers, Wilcox and his circle of relatives were warned and had been not there. McMurdo is furious and says he will contend with it. A few weeks later, news comes of Wilcox's dying.

These are just a number of the bloody deeds that occurred in the Valley of Fear; "by no means had the cloud above them been so darkish and hopeless as within the early summer season of the yr. 1875" (three hundred).

Analysis

Doyle does an intensive activity of depicting the threat of the Scowrers. There are beatings of crucial news editors, murders of neighborhood businessmen who get within the way, threats to participants of the hotel who provide positive complaint, and utter dismiss of the authority figures. It seems at this factor just like the Scowrers are unbeatable: just like the mafia, they have ties everywhere, and nobody wants to try and prevent them for worry of dropping their very own lives or having their households focused.

There truly is law enforcement, as embodied through Captain Marvin, however the law's efficacy at this factor inside the story is questionable. One of the maximum exciting things about Marvin is how he became delivered to American readers, instead of his introduction to British readers. For the previous, he sincerely says "Captain Marvin is my name" (264); for the latter he says, "Captain Marvin is my call—of the Coal and Iron [Police]." Before Marvin even says this within the American version Doyle introduces him thusly: "Just at the crowded hour one night time, the door opened and a person entered with the quiet blue uniform and peaked cap of the mine police" (164).

This is lots greater vital than it would seem on the floor in terms of what it manner contextually. Critic Marino Alvarez takes in this subject matter, suggesting that by way of truly the usage of the term "mine" Doyle implied a peacekeeping force rather than a regulatory strength managed through the colliers (mine owners). Marino also suggests that because Doyle and the Sherlock Holmes testimonies were so famous in America at the time, Doyle's American editor did not need to accomplice the novel with the particularly unpopular iron and mine police. Alvarez writes, "there is proof to suggest that the deletion...may additionally were to stem similarly incitement amongst miners and worker's and the American public approximately this non-public police enterprise." The Coal and Iron Police collaborated with the kingdom police as well as the Pinkertons for you to "quell liberties of those whom they perceived as either chasing a disturbance or had been perceived as capability disruptors."

Doyle had visited New York in 1914 earlier than the radical become launched there, and it's far probable that he and his editor discussed altering the words. The reading public have been developing greater vocally vital of past due about the Coal and Iron Police's methods, as well as different great abuses of people. Alvarez's argument for this reason seems achievable.

The individual of McMurdo is compelling at this factor within the tale, that's to mention before his proper identification is revealed. He is bold and brave, self-assured and arrogant. McGinty sees in him someone he can recognize. He does no longer appear to be fearful of law enforcement, any of the Scowrers, or anyone at the mines. He has little sympathy for those affected by the Scowrers' violent tactics, although he does stop Stanley Baldwin from killing Stanger. He seems to without a doubt love Ettie, but conceals from her his genuine individual. When she surprises him one night and catches a glimpse of his eyes she almost catches on, but he explains this away. It is ironic at this point that she loves a man who's just as violent as Baldwin.

Chapter 6—Danger

It was the height of the reign of terror. McMurdo, who had already been appointed Inner Deacon, with every prospect of some day succeeding McGinty as Body master, was now so necessary to the councils of his comrades that nothing was done without his help and advice. The more popular he became, however, with the Freemen, the blacker were the scowls which greeted him as he passed along the streets of Vermissa. In spite of their terror the citizens were taking heart to band themselves together against their oppressors. Rumours had reached the lodge of secret gatherings in the Herald office and of distribution of firearms among the law-abiding people. But McGinty and his men were undisturbed by such reports. They were numerous, resolute, and well armed. Their opponents were scattered and powerless. It would all end, as it had done in the past, in aimless talk and possibly in impotent arrests. So said McGinty, McMurdo, and all the bolder spirits.

It was a Saturday evening in May. Saturday was always the lodge night, and McMurdo was leaving his house to attend it when Morris, the weaker brother of the order, came to see him. His brow was creased with care, and his kindly face was drawn and haggard.

"Can I speak with you freely, Mr. McMurdo?"

"Sure."

"I can't forget that I spoke my heart to you once, and that you kept it to yourself, even though the Boss himself came to ask you about it."

"What else could I do if you trusted me? It wasn't that I agreed with what you said."

"I know that well. But you are the one that I can speak to and be safe. I've a secret here," he put his hand to his breast, "and it is just burning the life out of me. I wish it had come to any one of you but me. If I tell it, it will mean murder, for sure. If I don't, it may bring the end of us all. God help me, but I am near out of my wits over it!"

McMurdo looked at the man earnestly. He was trembling in every limb. He poured some whisky into a glass and handed it to him. "That's the physic for the likes of you," said he. "Now let me hear of it."

Morris drank, and his white face took a tinge of colour. "I can tell it to you all in one sentence," said he. "There's a detective on our trail."

McMurdo stared at him in astonishment. "Why, man, you're crazy," he said. "Isn't the place full of police and detectives and what harm did they ever do us?"

"No, no, it's no man of the district. As you say, we know them, and it is little that they can do. But you've heard of Pinkerton's?"

"I've read of some folk of that name."

"Well, you can take it from me you've no show when they are on your trail. It's not a take-it-or-miss-it government concern. It's a dead earnest business proposition that's out for results and keeps out till by hook or crook it gets them. If a Pinkerton man is deep in this business, we are all destroyed."

"We must kill him."

"Ah, it's the first thought that came to you! So it will be up at the lodge. Didn't I say to you that it would end in murder?"

"Sure, what is murder? Isn't it common enough in these parts?"

"It is, indeed; but it's not for me to point out the man that is to be murdered. I'd never rest easy again. And yet it's our own necks that may be at stake. In God's name what shall I do?" He rocked to and fro in his agony of indecision.

But his words had moved McMurdo deeply. It was easy to see that he shared the other's opinion as to the danger, and the need for meeting it. He gripped Morris's shoulder and shook him in his earnestness.

"See here, man," he cried, and he almost screeched the words in his excitement, "you won't gain anything by sitting keening like an old wife at a wake. Let's have the facts. Who is the fellow? Where is he? How did you hear of him? Why did you come to me?"

"I came to you; for you are the one man that would advise me. I told you that I had a store in the East before I came here. I left good friends behind me, and one of them is in the telegraph service. Here's a letter that I had from him yesterday. It's this part from the top of the page. You can read it yourself."

This was what McMurdo read:

How are the Scowrers getting on in your parts? We read plenty of them in the papers. Between you and me I expect to hear news from you before long. Five big corporations and the two railroads have taken the thing up in dead earnest. They mean it, and you can bet they'll get there! They are right deep down into it. Pinkerton has taken hold under their orders, and his best man, Birdy Edwards, is operating. The thing has got to be stopped right now.

"Now read the postscript."

Of course, what I give you is what I learned in business; so it goes no further. It's a queer cipher that you handle by the yard every day and can get no meaning from.

McMurdo sat in silence for some time, with the letter in his listless hands. The mist had lifted for a moment, and there was the abyss before him.

"Does anyone else know of this?" he asked.

"I have told no one else."

"But this man—your friend—has he any other person that he would be likely to write to?"

"Well, I dare say he knows one or two more."

"Of the lodge?"

"It's likely enough."

"I was asking because it is likely that he may have given some description of this fellow Birdy Edwards—then we could get on his trail."

"Well, it's possible. But I should not think he knew him. He is just telling me the news that came to him by way of business. How would he know this Pinkerton man?"

McMurdo gave a violent start.

"By Gar!" he cried, "I've got him. What a fool I was not to know it. Lord! but we're in luck! We will fix him before he can do any harm. See here, Morris, will you leave this thing in my hands?"

"Sure, if you will only take it off mine."

"I'll do that. You can stand right back and let me run it. Even your name need not be mentioned. I'll take it all on myself, as if it were to me that this letter has come. Will that content you?"

"It's just what I would ask."

"Then leave it at that and keep your head shut. Now I'll get down to the lodge, and we'll soon make old man Pinkerton sorry for himself."

"You wouldn't kill this man?"

"The less you know, Friend Morris, the easier your conscience will be, and the better you will sleep. Ask no questions, and let these things settle themselves. I have hold of it now."

Morris shook his head sadly as he left. "I feel that his blood is on my hands," he groaned.

"Self-protection is no murder, anyhow," said McMurdo, smiling grimly. "It's him or us. I guess this man would destroy us all if we left him long in the valley. Why, Brother Morris, we'll have to elect you Body master yet; for you've surely saved the lodge."

And yet it was clear from his actions that he thought more seriously of this new intrusion than his words would show. It may have been his guilty conscience, it may have been the reputation of the Pinkerton organization, it may have been the knowledge that great, rich corporations had set themselves the task of clearing out the Scowrers; but, whatever his reason, his actions were those of a man who is preparing for the worst. Every paper which would incriminate him was destroyed before he left the house. After that he gave a long sigh of satisfaction; for it seemed to him that he was safe. And yet the danger must still have pressed somewhat upon him; for on his way to the lodge he stopped at old man Shafter's. The house was forbidden him; but when he tapped at the window Ettie came out to him. The dancing Irish deviltry had gone from her lover's eyes. She read his danger in his earnest face.

"Something has happened!" she cried. "Oh, Jack, you are in danger!"

"Sure, it is not very bad, my sweetheart. And yet it may be wise that we make a move before it is worse."

"Make a move?"

"I promised you once that I would go some day. I think the time is coming. I had news to-night, bad news, and I see trouble coming."

"The police?"

"Well, a Pinkerton. But, sure, you wouldn't know what that is, acushla, nor what it may mean to the likes of me. I'm too deep in this thing, and I may have to get out of it quick. You said you would come with me if I went."

"Oh, Jack, it would be the saving of you!"

"I'm an honest man in some things, Ettie. I wouldn't hurt a hair of your bonny head for all that the world can give, nor ever pull you down one inch from the golden throne above the clouds where I always see you. Would you trust me?"

She put her hand in his without a word. "Well, then, listen to what I say, and do as I order you, for indeed it's the only way for us. Things are going to happen in this valley. I feel it in my bones. There may be many of us that will have to look out for ourselves. I'm one, anyhow. If I go, by day or night, it's you that must come with me!"

"I'd come after you, Jack."

"No, no, you shall come WITH me. If this valley is closed to me and I can never come back, how can I leave you behind, and me perhaps in hiding from the police with never a chance of a message? It's with me you must come. I know a good woman in the place I come from, and it's there I'd leave you till we can get married. Will you come?"

"Yes, Jack, I will come."

"God bless you for your trust in me! It's a fiend out of hell that I should be if I abused it. Now, mark you, Ettie, it will be just a word to you, and when it reaches you, you will drop everything and come right down to the waiting room at the depot and stay there till I come for you."

"Day or night, I'll come at the word, Jack."

Somewhat eased in mind, now that his own preparations for escape had been begun, McMurdo went on to the lodge. It had already assembled, and only by complicated signs and countersigns could he pass through the outer guard and inner guard who close-tiled it. A buzz of pleasure and welcome greeted him as he entered. The long room was crowded, and through the haze of tobacco smoke he saw the tangled black mane of the Body master, the cruel, unfriendly features of Baldwin, the vulture face of Harraway, the secretary, and a dozen more who were among the leaders of the lodge. He rejoiced that they should all be there to take counsel over his news.

"Indeed, it's glad we are to see you, Brother!" cried the chairman. "There's business here that wants a Solomon in judgment to set it right."

"It's Lander and Egan," explained his neighbour as he took his seat. "They both claim the head money given by the lodge for the shooting of old man Crabbe over at Stylestown, and who's to say which fired the bullet?"

McMurdo rose in his place and raised his hand. The expression of his face froze the attention of the audience. There was a dead hush of expectation.

"Eminent Body master," he said, in a solemn voice, "I claim urgency!"

"Brother McMurdo claims urgency," said McGinty. "It's a claim that by the rules of this lodge takes precedence. Now Brother, we attend you."

McMurdo took the letter from his pocket.

"Eminent Body master and Brethren," he said, "I am the bearer of ill news this day; but it is better that it should be known and discussed, than that a blow should fall upon us without warning which would destroy us all. I have information that the most powerful and richest organizations in this state have bound themselves together for our destruction, and that at this very moment there is a Pinkerton detective, one Birdy Edwards, at work in the valley collecting the evidence which may put a rope round the necks of many of us, and send every man in this room into a felon's cell. That is the situation for the discussion of which I have made a claim of urgency."

There was a dead silence in the room. It was broken by the chairman.

"What is your evidence for this, Brother McMurdo?" he asked.

"It is in this letter which has come into my hands," said McMurdo. He read the passage aloud. "It is a matter of honour with me that I can give no further particulars about the letter, nor put it into your hands; but I assure you that there is nothing else in it which can affect the interests of the lodge. I put the case before you as it has reached me."

"Let me say, Mr. Chairman," said one of the older brethren, "that I have heard of Birdy Edwards, and that he has the name of being the best man in the Pinkerton service."

"Does anyone know him by sight?" asked McGinty.

"Yes," said McMurdo, "I do."

There was a murmur of astonishment through the hall.

"I believe we hold him in the hollow of our hands," he continued with an exulting smile upon his face. "If we act quickly and wisely, we can cut this thing short. If I have your confidence and your help, it is little that we have to fear."

"What have we to fear, anyhow? What can he know of our affairs?"

"You might say so if all were as stanch as you, Councillor. But this man has all the millions of the capitalists at his back. Do you think there is no weaker brother among all our lodges that could not be bought? He will get at our secrets—maybe has got them already. There's only one sure cure."

"That he never leaves the valley," said Baldwin.

McMurdo nodded. "Good for you, Brother Baldwin," he said. "You and I have had our differences, but you have said the true word to-night."

"Where is he, then? Where shall we know him?"

"Eminent Body master," said McMurdo, earnestly, "I would put it to you that this is too vital a thing for us to discuss in open lodge. God forbid that I should throw a doubt on anyone here; but if so much as a word of gossip got to the ears of this man, there would be an end of any chance of our getting him. I would ask the lodge to choose a trusty committee, Mr. Chairman—yourself, if I might suggest it, and Brother Baldwin here, and five more. Then I can talk freely of what I know and of what I advise should be done."

The proposition was at once adopted, and the committee chosen. Besides the chairman and Baldwin there were the vulture-faced secretary, Harraway, Tiger Cormac, the brutal young assassin, Carter, the treasurer, and the brothers Willaby, fearless and desperate men who would stick at nothing.

The usual revelry of the lodge was short and subdued: for there was a cloud upon the men's spirits, and many there for the first time began to see the cloud of avenging Law drifting up in that serene sky under which they had dwelt so long. The horrors they had dealt out to others had been so much a part of their settled lives that the thought of retribution had become a remote one, and so seemed the more startling now that it came so closely upon them. They broke up early and left their leaders to their council.

"Now, McMurdo!" said McGinty when they were alone. The seven men sat frozen in their seats.

"I said just now that I knew Birdy Edwards," McMurdo explained. "I need not tell you that he is not here under that name. He's a brave man, but not a crazy one. He passes under the name of Steve Wilson, and he is lodging at Hobson's Patch."

"How do you know this?"

"Because I fell into talk with him. I thought little of it at the time, nor would have given it a second thought but for this letter; but now I'm sure it's the man. I met him on the cars when I went down the line on Wednesday—a hard case if ever there was one. He said he was a reporter. I believed it for the moment. Wanted to know all he could about the Scowrers and what he called 'the outrages' for a New York paper. Asked me every kind of question so as to get something. You bet I was giving nothing away. 'I'd pay for it and pay well,' said he, 'if I could get some stuff that would suit my editor.' I said what I thought would please him best, and he handed me a twenty-dollar bill for my information. 'There's ten times that for you,' said he, 'if you can find me all that I want.'"

"What did you tell him, then?"

"Any stuff I could make up."

"How do you know he wasn't a newspaper man?"

"I'll tell you. He got out at Hobson's Patch, and so did I. I chanced into the telegraph bureau, and he was leaving it.

"'See here,' said the operator after he'd gone out, 'I guess we should charge double rates for this.'—'I guess you should,' said I. He had filled the form with stuff that might have been Chinese, for all we could make of it. 'He fires a sheet of this off every day,' said the clerk. 'Yes,' said I; 'it's special news for his paper, and he's scared that the others should tap it.' That was what the operator thought and what I thought at the time; but I think differently now."

"By Gar! I believe you are right," said McGinty. "But what do you allow that we should do about it?"

"Why not go right down now and fix him?" someone suggested.

"Ay, the sooner the better."

"I'd start this next minute if I knew where we could find him," said McMurdo. "He's in Hobson's Patch; but I don't know the house. I've got a plan, though, if you'll only take my advice."

"Well, what is it?"

"I'll go to the Patch to-morrow morning. I'll find him through the operator. He can locate him, I guess. Well, then I'll tell him that I'm a Freeman myself. I'll offer him all the secrets of the lodge for a price. You bet he'll tumble to it. I'll tell him the papers are at my house, and that it's as much as my life would be worth to let him come while folk were about. He'll see that that's horse sense. Let him come at ten o'clock at night, and he shall see everything. That will fetch him sure."

"Well?"

"You can plan the rest for yourselves. Widow MacNamara's is a lonely house. She's as true as steel and as deaf as a post. There's only Scanlan and me in the house. If I get his promise—and I'll let you know if I do—I'd have the whole seven of you come to me by nine o'clock. We'll get him in. If ever he gets out alive—well, he can talk of Birdy Edwards's luck for the rest of his days!"

"There's going to be a vacancy at Pinkerton's or I'm mistaken. Leave it at that, McMurdo. At nine to-morrow we'll be with you. You once get the door shut behind him, and you can leave the rest with us."

Chapter 7—The Trapping of Birdy Edwards

As McMurdo had said, the house in which he lived was a lonely one and very well suited for such a crime as they had planned. It was on the extreme fringe of the town and stood well back from the road. In any other case the conspirators would have simply called out their man, as they had many a time before, and emptied their pistols into his body; but in this instance it was very necessary to find out how much he knew, how he knew it, and what had been passed on to his employers.

It was possible that they were already too late and that the work had been done. If that was indeed so, they could at least have their revenge upon the man who had done it. But they were hopeful that nothing of great importance had yet come to the detective's knowledge, as otherwise, they argued, he would not have troubled to write down and forward such trivial information as McMurdo claimed to have given him. However, all this they would learn from his own lips. Once in their power, they would find a way to make him speak. It was not the first time that they had handled an unwilling witness.

McMurdo went to Hobson's Patch as agreed. The police seemed to take particular interest in him that morning, and Captain Marvin—he who had claimed the old acquaintance with him at Chicago—actually addressed him as he waited at the station. McMurdo turned away and refused to speak with him. He was back from his mission in the afternoon, and saw McGinty at the Union House.

"He is coming," he said.

"Good!" said McGinty. The giant was in his shirt sleeves, with chains and seals gleaming athwart his ample waistcoat and a diamond twinkling through the fringe of his bristling beard. Drink and politics had made the Boss a very rich as well as powerful man. The more terrible, therefore, seemed that glimpse of the prison or the gallows which had risen before him the night before.

"Do you reckon he knows much?" he asked anxiously.

McMurdo shook his head gloomily. "He's been here some time—six weeks at the least. I guess he didn't come into these parts to look at the prospect. If he has been working among us all that time with the railroad money at his back, I should expect that he has got results, and that he has passed them on."

"There's not a weak man in the lodge," cried McGinty. "True as steel, every man of them. And yet, by the Lord! there is that skunk Morris. What about him? If any man gives us away, it would be he. I've a mind to send a couple of the boys round before evening to give him a beating up and see what they can get from him."

"Well, there would be no harm in that," McMurdo answered. "I won't deny that I have a liking for Morris and would be sorry to see him come to harm. He has spoken to me once or twice over lodge matters, and though he may not see them the same as you or I, he never seemed the sort that squeals. But still it is not for me to stand between him and you."

"I'll fix the old devil!" said McGinty with an oath. "I've had my eye on him this year past."

"Well, you know best about that," McMurdo answered. "But whatever you do must be to-morrow; for we must lie low until the Pinkerton affair is settled up. We can't afford to set the police buzzing, to-day of all days."

"True for you," said McGinty. "And we'll learn from Birdy Edwards himself where he got his news if we have to cut his heart out first. Did he seem to scent a trap?"

McMurdo laughed. "I guess I took him on his weak point," he said. "If he could get on a good trail of the Scowrers, he's ready to follow it into hell. I took his money," McMurdo grinned as he produced a wad of dollar notes, "and as much more when he has seen all my papers."

"What papers?"

"Well, there are no papers. But I filled him up about constitutions and books of rules and forms of membership. He expects to get right down to the end of everything before he leaves."

"Faith, he's right there," said McGinty grimly. "Didn't he ask you why you didn't bring him the papers?"

"As if I would carry such things, and me a suspected man, and Captain Marvin after speaking to me this very day at the depot!"

"Ay, I heard of that," said McGinty. "I guess the heavy end of this business is coming on to you. We could put him down an old shaft when we've done with him; but however we work it we can't get past the man living at Hobson's Patch and you being there to-day."

McMurdo shrugged his shoulders. "If we handle it right, they can never prove the killing," said he. "No one can see him come to the house after dark, and I'll lay to it that no one will see him go. Now see here, Councillor, I'll show you my plan and I'll ask you to fit the others into it. You will all come in good time. Very well. He comes at ten. He is to tap three times, and me to open the door for him. Then I'll get behind him and shut it. He's our man then."

"That's all easy and plain."

"Yes; but the next step wants considering. He's a hard proposition. He's heavily armed. I've fooled him proper, and yet he is likely to be on his guard. Suppose I show him right into a room with seven men in it where he expected to find me alone. There is going to be shooting, and somebody is going to be hurt."

"That's so."

"And the noise is going to bring every damned copper in the township on top of it."

"I guess you are right."

"This is how I should work it. You will all be in the big room—same as you saw when you had a chat with me. I'll open the door for him, show him into the parlour beside the door, and leave him there while I get the papers. That will give me the chance of telling you how things are shaping. Then I will go back to him with some faked papers. As he is reading them I will jump for him and get my grip on his pistol arm. You'll hear me call and in you will rush. The quicker the better; for he is as strong a man as I, and I may have more than I can manage. But I allow that I can hold him till you come."

"It's a good plan," said McGinty. "The lodge will owe you a debt for this. I guess when I move out of the chair I can put a name to the man that's coming after me."

"Sure, Councillor, I am little more than a recruit," said McMurdo; but his face showed what he thought of the great man's compliment.

When he had returned home he made his own preparations for the grim evening in front of him. First he cleaned, oiled, and loaded his Smith & Wesson revolver. Then he surveyed the room in which the detective was to be trapped. It was a large apartment, with a long deal table in the center, and the big stove at one side. At each of the other sides were windows. There were no shutters on these: only light curtains which drew across. McMurdo examined these attentively. No doubt it must have struck him that the apartment was very exposed for so secret a meeting. Yet its distance from the road made it of less consequence. Finally he discussed the matter with his fellow lodger. Scanlan, though a Scowrer, was an inoffensive little man who was too weak to stand against the opinion of his comrades, but was secretly horrified by the deeds of blood at which he had sometimes been forced to assist. McMurdo told him shortly what was intended.

"And if I were you, Mike Scanlan, I would take a night off and keep clear of it. There will be bloody work here before morning."

"Well, indeed then, Mac," Scanlan answered. "It's not the will but the nerve that is wanting in me. When I saw Manager Dunn go down at the colliery yonder it was just more than I could stand. I'm not made for it, same as you or McGinty. If the lodge will think none the worse of me, I'll just do as you advise and leave you to yourselves for the evening."

The men came in good time as arranged. They were outwardly respectable citizens, well clad and cleanly; but a judge of faces would have read little hope for Birdy Edwards in those hard mouths and remorseless eyes. There was not a man in the room whose hands had not been reddened a dozen times before. They were as hardened to human murder as a butcher to sheep.

Foremost, of course, both in appearance and in guilt, was the formidable Boss. Harraway, the secretary, was a lean, bitter man with a long, scraggy neck and nervous, jerky limbs, a man of incorruptible fidelity where the finances of the order were concerned, and with no notion of justice or honesty to anyone beyond. The treasurer, Carter, was a middle-aged man, with an impassive, rather sulky expression, and a yellow parchment skin. He was a capable organizer, and the actual details of nearly every outrage had sprung from his plotting brain. The two Willabys were men of action, tall, lithe young fellows with determined faces, while their companion, Tiger Cormac, a heavy, dark youth, was feared even by his own comrades for the ferocity of his disposition. These were the men who assembled that night under the roof of McMurdo for the killing of the Pinkerton detective.

Their host had placed whisky upon the table, and they had hastened to prime themselves for the work before them. Baldwin and Cormac were already half-drunk, and the liquor had brought out all their ferocity. Cormac placed his hands on the stove for an instant—it had been lighted, for the nights were still cold.

"That will do," said he, with an oath.

"Ay," said Baldwin, catching his meaning. "If he is strapped to that, we will have the truth out of him."

"We'll have the truth out of him, never fear," said McMurdo. He had nerves of steel, this man; for though the whole weight of the affair was on him his manner was as cool and unconcerned as ever. The others marked it and applauded.

"You are the one to handle him," said the Boss approvingly. "Not a warning will he get till your hand is on his throat. It's a pity there are no shutters to your windows."

McMurdo went from one to the other and drew the curtains tighter. "Sure no one can spy upon us now. It's close upon the hour."

"Maybe he won't come. Maybe he'll get a sniff of danger," said the secretary.

"He'll come, never fear," McMurdo answered. "He is as eager to come as you can be to see him. Hark to that!"

They all sat like wax figures, some with their glasses arrested halfway to their lips. Three loud knocks had sounded at the door.

"Hush!" McMurdo raised his hand in caution. An exulting glance went round the circle, and hands were laid upon their weapons.

"Not a sound, for your lives!" McMurdo whispered, as he went from the room, closing the door carefully behind him.

With strained ears the murderers waited. They counted the steps of their comrade down the passage. Then they heard him open the outer door. There were a few words as of greeting. Then they were aware of a strange step inside and of an unfamiliar voice. An instant later came the slam of the door and the turning of the key in the lock. Their prey was safe within the trap. Tiger Cormac laughed horribly, and Boss McGinty clapped his great hand across his mouth.

"Be quiet, you fool!" he whispered. "You'll be the undoing of us yet!"

There was a mutter of conversation from the next room. It seemed interminable. Then the door opened, and McMurdo appeared, his finger upon his lip.

He came to the end of the table and looked round at them. A subtle change had come over him. His manner was as of one who has great work to do. His face had set into granite firmness. His eyes shone with a fierce excitement behind his spectacles. He had become a visible leader of men. They stared at him with eager interest; but he said nothing. Still with the same singular gaze he looked from man to man.

"Well!" cried Boss McGinty at last. "Is he here? Is Birdy Edwards here?"

"Yes," McMurdo answered slowly. "Birdy Edwards is here. I am Birdy Edwards!"

There were ten seconds after that brief speech during which the room might have been empty, so profound was the silence. The hissing of a kettle upon the stove rose sharp and strident to the ear. Seven white faces, all turned upward to this man who dominated them, were set motionless with utter terror. Then, with a sudden shivering of glass, a bristle of glistening rifle barrels broke through each window, while the curtains were torn from their hangings.

At the sight Boss McGinty gave the roar of a wounded bear and plunged for the half-opened door. A levelled revolver met him there with the stern blue eyes of Captain Marvin of the Mine Police gleaming behind the sights. The Boss recoiled and fell back into his chair.

"You're safer there, Councillor," said the man whom they had known as McMurdo. "And you, Baldwin, if you don't take your hand off your pistol, you'll cheat the hangman yet. Pull it out, or by the Lord that made me— There, that will do. There are forty armed men round this house, and you can figure it out for yourself what chance you have. Take their pistols, Marvin!"

There was no possible resistance under the menace of those rifles. The men were disarmed. Sulky, sheepish, and amazed, they still sat round the table.

"I'd like to say a word to you before we separate," said the man who had trapped them. "I guess we may not meet again until you see me on the stand in the courthouse. I'll give you something to think over between now and then. You know me now for what I am. At last I can put my cards on the table. I am Birdy Edwards of Pinkerton's. I was chosen to break up your gang. I had a hard and dangerous game to play. Not a soul, not one soul, not my nearest and dearest, knew that I was playing it. Only Captain Marvin here and my employers knew that. But it's over to-night, thank God, and I am the winner!"

The seven pale, rigid faces looked up at him. There was unappeasable hatred in their eyes. He read the relentless threat.

"Maybe you think that the game is not over yet. Well, I take my chance of that. Anyhow, some of you will take no further hand, and there are sixty more besides yourselves that will see a jail this night. I'll tell you this, that when I was put upon this job I never believed there was such a society as yours. I thought it was paper talk, and that I would prove it so. They told me it was to do with the Freemen; so I went to Chicago and was made one. Then I was surer than ever that it was just paper talk; for I found no harm in the society, but a deal of good.

"Still, I had to carry out my job, and I came to the coal valleys. When I reached this place I learned that I was wrong and that it wasn't a dime novel after all. So I stayed to look after it. I never killed a man in Chicago. I never minted a dollar in my life. Those I gave you were as good as any others; but I never spent money better. But I knew the way into your good wishes and so I pretended to you that the law was after me. It all worked just as I thought.

"So I joined your infernal lodge, and I took my share in your councils. Maybe they will say that I was as bad as you. They can say what they like, so long as I get you. But what is the truth? The night I joined you beat up old man Stanger. I could not warn him, for there was no time; but I held your hand, Baldwin, when you would have killed him. If ever I have suggested things, so as to keep my place among you, they were things which I knew I could prevent. I could not save Dunn and Menzies, for I did not know enough; but I will see that their murderers are hanged. I gave Chester Wilcox warning, so that when I blew his house in he and his folk were in hiding. There was many a crime that I could not stop; but if you look back and think how often your man came home the other road, or was down in town when you went for him, or stayed indoors when you thought he would come out, you'll see my work."

"You blasted traitor!" hissed McGinty through his closed teeth.

"Ay, John McGinty, you may call me that if it eases your smart. You and your like have been the enemy of God and man in these parts. It took a man to get between you and the poor devils of men and women that you held under your grip. There was just one way of doing it, and I did it. You call me a traitor; but I guess there's many a thousand will call me a deliverer that went down into hell to save them. I've had three months of it. I wouldn't have three such months again if they let me loose in the treasury at Washington for it. I had to stay till I had it all, every man and every secret right here in this hand. I'd have waited a little longer if it hadn't come to my knowledge that my secret was coming out. A letter had come into the town that would have set you wise to it all. Then I had to act and act quickly.

"I've nothing more to say to you, except that when my time comes I'll die the easier when I think of the work I have done in this valley. Now, Marvin, I'll keep you no more. Take them in and get it over."

There is little more to tell. Scanlan had been given a sealed note to be left at the address of Miss Ettie Shafter, a mission which he had accepted with a wink and a knowing smile. In the early hours of the morning a beautiful woman and a much muffled man boarded a special train which had been sent by the railroad company, and made a swift, unbroken journey out of the land of danger. It was the last time that ever either Ettie or her lover set foot in the Valley of Fear. Ten days later they were married in Chicago, with old Jacob Shafter as witness of the wedding.

The trial of the Scowrers was held far from the place where their adherents might have terrified the guardians of the law. In vain they struggled. In vain the money of the lodge—money squeezed by blackmail out of the whole countryside—was spent like water in the attempt to save them. That cold, clear, unimpassioned statement from one who knew every detail of their lives, their organization, and their crimes was unshaken by all the wiles of their defenders. At last after so many years they were broken and scattered. The cloud was lifted forever from the valley.

McGinty met his fate upon the scaffold, cringing and whining when the last hour came. Eight of his chief followers shared his fate. Fifty-odd had various degrees of imprisonment. The work of Birdy Edwards was complete.

And yet, as he had guessed, the game was not over yet. There was another hand to be played, and yet another and another. Ted Baldwin, for one, had escaped the scaffold; so had the Willabys; so had several others of the fiercest spirits of the gang. For ten years they were out of the world, and then came a day when they were free once more—a day which Edwards, who knew his men, was very sure would be an end of his life of peace. They had sworn an oath on all that they thought holy to have his blood as a vengeance for their comrades. And well they strove to keep their vow!

From Chicago he was chased, after two attempts so near success that it was sure that the third would get him. From Chicago he went under a changed name to California, and it was there that the light went for a time out of his life when Ettie Edwards died. Once again he was nearly killed, and once again under the name of Douglas he worked in a lonely canyon, where with an English partner named Barker he amassed a fortune. At last there came a warning to him that the bloodhounds were on his track once more, and he cleared—only just in time—for England. And thence came the John Douglas who for a second time married a worthy mate, and lived for five years as a Sussex county gentleman, a life which ended with the strange happenings of which we have heard.

Epilogue

The police trial had passed, in which the case of John Douglas was referred to a higher court. So had the Quarter Sessions, at which he was acquitted as having acted in self-defense.

"Get him out of England at any cost," wrote Holmes to the wife. "There are forces here which may be more dangerous than those he has escaped. There is no safety for your husband in England."

Two months had gone by, and the case had to some extent passed from our minds. Then one morning there came an enigmatic note slipped into our letter box. "Dear me, Mr. Holmes. Dear me!" said this singular epistle. There was neither superscription nor signature. I laughed at the quaint message; but Holmes showed unwonted seriousness.

"Deviltry, Watson!" he remarked, and sat long with a clouded brow.

Late last night Mrs. Hudson, our landlady, brought up a message that a gentleman wished to see Mr. Holmes, and that the matter was of the utmost importance. Close at the heels of his messenger came Cecil Barker, our friend of the moated Manor House. His face was drawn and haggard.

"I've had bad news—terrible news, Mr. Holmes," said he.

"I feared as much," said Holmes.

"You have not had a cable, have you?"

"I have had a note from someone who has."

"It's poor Douglas. They tell me his name is Edwards; but he will always be Jack Douglas of Benito Canyon to me. I told you that they started together for South Africa in the Palmyra three weeks ago."

"Exactly."

"The ship reached Cape Town last night. I received this cable from Mrs. Douglas this morning:

"'Jack has been lost overboard in gale off St. Helena. No one knows how accident occurred.'

"'IVY DOUGLAS.'"

"Ha! It came like that, did it?" said Holmes thoughtfully. "Well, I've no doubt it was well stage-managed."

"You mean that you think there was no accident?"

"None in the world."

"He was murdered?"

"Surely!"

"So I think also. These infernal Scowrers, this cursed vindictive nest of criminals—"

"No, no, my good sir," said Holmes. "There is a master hand here. It is no case of sawed-off shotguns and clumsy six-shooters. You can tell an old master by the sweep of his brush. I can tell a Moriarty when I see one. This crime is from London, not from America."

"But for what motive?"

"Because it is done by a man who cannot afford to fail, one whose whole unique position depends upon the fact that all he does must succeed. A great brain and a huge organization have been turned to the extinction of one man. It is crushing the nut with the triphammer—an absurd extravagance of energy—but the nut is very effectually crushed all the same."

'How came this man to have anything to do with it?"

'I can only say that the first word that ever came to us of the business was from one of his lieutenants. These Americans were well advised. Having an English job to do, they took into partnership, as any foreign criminal could do, this great consultant in crime. From that moment their man was doomed. At first he would content himself by using his machinery in order to find their victim. Then he would indicate how the matter might be treated. Finally, when he read in the reports of the failure of this agent, he would step in himself with a master touch. You heard me warn this man at Birlstone Manor House that the coming danger was greater than the past. Was I right?"

Barker beat his head with his clenched fist in his impotent anger. "Do not tell me that we have to sit down under this? Do you say that no one can ever get level with this king devil?"

'No, I don't say that," said Holmes, and his eyes seemed to be looking far into the future. "I don't say that he can't be beat. But you must give me time—you must give me time!"

We all sat in silence for some minutes while those fateful eyes still strained to pierce the veil.

The Valley of Fear Summary and Analysis of Part II Chapters 6 & 7, and Epilogue
Summary

Chapter 6

It is the peak of the Scowrers' reign of terror, or even the citizens are trying to arm themselves and push back against it. McMurdo keeps to upward push within the business enterprise.

One Saturday night time before the inn assembly, Morris comes to see McMurdo. He is visibly afraid and worrying and says he has a mystery this is burning inside him. He eventually bursts out that a detective is at the union's path.

Astonished, McMurdo says there are always human beings seeking to get them. Morris replies that it's miles one of the infamous Pinkerton detectives and is consequently very critical. McMurdo earnestly grabs Morris and says he must tell him the entirety. Morris explains he had a pal returned East who sent a telegram asking how the Scowrers had been doing, and noting that he heard the Pinkertons and their fine detective, Birdy Edwards, have been at the case.

McMurdo feels as though an abyss is before him. He asks if Morris could realize what this Edwards gave the impression of and Morris says no; even his pal could now not recognize this. McMurdo unexpectedly bursts out that he knows who it's far, and vows to take of it. To

Morris's remedy he says he'll go away Morris's call out of something occurs subsequent.

Before the assembly McMurdo tells Ettie he's finally prepared to go, and to watch for his phrase soon.

That night time the meeting commences. This quiets anyone down; the policies state all people need to heed this enterprise before something else.

McMurdo explains that he has a letter telling him of Edwards and the Pinkertons, and that he is aware of precisely who the man is. A ripple of astonishment and worry sweeps the hall. McGinty says the man need to no longer be allowed to leave the valley. McMurdo agrees and asks go away to form a committee to speak about the plan.

That night time the motel's revelry is subdued; for the primary time the guys see the arm of the regulation accomplishing closer to them.

McGinty, McMurdo, 1st Earl Baldwin of Bewdley, and the other guys decided on for the committee meet to speak about the plan. McMurdo identifies the man as Steve Wilson, lodging at Hobson's Patch; Wilson changed into pretending to be a reporter. McMurdo then says his plan is to go to Wilson along with his "secrets" of the Lodge for a rate. This should occur at the trusty (and deaf) Widow MacNamara's residence. The seven guys will meet there through 9; Edwards will display up, and they'll take care of him.

Chapter 7

McMurdo and McGinty speak approximately the lure they are placing. McGinty frets over whether or not or no longer has McMurdo already informed all of us anything. He wonders if Morris is involved; McMurdo tells him it's far not going, however they should cognizance on Edwards right now besides. He then proceeds to give an explanation for how the plan will paintings: Edwards comes to the house at ten that night; the Freemen cover while he places Edwards at his ease; he then jumps on Edwards and holds him until the others rush in. McGinty likes the plan and compliments McMurdo.

At the residence McMurdo prepares his weapon and tells Scanlan, who confesses he does not like those bloody deeds, to live far from the house that night time.

The men arrive and wait; bloodlust is in their eyes. Three knocks sound at the door and McMurdo hushes them to be quiet and goes into the other room. They pay attention him speaking to a man and anxiously wait for their cue.

McMurdo seems on the door and the men see his fierce eyes, company expression, and glow of power. He proclaims that he is Birdy Edwards. For ten seconds there's silence, then numerous rifles crash thru the glass windows. The police surround the men and point weapons at them; the irate McGinty can do nothing.

Before the guys are hauled off, McMurdo speaks to them of his dangerous recreation. He can inform that they may be angry, but over sixty extra Scowrers could be rounded up and jailed. The law changed into never after McMurdo: Captain Marvin knew him; he joined their "infernal lodge" (317) to show them. Perhaps a few will say he is as horrific as there, but he does now not care what people say. He stored Stanger's life; he warned Wilcox and his own family.

McGinty bursts out that he is a traitor; the amused McMurdo says he does now not mind the epithet, and comments that others might name him a deliverer. He will die easier knowing that he has finished properly.

McMurdo and Ettie depart the Valley of Fear. The Scowrers are defeated and scattered; McGinty dies on the scaffold. Stanley Baldwin escapes, though, and vows to kill "McMurdo." He consequently follows them to Chicago and California (wherein Ettie dies) and then to England.

Epilogue

John Douglas is acquitted by the English regulation. Holmes warns him to get out of England, although, due to the fact there are worse forces at paintings. One day Holmes gets a letter that handiest says "Dear me, Mr. Holmes. Dear me!" (319.) Watson is careworn, but Holmes is quiet.

Not lengthy afterwards, Cecil Barker arrives. Clearly distraught, he says Mrs. Douglas cabled to say Douglas changed into lost at sea. It appears he was murdered, but there's no proof.

Barker thinks the Scowrers killed Douglas, however Holmes knows its miles Moriarty, hired to kill Douglas. The man by no means leaves a fee unfulfilled. Barker rages and asks if every person can do whatever about Moriarty. Holmes really says to offer him time.

Analysis

The novel involves a near with the revelation that McMurdo, Birdy Edwards, and John Douglas are all of the identical individual; it additionally adds a traumatic coda in that Moriarty has Douglas killed on behalf of the Scowrers who employed him. Moriarty's involvement seems a touch flimsy, however it emphasizes how linked, green, and lethal the Professor virtually is.

However, everyone hoping to learn extra about Holmes's enigmatic foe is certain to be disenchanted. Critic Catherine Wynne ties this in to the bigger Irish issue: "Occlusion of crook Irishness is more express while we observe Moriarty's faction, which retains its decidedly nebulous and pernicious satisfactory during the canon. Moriarty's business enterprise is by no means described, in no way named." She thinks Holmes's rationalization of ways Moriarty changed into involved is unsatisfactory and "that the master crook's reputation rests on the annihilation of a center-elderly and retired Pinkerton detective is improbable or certainly spurious. Rather, Moriarty's choice for Douglas' dying is based upon Moriarty's alignment with American, and by means of extension Irish, mystery societies, drastically Fenianism and its counterpart Clann-an-Gael. Doyle, then, is unobtrusively allying Moriarty and his criminal organization with Irish physical force separatism."

Wynne connects Moriarty's shady company to that of criminal Irish companies. This aligns with how Holmes describes Moriarty's modus operandi: "I may tell you that Moriarty regulations with a rod of iron over his human beings. His area is incredible. There is only one punishment in his code. It is demise" (177). However, this isn't always a blanket condemnation of all Irish groups or the Irish nationalist groups. Wynne writes of the way Doyle's entire oeuvre is a move toward rapprochement together with his Irish lineage. The "early short testimonies have a look at militant Irish nationalism while attempting a few information of the social situations that propagate such extreme political moves. The Holmes stories investigate the nature of the name of the game society: Moriarty's criminal gang, the Pennsylvanian Scowrers who invoke Irish Molly Maguireism and in the end Fenianism"; Moriarty is the link to Fenianism, and he demanding situations the detective inside the equal way Irish militancy posed a task for Doyle.

Ultimately, although, after The Valley of Fear, the tale "The Final Bow," Wynne says, "sooner or later shatters the idea of identarian cohesion and racial purity." Holmes leaves off his detective paintings and "Doyle retreats into the sector of spiritualism—an international in which the conflicting demands of British imperialism and Irish nationalism would haven't any vicinity."

Finally, the remaining chapters provide readers a thrilling moral question in whether or not or now not McMurdo's undercover movements are justified, and he answers this to a volume while he says, "Maybe they'll say that I become as horrific as you. They can say what they like, so long as I get you" and "there's many a thousand in order to name me a deliverer that went right down to hell to save them" (317). McMurdo beat, terrorized, and perhaps even killed, but he justifies this with the aid of saying that it's far fascinated by the greater appropriate. And it's far certainly tough, given this sort of black-and-white depiction of the Scowrers, to shield the ones whom McMurdo deceived.

The Valley of Fear Glossary

Afoot

In preparation or progress

Almanac

An annual calendar containing important dates and statistical information such as astronomical data and tide tables

Cipher

A secret or disguised way of writing; a code

Coruscation

Twinkling

Disparity

A great difference

Dour

Relentlessly severe, stern, or gloomy in manner or appearance

Evasive

Tending to avoid commitment or self-revelation, esp. by responding only indirectly

Exiguous

Very small in size or amount

Gamekeeper

A person employed to breed and protect game, typically for a large estate

Garrulous

Excessively talkative, esp. on trivial matters

Meagre

Lean; thin

Nugget

A small lump of gold or other precious metal, found ready-formed in the earth

Pagination

The sequence of numbers assigned to pages in a book or periodical

Gawky

Possessing a sly sense of humor

Predominant

Present as the strongest or main element

Remonstrance

A forcefully reproachful protest

Scrutinize

Examine or inspect closely and thoroughly

Shrewd

Possessing sharp powers of judgment

Solarium

Something furnished on someone as a form of compensation

Stratum

A layer or a series of layers of rock or earth

Buxom

Plump, curvaceous, healthy, and hale (usually in reference to a female)

Enigmatic

Mysterious; cryptic

Curt

Brusque in speech

Altercation

A fight

Colliers

Coal miners

Hue and cry

A loud cry, protest, or alarm

Valise
A suitcase

Made in the USA
Middletown, DE
04 February 2024

49083939R00175